THE TROUBLESHOOTER

NORCROSS SERIES

ANNA HACKETT

The Troubleshooter

Published by Anna Hackett

Copyright 2020 by Anna Hackett

Cover by Lana Pecherczyk

Cover image by Wander Aguiar

Edits by Tanya Sara

ISBN (ebook): 978-1-922414-12-0

ISBN (paperback): 978-1-922414-13-7

At Star's End – One of Library Journal's Best E-Original Romances for 2014

The Phoenix Adventures – SFR Galaxy Award Winner for Most Fun New Series and "Why Isn't This a Movie?" Series

Beneath a Trojan Moon – SFR Galaxy Award Winner and RWAus Ella Award Winner

Hell Squad – SFR Galaxy Award for best Post-Apocalypse for Readers who don't like Post-Apocalypse

"Like Indiana Jones meets Star Wars. A treasure hunt with a steamy romance." – SFF Dragon, review of *Among Galactic Ruins*

"Action, danger, aliens, romance – yup, it's another great book from Anna Hackett!" – Book Gannet Reviews, review of *Hell Squad: Marcus*

Sign up for my VIP mailing list and get your *free box set* containing three action-packed romances.

Visit here to get started: www.annahackett.com

CHAPTER ONE

O kay, this night had *not* turned out the way she'd planned.

Gia Norcross raced along the balcony, her Aquazzura heels clicking, her Alberta Ferretti dress flowing out behind her.

Not to mention the Ruger in her hand, and the bad guy chasing her.

Yes, her night had *not* gone according to plan.

She reached a set of stone stairs and flew down them. They led her into a tiny, shadowed courtyard at the back of San Francisco's Hutton Museum. The courtyard was ringed by trees starting to lose their leaves. A fountain burbled quietly in the center of the space.

Ordinarily, it was a peaceful spot. Gia had eaten lunch here a few times with her best friend, Haven McKinney. Haven was the curator of the Hutton, and Gia's oldest brother, Easton, owned the museum.

Gia darted under the trees, and sank into the shadows. She kept a tight grip on the Ruger. The handgun was small and light, making it easy to conceal and use.

She was a Norcross. She knew how to shoot. All three of her brothers were former military. Two of them had been in some classified, beyond-black-ops, special forces team. They'd not given her much choice about being able to shoot and defend herself.

Gia took a deep, calming breath to counter the adrenaline pumping through her system. Tonight was supposed to have been a relaxing and enjoyable evening at the museum's charity gala.

It had all started out fine. She'd been so happy watching Haven and Gia's youngest brother, Rhys. The pair were so in love they practically had little cartoon hearts floating around their heads. Haven had been in danger recently, when a multi-million-dollar painting had been stolen from the museum. Add in a very bad ex-boyfriend and the Russian mafia, and things had been messed up.

Needless to say, Haven had been in danger, and Rhys had stepped up to keep her safe. Haven could no longer ignore the sizzling attraction between her and Rhys.

A scrape of sound and Gia froze.

A large shadow moved in her peripheral vision. *Shit.* He was down here already. She hadn't even heard him.

The man moved stealthily through the courtyard.

Hunting her.

Gia's pulse spiked, followed by a punch of fear. She shoved it down. She had no time to be afraid.

This asshole had threatened Gia's old friend. Willow

had messed up, for sure, but Gia wasn't going to let her get hurt.

Willow had come to Gia looking for a place to stay. Gia sighed. She couldn't seem to say no to her old high school bestie. Of course, Willow had neglected to mention she'd stolen something from a not very nice guy. And he'd sent a *really* not nice guy to retrieve it.

He'd found her and threatened her, but Gia had intervened with her Ruger and sent him packing.

But the man's eyes had promised retribution.

And that brought them to now.

Unfortunately, the bad guy had found her at the gala. She'd spotted him in the crowd, and Gia had known she needed to get him out of there before he hurt someone.

Before her brothers got involved.

Her stomach jittered. She hadn't expected the idiot pull a gun on her on the balcony, in full view of a wall of glass windows and every guest at the party.

Her brothers would be here in minutes. She needed to take care of this.

That's what Gia did. She tidied up messes, helped people, made things right. Her PR firm was the best in San Francisco, and there were more than enough people and messes to keep her busy.

The man turned.

Gia darted out and kicked him. She felt her heel dig into his leg. He staggered and grunted.

She landed another kick to his leg, and he went down on his knees.

She pressed her gun to his temple and he froze.

"Don't move," she warned.

"You won't shoot me." He had a normal voice, nothing distinctive about it. He looked the same, as well. Ordinary. It probably made it easy to do your boss' dirty work when you blended into the crowd.

"You don't know me," she said. "You have no idea what I'm capable of." She sank confidence and authority into her voice. It was her "work" voice. "Leave me and Willow alone."

"My boss wants his gems back."

"Gems?"

"Yeah. Your friend helped herself to a bag of precious stones. Sapphires, emeralds, rubies."

Stupid, stupid Willow. All she'd told Gia was that she'd been seeing this guy, and then things had gone bad. Now she'd stolen *gemstones* from him. *God, Willow.*

"I'll talk to her."

"That's not good enough. Mr. Dennett needs more than that."

"I'll *talk* to her." Gia emphasized the words. "He'll get his gems back."

"I think it's better if you come with me. Your life might convince your friend."

The man exploded upward. He knocked the gun out of Gia's hand and it clattered to the stone paving.

Crap.

He rushed her. Gia dodged, well aware that he was bigger and stronger than her.

But Gia was smarter.

He reached for her, pushing against her shoulder. She let herself stagger and let out a gasp.

He grabbed a handful of her dress. *Better not ruin it,*

asshole. "Please... Please don't hurt me." She made herself cower.

"Come without any trouble and—"

Gia rammed the side of her stiff palm into his throat. He let her go and gagged.

She jammed her thumbs into his eyes and he growled, doubling over. Next, she grabbed his head and rammed her knee up, smashing into his nose.

She heard a crunch, and he cursed viciously.

She had to admit to feeling a bit of satisfaction. She'd always hated bullies who intimidated with their size.

She looked for her gun. *Where the hell was it?* Spotting the glint of something in the low light, she raced for it.

There was a bellow behind her, and the man charged. He tackled her, and they hit the ground hard.

The air whooshed out of Gia and pain exploded in a dozen places. *Ow.*

"Bitch, you'll pay for that."

She struggled, kicking at him. He was half on her body, pinning her down. Her dress hampered her movement. "You came after *me*, and you're pissed I fought back? Grow up."

He rose, and picked her up like a football, pinning her to his side. He let out an annoyed grunt.

He strode across the courtyard, skirting some construction work where a low stone wall was being rebuilt.

"You don't want to do this," she said. "You *really* don't want to meet my brothers." Speaking of her brothers, where the hell were they?

The bad guy grunted.

"Don't say I didn't warn you," she said breezily.

"Shut up," he bit out.

She tried to elbow him.

He reached over and slapped her face. *Ouch.* She pressed a hand to her cheek. *Asshole.*

The attack came out of nowhere.

There was the tiniest flash of movement and suddenly Gia was free. She hit the ground, landing on her hands and knees.

Her assailant staggered back, and a tall, dark, lean shadow attacked him.

Gia's heart leaped into her throat. She watched the vicious kicks and methodical punches. Her rescuer was almost elegant in the way he moved as he destroyed his opponent.

Except there was too much brutal power in his blows to be elegant.

Even in the darkness, she knew who it was.

She swallowed an inner groan. Of course, it had to be *him.* The bane of her existence. Her nemesis.

A shaft of light caught his face.

It was a hell of a face. Saxon Buchanan was not one of her brothers. He was her brother Vander's best friend, and Gia had known him half her life.

He was tall, with a muscled body that almost hid his strength. His collection of well-cut suits—which included the designer tuxedo he currently wore—disguised just how muscular and strong he was. It somehow minimized his broad shoulders and powerful legs. Her gaze moved back to his face.

Saxon had been in the military with Vander. He was from a wealthy, San Francisco family that went back generations, and they'd forbidden him to join the Army. He went anyway.

Saxon made his own rules.

He finished hitting her attacker and the man curled into a ball on the ground.

Saxon's head lifted, his gaze on her. The light caught his hair, and she couldn't decide if it was dark blond, or golden brown.

"You have some explaining to do," he said.

She sniffed.

His good breeding showed in the most handsome face she'd ever seen— strong jaw, straight nose, aristocratic features, and green eyes. Those eyes flared. He strode toward her and grabbed her forearms.

His long fingers on her skin sent a sizzle of sensation up her arms. She gasped. "I just needed some air."

A muscle ticked in his jaw. "Now isn't the time for clever words and games, Gia."

"Everything's fine. I had it under control."

Saxon made a harsh sound. "Under control? He was about to carry you out of here."

Wow, Saxon was really pissed. He was usually Mr. Cool and Suave, so it was interesting to see the tension in his face and body.

"It was *fine*." Damn, he had a habit of seeing her at her worst and rubbing it in.

He snorted. "What have you gotten yourself mixed up in?"

"None of your business." She went toe to toe with

him. She hated that he towered over her measly five feet, four inches. "You always try to stick your nose into my business. I already have three brothers. I don't need another one."

Saxon glared at her. "Believe me, I don't think of myself as your brother."

They stared at each other, gazes locked. Then one of his hands slid up and cupped her cheek. Her traitorous body shivered.

"I just saved you, and this is the thanks I get?"

"Thanks." She was well aware she didn't sound very grateful. She struggled for some control. "I had it in hand."

He glanced at the man, then back at Gia. "Willow dragged you into something."

Gia lifted her chin. "Like I said, none of your business."

Saxon leaned closer. "Contessa, after seeing this asshole shoot at you, I'm making you my business."

What? "Don't use that ridiculous name."

"What the fuck is going on?"

The deep voice, with a lethal edge, made goosebumps rise on Gia's bare arms.

She turned her head and saw Easton first. Her older brother wore a tuxedo and looked gorgeous. Their Italian-American heritage showed through in Easton's dark hair and good looks. He had an air of authority, every inch the big brother and successful businessman. He frowned at the attacker, then scanned her, relief on his face.

But it was Vander who'd spoken. He stood half in the

shadows, like the darkness wanted to cling to him.

He stepped forward. Vander had badass deeply embedded in his DNA, and it had been there even when he was a kid. Despite loving him to bits, there were times when he scared her.

He was intense, and he thrived on control, and she was well aware that he was dangerous.

His tuxedo didn't hide any of that.

Saxon gave her a little shake. She looked up at him and she gave a start.

She realized that he had the same dangerous glint in his green eyes. He just hid it better than Vander.

She cleared her throat. *Time to face the music.*

SAXON BUCHANAN WAS PISSED as hell.

He saw the man on the ground move and shot him a glare. The guy stilled. The asshole had fired on Gia. Tried to abduct her. Had put her in danger.

Saxon's fingers flexed on her arm. *Big mistake.*

He looked down at Gia. As always, her stubborn jaw was lifted as she faced down Vander. And as usual, Saxon felt the competing urges to hit that jaw, or bite it.

The thought of biting Gia Norcross—in many and varied locations—fired his blood.

Fuck.

He shut the thought down as best he could. He'd had years of practice. He tried to remember her as the opinionated, twelve-year-old from the first time he'd met her. At sixteen, after being booted out of his expensive private school, Saxon had been sent to a local high school. Despite their differences, he and Vander had clicked. He'd spent as much time in the Norcross family home as he could. It had been much better than the stifling mausoleum his parents called home.

He'd watched Gia transform from his best friend's pesky sister into a gorgeous, feisty, smart woman.

It'd been uncomfortable at first—the flashes of lust he'd had for her when she'd grown breasts. *Definitely* not appropriate.

But as always, she'd been off-limits—far too young, and Vander's little sister.

Vander wasn't related to Saxon by blood, but they were brothers in every other sense. Saxon had vowed that he would never, ever cross the boundary with his best friend's sister.

It didn't help that he and Gia seemed to irritate each other without barely trying. Damn, Saxon loved seeing her chocolate-brown eyes fire up.

She was no longer underage, but after ten years in the military, and a lot of those in Ghost Ops doing the dirtiest, meanest, and hardest jobs the government needed done...

Saxon blew out a breath. Not to mention his fucked-up family. He had baggage he'd never, ever unload on a woman. He liked his relationships brief, uncomplicated, and simple.

And Gia would always be Vander's little sister.

But seeing that asshole draw a gun on her...

Seeing her in danger.

Something inside Saxon had cracked open. He would pull out all the stops to keep Gia safe.

"Willow has a thing," Gia said.

Vander cursed and Easton looked up at the night sky, jaw tight.

Saxon *knew* it. That woman was trouble.

Vander cocked his head. "Willow dragged you into this mess, which ends up with you getting shot at and almost snatched."

"Yes." Gia's chin lifted another inch.

"Cut her loose," Vander bit out. "I'll get word out to whoever's after her that you are *not* involved."

The man on the ground finally shook off his grogginess and raised his head. He looked at Vander and went still. "You're Vander Norcross."

Vander just stared at him.

"And she's his sister," Saxon added.

"Fuck," the man breathed. Then he gathered himself. "It won't stop my boss. He wants his gems back."

"Gems?" Saxon cut a glance to Gia.

She sighed. "Willow was seeing a guy. They had words—"

"He dumped her drug-addicted ass," the man said.

"She took a bag of precious stones from him," Gia said.

"Jesus," Vander scowled. "Cut her loose."

"Vander, no." Gia grabbed her brother's arm. "You know she had a rough childhood. She—"

"Is an adult," Saxon said, interrupting her. "She can't keep using that as an excuse to fuck up."

Gia's eyes narrowed. "You might've grown up with a set of silver spoons shoved in your mouth, but she didn't."

"She's trouble, Gia," Easton said. "Always was, even though you couldn't see it. Your loyalty is admirable..."

"No, it's not," Saxon said. "It's stupid."

Those brown eyes—surrounded by ridiculously long lashes—flared hot. "You never miss a chance to tell me I'm stupid."

"Contessa—"

"No." She cut her hand through the air. "Willow has no one. Anyway, she's gone now. If she calls, I'll tell her to return what she stole."

Shit. Saxon did admire Gia's loyalty, but he was still mad. He knew that whoever Gia loved, she protected them fiercely.

Vander crouched by the man. "Who's your boss?"

The man didn't hesitate. "Kyle Dennett."

Saxon barely controlled his sneer. An upstart trying to make a name for himself in the San Francisco drug trade. The guy had a few legit businesses—bars, a club. But you didn't have to dig far below the veneer of businessman to find filth.

"You tell him that Gia is off your radar, otherwise he'll deal with me," Vander said.

The man nodded.

Saxon stepped closer, then noticed something. He gripped Gia's chin and tilted it up.

"Hey, hands off—" She tried to jerk out of his hold.

"Your cheek is swelling."

Three sets of male eyes swung to the man. He looked

like he was hoping the ground would open and swallow him up.

"Did you hit her?" Saxon asked softly.

Gia cleared her throat. "Guys—"

Saxon gripped the back of the man's shirt and started dragging him across the courtyard.

"Saxon!" She moved to follow.

Then Saxon heard her make a sound.

"Let go of me, Easton!"

Saxon delivered a hard punch to the man's face. He groaned. Saxon felt icy, deadly calm spread over him.

Suddenly, the man leaped up and attacked. He kicked Saxon's knee and Saxon staggered, but caught his balance.

The man launched at Saxon. Clearly, the guy had been play-acting, and wasn't as hurt as he'd seemed.

"Do something!" Gia cried.

"Sax has it," Easton murmured.

Dennett's man lunged forward, and Saxon let him get a hit in. His fist rammed into Saxon's gut. But that got the man close, and Saxon followed through with a hard jab to the face, then a chop to the back of the man's neck. Saxon put all his strength into it.

With a groan, the man went to his knees, blood streaming down his face and soaking into his shirt.

"Hurt her again, and this will seem like just a bit of fun," Saxon warned.

Then Saxon turned, tugging the hem of his jacket and dusting it off.

Gia was staring at him, her gaze running over his

body like she was looking for injuries. Then she looked behind Saxon. Her face changed and he tensed.

Suddenly, she broke free of Easton. She was right near the construction and scooped up a hunk of rock. She threw it.

For a second, Saxon thought she was throwing it at him.

The rock sailed right past him and as he swiveled, he saw the chunk of stone hit Dennett's guy right between the eyes.

He howled, and dropped the gun that he'd pulled from somewhere.

The Norcross brothers raced forward, and soon had the man on his belly, hands zip tied.

Saxon stared at Gia. He saw fear on her face before she quickly hid it.

"*Bastardo.*" She spat at the man on the ground.

Saxon's lips twitched. Mrs. Norcross was Italian-American, and had clearly passed on some curses to Gia.

God, she was beautiful. A tiny Italian goddess.

"Gia." Saxon desperately wanted to touch her, but couldn't risk it.

He'd want more, take more.

He was pretty sure her brothers wouldn't like him kissing the hell out of her in front of them.

"Lucky you were so damn good at softball, Gia," Easton said.

Vander and Easton heaved the man up.

"I'll take care of this." Vander shot Gia an unhappy look. "You fucking deal with Willow, Gia. She's out of your life."

With one hand clamped on the groggy thug's arm, Vander dragged the man away.

"I'll check on Rhys," Easton said. "He's with Haven, and mom and dad, keeping an eye on things inside. I'll let everyone know that you're okay." Easton swiveled and headed up the steps back to the gala.

"I'll take you home," Saxon said.

Gia wrapped her arms around herself, her face pale. "I have my driver."

"I'll take you home," he said again.

"No." She shook her head. "I've had enough for tonight. I want to be alone."

"You need to cut Willow off, Gia."

"Don't start, Saxon."

He grabbed her arm. "Her mess could have gotten you killed. Tonight could have turned out very differently."

Gia looked sad and tired. "She's my friend."

"She's not a very good one."

"Enough. *God*. You're always questioning my judgment. Back off, Saxon. I'm not a brainless doll."

No, she was one of the smartest, savviest people he knew. But he didn't want her hurt. Willow would take advantage, like she always did.

"I never said you were brainless, but sometimes you make bad choices when it comes to those you care about."

"And you never let me forget it." Her hands balled into fists. "Quit picking on me!"

He reached out and tugged on one of her curls. He loved her thick mass of curly, dark hair. "Contessa, if I didn't pick on you, you'd feel deprived."

She made an annoyed sound and knocked his arm away. "Leave me alone, Saxon Buchanan!"

He waited a beat. She usually got creative when she started ranting. "That all you've got?" Damn, arguing with her got his blood pumping.

Her nose wrinkled. "I was hoping for something more dramatic than that, but that's the best I've got. I'm tired and sore." She stormed off, her dress flaring behind her.

Saxon shook his head. It was getting harder and harder to ignore how he felt about Gia. He'd been trying to leave her alone for years. His hands flexed.

Gia Norcross had been off-limits for a long time.

But tonight, that changed.

CHAPTER TWO

S he was going to need more concealer.

In her lovely bathroom, her little sanctuary, Gia dabbed on her makeup.

She was headed to work shortly, had a full day ahead of her, and needed to hide two sleepless nights and her bruises.

She hadn't slept much Saturday night after the gala, and she'd spent Sunday locked in her apartment, ignoring the world, and worrying about Willow. Everyone had called to check on Gia, and she'd done her best to reassure them she was all right. Last night, she'd been exhausted and sure she'd sleep. Instead, she'd had nightmares of Dennett's man chasing her...but as she ran, he'd morphed into a steely-eyed Saxon, which had strangely scared her more.

Finally, Gia had fallen into a restless sleep in the early hours, then slept through her alarm. Which meant she was late. She *hated* being late.

She blew out a breath and studied her reflection.

That would have to do. She walked into her bedroom, wearing only her black bra and panties. Gia loved lingerie. She owned zero pairs of granny panties, and she had more bra and panty sets than she'd ever 'fess up to. She stepped into a sleek, navy-blue dress, and pulled her hair up into a twist.

She dug around in her walk-in wardrobe, and found a pair of navy Jimmy Choo pumps.

Then, her cell phone rang.

Cursing, she ran into the kitchen. She could run in heels just fine. She was the shortest in her family, so she'd been trying to compensate for years. Hell, she could probably run a marathon in heels. Okay, maybe not a marathon since she hated running.

She snatched her phone off the kitchen island. It was Haven.

"Hi, girlfriend. I told you yesterday, I'm fine."

"G, I'm the queen of telling people that I'm fine when I'm not. Don't kid a kidder."

Gia sighed. "Fine. I didn't sleep well. I'm worried about Willow."

"But not yourself," Haven said dryly.

"And I want to skewer Saxon with a fork and watch him bleed."

"Hmm."

Haven had a funny tone to her voice. "What does that mean?"

"It means *hmm*."

"Haven—"

"It means that after thirty seconds around you two, I

feel the need for a cigarette. And I've never smoked in my life."

Gia sniffed. "I've no idea what you're talking about."

"You know, Gia. You're the smartest woman I know."

"He's like an annoying older brother." *Liar, liar, Gia Gabriella.* She'd never, not once, thought brotherly thoughts about Saxon Buchanan.

"Hmm," Haven said again.

"I'm ignoring that and hanging up now. I have to get to work."

"I won't forget. One night, I'm going to get you tipsy on your favorite Syrah, and you're going to tell me all about your supernova sexual tension with the oh-so-sexy Saxon."

"Nothing to tell. Okay, bye."

Shoving all thoughts of Saxon down deep and clanking a big padlock on them, Gia grabbed her things and strode out of her apartment.

She lived in a gorgeous building in SoMa. Between her apartment and her business, she owed way too much to the bank, but thankfully, Easton was a financial whiz. After he'd left the Army Rangers, he'd dedicated himself to making money. He managed all her investments, and Firelight PR turned over a tidy profit.

Her car was waiting out front. Her driver, Rob—a buff man in his late forties—opened the door for her.

"Morning, Ms. Norcross."

"Good morning, Rob. How's Katie today?"

The man grinned. "That florist you suggested did the trick. She loved the flowers, and forgave me."

"Wonderful news." Gia slid into the back seat of the Mercedes.

Rob had lost his first wife five years ago to cancer. He'd found navigating the dating scene hard, but had ended up falling for the sweet, forty-something school-teacher who lived next door to him.

The car slid into traffic. Gia's office was downtown, so there wasn't far to go, but she got a lot of work done on her phone on the drive.

Gia was happy for Rob and Katie. And Haven and Rhys. Gia had no time for a man, and had yet to meet one who could keep up with her. So many felt intimidated, or were needy, or competitive. The last guy she'd dated could not handle the fact she made more money than he did.

Lifting her phone, she opened her emails. Work was all she needed.

She started sorting through the urgent stuff that needed her attention. She had her assistant cull lots of them. She also had a great team at Firelight PR. She *loved* her job.

She did work for Easton, especially for the Hutton. She did work for Vander when he let her. Norcross Security at least had a website, but much to her dismay, no social media presence. Vander had made it very clear that he'd never post on social media.

She saw an email from a Kenneth Grahame and froze. He was the author of an old English children's story, *Wind in the Willows*.

Willow.

She opened it. There were only two words. *I'm okay.*

Gia closed her eyes. Her friend was okay. Of course, Willow hadn't thought to ask about Gia.

Willow had survived a tough upbringing. Her mom had been an alcoholic, and her dad had just been plain mean. They hadn't been poor, but they'd been definitely on the bottom rung of middle-class, and clinging to it desperately. Willow had always resented that she'd had to go without. And when times were tough, her dad had coped by hitting Willow and her mom sometimes.

Willow always had an edginess to her, like she was looking for where the next blow might come from, or searching for her next escape route. She'd been wild, and still was. Teenage Gia had been in awe of her.

Now, grown-up Gia was just worried about her friend. They weren't as close as they had been. Willow had a drug problem, and Gia had paid for rehab twice. Her heart twisted. Willow had stayed four days the first time, and two days the second time around.

Her brothers and Saxon wanted Gia to cut her off, but then Willow would have no one.

Gia remembered that Willow had been the one who'd taught Gia to use makeup. They'd giggled together about boys. She'd helped Gia get revenge on Nancy Butler, who'd kissed Gia's boyfriend at school. There'd been a lot of toilet paper involved.

She smiled, remembering those days. Willow was also the only person a young Gia had confessed to that she had a deep crush on her brother's best friend. Yeah, she'd crushed hard on the gorgeous, beautiful, golden Saxon Buchanan...for about thirty seconds. She'd been twelve and full of budding hormones. He'd been sixteen, and took every chance to tease Gia—about her hair, about being on the debate team, about her boyfriends, about everything.

Argh, he made her lose her temper quicker than anyone she'd ever known. Over his and Vander's last few years at school, Saxon had become her nemesis. Whenever they'd been in the same room, they'd argued. He'd teased her and she'd shouted at him. The man thought he was better than everyone else, and he was so damn bossy. She'd watched him work his way through all the cheerleaders at school with ridiculous ease. It had been Gia's sworn duty to keep the man's ego from growing to epic proportions.

She might have shed a tear or two when he'd enlisted with Vander and they'd both joined the Army. Not that she'd *ever* tell Saxon that.

She'd seen him occasionally when he and her brothers were on leave from Delta Force. Even then, Saxon had excelled at annoying the hell out of her. The man knew just what buttons to press, the arrogant know-it-all.

Gia shook it all off as the car stopped. "Thanks, Rob."

"Call me if you need me."

She strode into the building. She loved the bright, airy lobby. Firelight PR took up two floors, and she kept tapping on her phone as she rode the elevator up.

"Morning, Janine," she said to the receptionist at the high, polished reception desk.

"Good morning, Ms. Norcross." The bubbly blonde smiled back.

Gia strode through the open-plan office area. Phones

were ringing, keyboards clacking, and several people surrounded a whiteboard, having a spirited debate.

Ah, yes, she loved her work.

She neared her corner office, and outside, her assistant Ashley Wu rose from her desk. She was two years older than Gia, with the long lean body of a dancer. She was also the most organized woman on the planet.

"Morning." Ashley held out a takeout coffee cup.

"I knew there was a reason I employed you." Gia sipped and groaned.

"Late night?" Ashley's long, dark hair was black at the top, but slowly changed colors to a silver-pink at the ends.

"Rough night," Gia corrected. "Caffeine will be my God today."

"How was the gala?"

"Great."

Ashley lifted a newspaper off her desk. "Uneventful?"

Gia saw the headline. *Shootout at Museum Charity Gala*.

"Hmm." Gia drank some more coffee.

"It says that a woman in a gorgeous blue Alberta Ferretti dress and a man pulled guns and fired on each other."

Oh, crap. "Really?"

"Gia, I helped you pick out that dress. I'm guessing Easton pulled a ton of strings for your name not to be in here." Ashley stabbed the paper.

"My brothers handled it."

Ashley got a dreamy, faraway look on her face.

"Ash?"

"Sorry, just a little daydream about your brothers handling me. All three of them, at the same time."

"Ew, stop fantasizing about my brothers." Gia had suffered her entire life having three hot brothers. "And Rhys is taken now."

"I hate Haven," Ashley said good-naturedly. "That lucky bitch."

Smiling, Gia crossed to her office.

It was airy, elegant, with pops of color. The windows at one end let in lots of light. Behind her wide, pale-wood desk she had built in shelves that flanked a colorful painting done in splatters of pink, yellow, blue, and green. Two comfy, yet stylish, white guest chairs sat in front of her desk. At the other end of the space was a sleek, feminine chesterfield sofa with lots of colorful pillows.

She dumped her bag on her desk. "I don't want to talk about the museum. Everything is fine."

Ashley's nose wrinkled.

Gia raised a brow. "Okay, what have we got today?"

"Meetings, meetings, and more meetings." Ever efficient, Ashley lifted her tablet. "You have a nine AM call about the Rivera account. Potential new client coming in at ten. She's expanding her chain of sports bars and wants a full workup for the launch and branding. Eleven AM, team workshop. And then you have a lunch meeting." Ashley winced.

Gia sat. "With?"

"Neil Robinson."

Now Gia groaned. She'd had one meeting with

Robinson. He was an up-and-coming businessman, and he'd asked her out about thirty times during that meeting. She'd told him no, repeatedly, and stressed that she didn't date clients. For the next meeting, he'd demanded a dinner meet, but she'd managed to talk him into lunch.

"Do we really need his account?" Ashley asked.

"I can handle him."

Gia's morning was a whirlwind. She thrived on it. She loved working with people. She loved solving problems. She loved being productive.

At 12:25, she walked into the EPIC Steak restaurant on the waterfront in the Embarcadero. The place had great food, lots of leather and industrial-metal accents, and a killer view.

Neil Robinson rose from a table near the windows, the Bay Bridge behind him, and a wide smile on his face.

He was handsome, in a clean-cut way—maybe six feet tall, with a trim body that he clearly kept in shape. But Gia spent time with men who kept in military shape. She had a secret obsession with powerful thighs, hard abs, and brawny arms. Not to mention a little ink.

Pretty and glossy didn't really do much for her unless it came with an edge.

"Gia, a pleasure. You look beautiful."

Ugh. Neil just couldn't get "business meeting" into his head.

"Neil."

She sat and he took the seat beside her. "I'll get you a drink. Wine?"

"I don't drink at business meetings."

His smile faltered, then reformed. "Oh, but this is business *and* pleasure."

"I'll have a soda with a twist of lime, please."

He didn't look happy, but he passed her order onto the waitress.

"So, let's get down to business," Gia said.

Neil smiled, and under the table, he put his hand on her thigh.

She kept her face bland, and shifted his hand away. This was going to be a long, annoying lunch.

———

SAXON STRODE toward the double-door entrance to EPIC Steak.

Gia's assistant had told him where to find her. He scowled. She should have stayed at her office. He'd arrived at her apartment this morning, and tailed her and her driver to her office.

Vander had sent a pretty strong message to Dennett to stay away from Gia. But until Willow returned the gems, or Dennett confirmed he was no longer targeting Gia, Saxon wouldn't consider her safe.

A statuesque brunette walked past him and shot him a lingering look.

He ignored her and moved on. He'd spent his morning digging up dirt on Kyle Dennett. He didn't like what he was finding.

Norcross Security operated on both sides of the legal line. Occasionally, they had to work with scum to get the info they needed to get a job done successfully. Saxon had no qualms about dipping his toe into the gray. His time in the military, especially in Ghost Ops, had taught him that right and wrong could get pretty fucking subjective in shitty situations. He had his own code, and he followed it.

"Saxon."

The cool, female voice made him fight back a sigh. He glanced up at the woman who'd just exited the restaurant. "Mother."

Tall, impossibly thin, and decked out in Chanel, his mother looked ten years younger than she was. Her blonde hair was perfectly styled an inch above her shoulders.

She eyed his rolled-up sleeves and ink with distaste. "I just finished lunch with friends from the country club. What are you doing here?"

It was Monday, what did she think he was doing? "I'm working."

Her nose wrinkled.

Saxon knew she was about to launch into a tirade. His parents made it very clear how they felt about him working, especially in security.

No, they'd much rather he skimmed off his trust fund, married a socialite, and did nothing.

"Sorry, Mother, I'm busy. I have to go." He dutifully kissed her cheek. "You look fabulous, as always."

Vanessa Buchanan had a killer plastic surgeon.

"Very well. You should come for dinner sometime."

At that loving, heartfelt invitation, he nodded and pushed through the doors.

At the hostess desk, a stylishly dressed redhead in her

twenties shot him a welcoming smile. "Hello, welcome to EPIC Steak."

"The Norcross table."

The woman's smile dimmed. "They're seated by the windows, but I believe all the guests have arrived."

Saxon spotted Gia straightaway. Her curls were tamed up into a twist, exposing her slender neck. So fucking sexy.

He strode toward them. Then he saw the asshole in a suit with shiny hair lean closer to her. Saxon had the right line of sight to see the man slide his hand onto her leg.

Saxon's gaze whipped back to Gia's face. Was she on a date?

No. Her face was composed, her professional look. Only someone who knew her well would sense the temper brewing.

She moved the asshole's hand, clearly attempting to redirect the conversation.

Saxon strode closer, coming up behind them.

"Neil, this is a business meeting. I expect you to act professionally, if you want to work with Firelight PR and have us take on your account. Please keep your hands to yourself."

"Gia, you must feel our attraction." The man leaned in. "I want you naked. I want to fuck you." His hand went sliding under the table again.

Saxon saw red.

He gripped the idiot and yanked him out of his chair.

The asshole yelped, and the chair tipped over. The guests at nearby tables gasped.

Gia shot to her feet. "Saxon!"

"She said hands off, asshole."

The suit straightened. "Who the hell are you?"

"The guy who'll make sure you keep your hands to yourself."

Mr. Shiny Hair frowned and looked at Gia. "Are you with this guy? Everyone I spoke with said you were single."

Gia made a sound that Saxon knew well. She was heading toward losing it. She'd made that sound with Saxon too many times to count.

"Whether I'm seeing anyone or not is none of your business, Neil. As I've told you *repeatedly*, and you haven't listened, I'm not interested in you personally, only professionally."

"So, you are fucking him?"

Saxon growled and took a step forward. Gia slapped a hand to his chest. "Not one more step, Saxon." She turned to the man. "It wouldn't matter if I was sleeping with the entire lineup of the San Francisco 49ers. Who I sleep with is *none* of your business." She drew in a breath. "I don't think you're the right fit for Firelight PR, Neil. I'd be happy to give you some recommendations for other firms."

"Fuck you. I've wasted weeks on you."

Saxon lunged and punched the guy in his glossy teeth.

With a cry, Neil flew back into several chairs, knocking them over. He flopped around on the ground.

"Just great." Brown eyes skewered Saxon. "You can't solve everything with your fists, you know?"

"Why not?"

She glanced at him, her look withering, then turned and tossed her napkin on the man on the floor. "Goodbye, Neil. Don't call me again."

Then Gia took Saxon's hand and dragged him out of the restaurant.

Gia nodded at the open-mouthed hostess. "Sorry for the drama. Please put the drinks on my account."

She towed Saxon outside and spun to face him. "Why are you here? How dare you barge your way into my business meeting and punch my potential client in the face."

"He was an asshole."

"I'm aware of that."

"I need to talk to you."

"So pick up the phone."

"Would you have answered?'

Her nose wrinkled. "Possibly." She sighed. "Let me call my driver."

"I have my car." He pressed a hand to the small of her back, sending electricity tingling across his fingers. She was a tiny, curvy package. He wanted to tug her curls out of the tidy roll they were trapped in.

"So, you like having potential clients paw you?" There was an edge to his voice, but he couldn't seem to tone it down.

"No. I was dealing with it."

"Like you were dealing with things Saturday night?"

Her glare was hot enough to melt metal. "Finesse takes time, Saxon. You don't have to resort to violence in one millisecond."

"You shouldn't have left the office."

"God, you're so bossy."

"Your point?"

"Take the time to *talk* to people, Buchanan. Ask, explain, use your pleases and thank yous. You know, act like a nice person."

He raised a brow.

She huffed out a breath. "You are *aggravating*."

"Right back at you, Contessa."

"Why shouldn't I have left the office?" she asked, with exaggerated patience.

"It's not safe yet. Until Willow returns the gems, there's still a risk Dennett will target you."

Saxon stopped by his dark-blue Bentley Continental GT.

Gia faced him. "Dennett knows I don't have them, and that he risks going up against Vander and Norcross Security if he pursues this. He won't come after me again, which is why Vander didn't order me to stay at the office."

Saxon pressed his hands to the car either side of her, caging her in. "That's not a risk I'm willing to take, Gia."

She swallowed, and the air between them charged.

Oh yeah, Gia Norcross liked to irritate the fuck out of him, but she felt the incessant, always-simmering attraction between them.

Saxon leaned an inch closer and their breath mingled. "I'll do whatever it takes to keep you safe."

She eyed his lips. "Because I'm Vander's sister?"

"Yes. And because I've known you half my life. And because I want to keep that curvy little body of yours in one piece."

She pressed a hand to his chest. "Step back."

He hesitated, then did as she asked. They were exposed on the street, but soon, very soon, he'd get Gia alone and make things clear to her. He reached past her and opened the car door for her.

After he closed the door, he circled the car and slid inside.

"Why are you so worried about this Dennett guy?" she asked.

Saxon expertly pulled into traffic. "He's trying to make a name for himself."

"Doing?"

"A bit of this, a bit of that. Drugs. Prostitution."

"God, why are there so many assholes in the world?" she grumbled.

Saxon noted that she was stroking the leather seat. He watched those neat, painted nails and thought of them stroking other things. "You like my car?"

"It's a nice car." She glanced at him. "Only the best for Saxon Buchanan."

Everyone liked to give him hell about liking the best. So what if he liked his cars expensive, his suits tailored, and his sheets one-thousand thread count? He could afford it, and he'd spent ten fucking years on missions sleeping in clothes he'd worn for days, smelling ripe, in the middle of warzones. "Well, I wouldn't buy a shit car."

She snorted. "So, Dennett's making a name for himself."

"Proving himself. Making an impression with people he'd like to work with. Makes him unpredictable. If word gets out that his junkie ex-girlfriend stole a bag of precious stones, his rep takes a hit."

"Hmm." Gia tapped her nails on the dash.

"And the bag of stones is worth two hundred and fifty grand."

"What?" Her mouth dropped open.

"Your friend didn't just steal a few baubles."

Gia looked out the window. "Goddamn you, Willow."

"She contact you?"

Gia touched her earlobe. A tell.

"Gia," he growled.

"She sent an email to let me know that she was safe."

He growled again. "Willow thinking only of Willow."

"She wasn't always like that."

"She was. She was always jealous of you."

"What?" Gia frowned.

Saxon pulled up in front of her office building.

"Get inside, Gia. No more lunch dates. Head straight home after work, and once Vander has confirmation you're clear of Dennett, then you can wander the streets."

"You love telling people what to do, don't you?"

He considered for a second. "Yeah."

She opened the door and smiled. It wasn't a pleasant one. "Any other orders, Master Buchanan?"

He smiled. "Yes, you can call me Master Buchanan all the time, now."

She got out, flashing her slender legs, which his cock definitely noticed. She shot him one more glare, then slammed the door.

He watched her stride inside, hips swinging. He blew out a breath and gripped the wheel.

His hunger for Gia Norcross was no longer under control. Once she was safe, he was making her his, one way or another.

CHAPTER THREE

G od, she was tired.

After her lovely lunch with Neil, and the confrontation with Saxon, she'd gotten back to an afternoon of problems. A client caught up in a Twitter storm. Another client caught in a scandal involving a woman who was definitely not his wife.

Gia was tired to the bone and her face was throbbing.

She unlocked her apartment door. At least she didn't look as bad as poor Haven had. During a theft at the museum, when a Monet had been stolen, her friend had been beaten. Haven's bruises had lasted for days.

Haven had powered through, and she'd had Rhys at her side.

Gia was going to have a glass of red wine, and then sleep. She'd power through tomorrow.

She dumped her things on the island and kicked off her shoes.

Home. She loved her light, beautiful two-bedroom apartment. She had a gorgeous kitchen she didn't have enough time to use. A spa-like master bathroom that was her favorite room in the place. And a balcony with great views.

SHE SMILED, feeling a sense of peace wash over her. She'd picked out every little thing. Her apartment was her sanctuary. The place where she could shed her kick-ass, successful PR persona, and just be herself. There was nothing to prove, no one to impress.

A quick *rat-a-tat-tat* knock on her door made her frown. Someone had gotten past the doorman.

She checked the peephole and her pulse leaped.

Willow.

Gia wrenched open the door. "Will."

Her friend pushed in. Willow's face was twitchy, her blue eyes bright. She shoved her hair back. In high school, it had been thick and blonde, now it was stringy and the color of dishwater.

Willow was tall and far too thin. She paced into Gia's apartment and whirled.

Gia studied her friend's face carefully and let out a breath. "You're high."

"I'm in a fuck load of trouble, Gigi. I needed to chill a bit, take the edge off."

"You got yourself into this situation by stealing a quarter of a *million* dollars of gems that aren't yours."

Willow shifted her beaten-up running shoes. "Dennett's got loads of money. Why shouldn't I get some?"

"Because it's *his*." Even if it was ill-gotten. "You stole from him."

Willow shrugged a thin shoulder. "I thought you'd take my side."

Crap, Gia had been taking Willow's side for years. Excusing her friend's poor choices. Saxon's voice rang in her head.

God, had she been enabling Willow?

"Dennett's man came after me," Gia said. "He threatened me. You need to return the gems."

Willow went silent, chewing on her lip. "You look okay."

"He pulled a *gun* on me. He shot at me."

"Your brothers won't let anything happen to you. And that golden-boy snob would take a bullet for you."

"Saxon?"

"Yes," Willow sneered. "He won't let anything happen to his precious princess."

"Saxon is just—"

"Has fucking wanted you since before you were legal."

The words sent a jolt through Gia.

"That blue-blooded asshole wouldn't look at me twice, but you..." Jealousy laced Willow's voice.

Gia dragged in a breath. Right now, this wasn't about Saxon. "Look, focus on Dennett. You need to—"

"His guys have been tailing me all day." Willow wiped a hand across her mouth. "I need—"

Gia straightened. "Did they follow you here?"

"Pretty sure I lost them." Willow pulled a small, black bag from her pocket. "Look, Gigi, I just need to stash these here. Just for a bit."

"Willow, no." Her brothers and Saxon would lose their minds.

"I need to make things right. *Please.* Just hide them for a few hours and I'll fix this, Gigi."

Willow threw her arms around Gia in a tight hug. She was so thin, and the desperation wafted off her.

"Okay." *You're an idiot, Gia Norcross.* "Just for a few hours, Will."

"Thank you." Her friend smiled, the old Willow shining through.

Gia took the bag. It felt far too light for two hundred and fifty thousand dollars.

"I'm going to make this right." Willow opened the front door. "You'll see."

Then she was gone.

Gia dropped heavily onto her lovely suede couch. The temptation was too much and she opened the bag.

She gasped. *Oh, wow.*

The stones were cool on her palm. Blood-red rubies, deep-green emeralds, jewel-blue sapphires, some large, pale-pink stone.

She gave herself a second to imagine a set of ruby earrings, or a gorgeous emerald necklace.

Then she shoved the gems back in the bag. She moved over to the floating shelf on her living room wall. She popped a panel on the side and slid the bag inside the hollow wood. She set the panel back in place.

She really wanted that glass of wine, but if her brothers found out that she had the gems and she hadn't told them...

If Saxon found out, he'd ride her for days for being stupid.

She needed to visit Norcross.

Saxon's warnings echoed in her head. She bit her lip. She didn't believe Dennett was stupid enough to go up against her brothers. Still, she needed to be smart. She'd change, and get an Uber straight over to the Norcross office.

Hurrying into her bedroom, she stripped her work dress off and pulled her hair out of its twist. She pulled on her yoga gear—black leggings, lilac top, and her favorite hoodie sweatshirt that she only wore at home. The gray fabric settled comfortingly around her. No one would expect stylish Gia Norcross to be wearing a hoodie.

As she walked through the living room, she glanced at the shelf and felt the weight of those damn gems. She wanted them gone, and she wanted Willow safe.

Gia grabbed her keys and phone. She decided to be extra careful and take the stairs. Dammit, Saxon had her imagining the bogeyman everywhere.

In the lobby, she pulled the hood up over her hair and swiped the Uber app on her phone.

The car arrived, and as far as she could tell, no one was paying her any attention.

It was a short ride to South Beach, where Vander had purchased an old warehouse several years back to house the Norcross office—then completely gutted and renovated it. Now, the bottom level of the warehouse housed the fleet of BMW SUVs that the Norcross team used, a high-tech gym, and cells. Okay, technically, holding rooms. The next level was mostly open plan, with glass-walled offices that the guys barely used. Every time she'd visited, the Norcross men were in the field doing badass security and investigations stuff. Sitting at a desk was not their favorite thing to do.

She'd helped Vander pick out the interior for the office. The inside had a concrete-and-steel, industrial vibe that suited Vander. The upper floor and roof terrace were Vander's private domain and home.

Gia slipped out of the Uber with a thank you, and headed down the street, looking quickly toward the warehouse.

Suddenly, a small, wiry body raced out of an alley and slammed into her.

"Hey!" she cried.

The man, only inches taller than her, pulled a knife. "Give me the bag."

"I don't have a bag."

"The gems," he barked.

Oh, shit. He must be one of the guys who'd been following Willow.

"She gave them to you," the man snapped. "I want them."

Gia stiffened. Then in her haughtiest voice, she said, "I have no idea what you're talking about."

The knife slashed and Gia felt a sting of pain on her forearm.

Anger exploded inside her. She'd had a crappy, trying few days. Her mama liked to say that Gia had inherited her fiery, Italian temper from her.

Gia struck. She chopped her hand into her attacker's arm. With a shout, his knife dropped to the pavement.

She kicked him in the crotch, but he deflected at the last second and she caught his thigh. She kept attacking. She'd been taught well, but she knew she would never be as strong as a male attacker. She had to attack fast and hard, before he realized that she meant business.

She rammed her elbow into his neck and he coughed. Then he reached out and grabbed her hoodie and hair, and yanked.

Ow. Ow. Ow. Tears threatened. Her scalp felt like it was on fire. She jerked her arms up violently, breaking his hold, and probably losing a few strands of hair in the process.

But now he attacked full force.

His body drove into hers, slamming her into a nearby brick wall. It knocked the wind out of her.

He snatched the knife off the concrete and pressed it to her throat.

Gia froze. *Oh, shit.* She felt the sting on her neck. Her first worry was about what germs and grime might be on the blade.

The man's eyes glittered with rage. *Screw this.* She rammed her knee up between his legs. Really hard.

He made a horrible noise and she almost felt sorry for him. He dropped the knife again, and she shoved away from him.

The man raised his head, and she saw the frightening promise of retribution on his face.

"Hey!" a deep male voice roared.

Her attacker spun and awkwardly ran off, hunched over and hobbling.

Gia picked up the switchblade. "I'm keeping this, asshole."

A tall man appeared beside her.

Ace Oliveira, Norcross' guru of all things tech and electronic, looked *nothing* like any geek she'd ever seen. He was tall, dark, and Brazilian. His long, dark hair was pulled back in a sexy ponytail, showcasing the angles of his handsome face. His body was long, rangy, and muscled.

"Gia, you okay?"

"Yes." But the shaking was setting in. "I'm okay."

His dark eyes were concerned. "You're bleeding."

She swiped a hand across her neck. "Um, I think I'll head home."

Ace's gaze narrowed.

"Can you...um, forget you ever saw this?"

"No." He took her arm, his grip strong, and herded her toward the Norcross office.

Shit, she was afraid of that.

SAXON HAD JUST FINISHED up with some searches on his laptop—tapping a few PI databases—when he heard the dangerous snap of Vander's voice.

"What the fuck?"

Pushing back from his desk, Saxon strode into the central open area of the Norcross office.

Ace and Vander were scowling at a small woman with her back toward Saxon and a hood over her head.

But he'd recognize that curvy little ass anywhere. Hell, he'd dreamed about it constantly.

"Gia?"

She turned.

Saxon's blood ran cold.

Blood was smeared across her neck and on one arm of her sweatshirt.

He advanced and she held her hand up. "I'm fine—"

Saxon crossed the space in a few strides. He cupped her cheek, tilting her head back.

"Guy with a knife attacked her out front," Ace said.

Saxon's blood ran from ice cold to boiling hot. "I told you to stay in your office, or at home."

She dragged in a breath. "I know—"

"I told you that you were still in danger."

"You said that I *might* be in danger." That chin lifted. "I got an Uber, and I wore different clothes."

Saxon studied the line marring her delicate throat, and something ugly churned in his gut. If the bastard had cut her any deeper—

Saxon gripped her arm. "How did that work out for you?"

The anger in his voice made her stiffen.

Vander frowned. "Saxon."

"I'll get her cleaned up." He towed her across the office. She tried to pull her arm away. "Don't test me right now."

Vander was watching them, his gaze like a laser. "I

think I need to send Dennett a stronger message." Vander hit the stairs and was gone like smoke.

Gia's eyes widened. "What does that mean?"

"Don't worry about it." Saxon pulled her into a small room they kept stocked with medical supplies. They didn't often get injured, but it happened, and none of them liked a trip to the ER.

There was a double bed pressed against the wall, and he made her sit.

"You don't need to worry about Vander."

"But I do. He's my brother." Her brown gaze met his. "And I know you worry about him, too. He's so..."

"Badass?"

"Closed off. Remote. He never smiles anymore."

Yeah, well, Saxon was well aware of the things Vander had done as part of Ghost Ops. The decisions he'd been forced to make. The men he'd lost.

"He's home." Saxon pulled out the medical kit. "He has his family."

When he looked up, he found her watching him.

"Does your family help you?" she asked quietly.

Saxon snorted. "I try to see them as little as I can."

Something moved in her dark eyes. "I thought...well, you're an only child and your family's rich. I figured you were spoiled and indulged."

"Why do you think I spent so much time at your house when I was younger? I can't stand my parents."

"Oh. They're...difficult?"

Difficult? He fought back a laugh. "If you mean, cold and self-absorbed elitist assholes, then yes." He pulled out an antiseptic pad and started wiping her neck. His anger came back full force. "Dammit, Gia."

She winced. "I've scratched myself worse than this."

It wasn't deep, but it could have been worse. Way worse. *Fuck.*

He spread some cream over the cut, shocked to find his damn hands weren't steady. The thought of Gia hurt, of her dead. His chest felt like a rock was sitting on it.

"I told you not to wander the streets."

"Okay, okay. Get the 'I told you so' out."

"This isn't the time for jokes."

She sighed. "I know."

That's when Saxon felt the small tremors running through her. Her skin felt cold. "You're okay now. You're safe."

She pulled in a shuddering breath and nodded.

He pushed up the bloody sleeve of her sweatshirt. There was a smaller, but deeper cut on her forearm, and he cleaned it next.

She pouted, staring at the tear in the fabric. "This is my favorite sweatshirt."

He stared at the blood smeared on her skin. It blasted through the last of his self-control. "He could have killed you." Saxon exploded upright and gripped the back of his neck. "He could have stabbed you, cut an artery—"

"I'm fine, Saxon." She watched him steadily.

He growled. Her face was cool, and he could see her practically pulling herself back together. So damn tough.

He wanted to punch something. He dropped back on the bed and carefully put some cream on the cut. Her skin was a smooth, beautiful bronze.

Her breath hitched. He looked up and saw her watching him. His gut clenched. "Don't look at me like that."

"Mostly you annoy the crap out of me. This is my annoyed look."

"That's not your annoyed look." He pressed a bandage over her arm.

Then he reached up and touched her neck. He felt the pound of her pulse, feathered his thumb over it.

She was alive.

His body shuddered.

Gia licked her lips. "Saxon?"

"Not going to let anyone hurt you again."

"Okay."

He didn't think. He let his instincts drive him—something he never allowed. He dragged her into his lap and heard her gasp.

Her eyes were huge. "Saxon?"

He covered her mouth with his, pulling her as close as he could.

Her hands pressed to his chest, and he felt the bite of her nails, and then they were sliding into his hair.

He slid his hands up her slim back and she straddled him. This kiss was all tongues and teeth. Heat and need. Like they were trying to eat each other.

She moaned—a throaty, needy sound.

Blood pounded through Saxon, and his cock was as hard as steel. Then he moved his hand and heard her hiss. He'd touched her injured arm.

Hell. She was hurt and he was pawing her. He drew back, both of them panting.

"This... God..." she said breathlessly. "I don't like you."

"Yeah, same, Contessa."

He was sure both of them heard the lies. They liked each other just fine, they just didn't *want* to like each other.

Then Gia cupped the back of his head and yanked him back to her. They kissed again, just as hot and hungry. She moaned into his mouth.

When she lifted her head, she touched her lips, her face dazed. "Oh, God, what are we doing?"

"Acting on something we both know has been there for a long time."

Fear shot through her eyes. "No."

"Yes."

She tried to pull away, but he held her tight.

"Saxon, this is *crazy*. You're my brother's best friend, we don't like each other, we drive each other insane, and—"

"I'm claiming you, Gia. I've wanted you a fucking long time, and I'm not letting the excuses get in the way anymore."

"What?" she squeaked.

"You're mine. This is the start of you and me."

She shook her head. "No way."

"Yes." He tightened his grip.

Her curls flew as she shook her head wildly. "You've bumped your head or something."

"Nope." He captured her face in his hands and looked into her eyes. "You know, Gia. You've fucking known from the first moment we laid eyes on each other."

She closed her eyes. "I'm in some crazy dream, or maybe I bumped *my* head."

He grinned. "I remember you used to close your eyes and hope I'd go away when you were a teenager. A pretty teenager who I had to fucking stay away from."

Gia's eyes snapped open. She held up a hand like a traffic cop. Gia's "hand" was legendary. "Saxon, I can't deal with this right now."

He nodded. "I know. Right now, my number one priority is keeping you safe."

She gently pulled free of his hands. "Um, I have something to tell you. Promise you won't get mad."

His gaze narrowed. "No."

"Saxon, *please.*"

He blew out a breath. "Well, you've been in a standoff with a man with a gun, and now you've been in a knife fight, so what else? Have you been wrestling tigers? Taken on a tank with a nail file?"

She shot him a look designed to shrivel a man's testicles. "No. Willow came to see me."

Saxon scowled. *That woman.* He wanted to shake Gia.

"She came to my place. She said guys were after her. Dennett's men."

"And she fucking led them right to you." Fury was like an acid burn in his veins.

"Saxon." Gia's hands moved to his forearms. "She gave me the gems."

He cocked his head. "Say again?"

"The gems. They're at my place."

He cursed. Then he rose, setting her on her feet.

"Come on. I'll take you home and get the stones, then we're coming back here, and those rocks are going in Vander's safe."

Gia nodded, gnawing on her bottom lip.

Shit. He wanted to kiss her again. He wanted to devour his best friend's little sister.

She fiddled with her curls. "I promised her that I'd take care of them until she could organize a safe handoff to Dennett."

Saxon growled. "That plan has changed. Vander and I will get them to Dennett."

Gia's shoulders sagged. "Maybe that's for the best."

"You are not fucking having any more knives at your throat." He took her hand, lacing their fingers together. He pulled her out of the medical room.

"This is the perfect chance for you to berate me for my misguided decisions," she said quietly.

Saxon stopped and spun. She collided with him.

Holding her biceps, he lifted her up to meet his gaze. "I won't let anyone mar that smooth skin of yours. Or spill your blood. Or hurt you."

She stared at him.

"You irritate me, but I admire your damn loyalty, Gia. You take care of the people you love. I don't want you hurt."

"Saxon—"

The breathless tone of her voice burrowed into his skin. He started moving again before he did something that he'd regret. Something more than just kissing her senseless.

She straightened. "There isn't going to be an *us*,

49

Saxon. I can't be with you. We'll burn out and leave a trail of destruction behind us. It isn't worth the risk."

"We'll talk about it later."

"No, we won't."

"Yes, we will."

She made a cute growling sound, and with a smile, he led her down to the garage. He shoved her into a black Norcross BMW X6.

As he drove to her apartment building, he could see that she was still worried about her friend. Willow didn't deserve it, in his opinion.

They rode the elevator up in silence and got out on her floor. Saxon scanned the hall. There was nobody around.

Then Gia gasped.

Saxon turned his head and saw her apartment door ajar.

"Oh, no." She raced forward.

"No." He stopped her and pulled his HK VP9 out of his shoulder holster. "Let me check."

He pushed the door open.

Gia peered around him. "No!"

The apartment had been ransacked.

Everything was tipped over and smashed. The TV was a broken, shattered twist. Chairs were splintered. Paintings had been pulled off the wall and destroyed.

"*Bastardo*!" She shoved past him. "*Cazzo*!"

Saxon stuck to her like glue and quickly checked the bedroom. The mattress was half pulled off the bed and slashed open. Clothes littered the floor, and her fancy, walk-in wardrobe looked like a tornado had ripped through it.

Gia broke out in a string of rapid-fire Italian. He was pretty sure they were curses. No doubt salty and creative.

In the bathroom, the shower door was shattered, and bottles and pots of creams and lotions were scattered across the tile floor. Clearly a perfume bottle had been broken, because the rich scent of Gia's perfume filled the air.

Whoever had done it was long gone.

Gia picked her way through the destruction, her hands curled into fists.

Her face was blank, and her skin was pale, except for two bright-pink spots on her cheeks. Her mouth was a flat line.

As she moved back into the living room, she stared at the wall.

A shelf hung drunkenly and had been busted open.

"Gia?"

"The gems." She looked at him. "They're gone."

CHAPTER FOUR

S he picked out some clothes that hadn't been torn up or tossed around and shoved them in a bag.

Gia felt sick to her stomach. Her place, her home, her sanctuary had been invaded and desecrated.

"Appreciate it, Hunt," Saxon's deep voice said from the living room.

He was on the phone. Hunt was Detective Hunter Morgan, an old Army buddy of Vander and Saxon's who now worked for the SFPD.

When she paused in the doorway, Saxon slid his cell phone away. His gaze moved over her. "Police are on their way."

She nodded.

"You packed some things?"

"What was salvageable." No way she wanted to touch anything some asshole had ruined or pawed through.

Once two officers from the SFPD arrived, and she and Saxon had given a highly edited statement, she let

Saxon shuffle her into the SUV. She was chilled and a little shell-shocked.

She listened to him call Vander in the vehicle, and she stared out at a night-drenched San Francisco.

"Fuck," Vander bit out. "Gia okay?"

Saxon glanced at her, and she felt the weight of his gaze.

"She will be."

"You called Hunt?"

"Yeah. Officers are there now. They're going to dust for prints and check the building's security feed."

"Good. Sax, I just spoke with Dennett. He doesn't have the gems."

Saxon cursed.

Gia twisted her hands together. "Then who broke into my place?"

"Someone else who wanted the stones," Saxon said grimly.

Oh, no.

"Take Gia to my place," Vander said.

"Whoever's involved knows who she is," Saxon said. "If they're looking for her, they'll expect her to stay with one of you guys." A pause. "She can stay at my place. You know it's secure."

What? Gia looked at Saxon's profile.

It didn't take much to remember that kiss. That hot, hungry, all-too-delicious kiss. It would be so very easy to lose herself in Saxon Buchanan, but Gia couldn't afford to do that. Her heart knocked against her ribs. She knew he was a danger to her.

She couldn't stay with him.

She cleared her throat. "I don't think—"

"Take care of her," Vander said.

"You don't need to tell me that," Saxon fired back.

Gia made an annoyed sound. "Hello, grown woman here. Who makes her own decisions."

They ignored her and kept talking. She crossed her arms and stared out the window.

"We need to find those fucking gems," Vander said. "Call me if you need me."

Saxon drove into Nob Hill. The wealthy suburb was home to historic mansions and swanky hotels. The big four railway barons—the Nobs—had made their homes here in the 1800s. She was pretty sure the Buchanans could track their family tree back that far. She knew Saxon's parents had a mansion here.

He stopped in front of a four-story, cream house with charcoal trim. It was deceptively simple, sandwiched in between two larger buildings. She watched the garage door slide open.

Gia was well aware of what real estate cost in the area. They drove down into an underground garage, and he parked the X6 beside his Bentley. She climbed out, her running shoes squeaking on the polished-concrete floor. There was room for four cars, and at the back were some closed doors, storage space or maybe a gym.

"Come on." He got out and reached for her bag.

They headed up some stairs and came out on the lower floor of his home. Beautiful marble floors opened up to a magnificent, curving staircase with a polished, wooden handrail. As they headed up the stairs, she glimpsed a high-tech media room and a glassed-in wine cellar.

He dropped her bag on the next level, but kept heading upward. They passed a third level before they finally reached the top. Gia walked into the open-plan living area and kitchen, gob-smacked. She'd never been to his place before. Saxon lived in her dream house, dammit.

The floors were warm wood and she watched as he strode into a giant, white kitchen with a huge, stone island. Off to the side was a long, steel table, with a banquette built in on one side.

The entire space was light, sleek, and spacious.

Gia walked toward the modern, cream couches situated to face a flat-screen TV on the wall. To the side, huge sliding doors framed a perfect view of the city—downtown, the Coit Tower, the Bay Bridge, and the water.

She realized now why the house had the living area at the top. To maximize the views. She did a slow circle. On the other side of the space was a wooden deck with potted trees and plants, and comfy-looking outdoor furniture.

"Your home is incredible," she said. "Beautiful."

He looked up from the mail he was reading at the island. "Glad you like it."

There was something in his tone that she couldn't quite read. "How many bedrooms?"

"Four. The master takes up the entire level below. The second level has three bedrooms."

She swallowed. It was a big house for a single guy.

She looked at him. He'd shed his jacket and tossed it over a stool. As she watched, he rolled the sleeves of his blue shirt up, showing off his tattooed forearms.

Badass in off-mode.

Her belly flooded with heat, and memories of their kiss swamped her. *Saxon had kissed her.* And it had been the hottest kiss of her life. Places inside her were still tingling.

She watched him pull out some glasses, then a bottle of amber liquid. He poured a splash into each glass, then walked over and handed her one.

He touched the rim of his glass to hers. "I think you need this."

She nodded and then she tossed it back. The whiskey burned down her throat.

"My apartment." Her voice cracked. *Oh, God.*

He reached out and touched her hair. "Willow led them straight to you."

"She didn't mean to—"

"Stop making excuses for her."

Gia made an angry sound and stalked to the windows. "I know she screwed up, but she's my friend."

"You're too damn loyal."

Gia spun. "I'm not like you." She flung a hand out. "Do whatever you want, have fun, stay removed, then move on." She'd seen the way he discarded women. Usually glossy, leggy blondes.

A muscle ticked in his jaw.

She had no right to judge his lifestyle. She sighed. "I'm poor company tonight, Saxon, and I'm in a really bad mood. God, I've lost all of my things." She set the glass down on the table and pressed her face to her hands, despair and sadness tangling through her. "My apartment meant something to me."

Suddenly, strong arms wrapped around her, holding her tight.

Desperate for more, she pressed her face to his firm chest and held on. Her hands clutched the back of his shirt, fisting against hard muscles. She breathed him in. Saxon's scent always made her think of thunderstorms and crashing waves.

"It's just stuff, baby," he murmured.

She nodded. God, she was getting comfort from Saxon Buchanan.

Then she heard a cell phone ringing and realized it was hers.

She pulled away. When she grabbed the phone, she saw a number she didn't recognize. "Hello?"

"Gia."

Her hand clenched. "Willow."

Saxon's face hardened.

"Oh, God, Gia." Willow sounded panicked.

"Are you all right?"

"I need the gems. Now."

Gia's belly turned in a sickening circle. "Someone broke into my place, Will." Saxon's hand landed on her shoulder, squeezed.

Willow's breath hitched. "Gia..."

"They followed you, Willow. They attacked me and ransacked my place. I'm sorry, but the gems are gone. And it wasn't Dennett."

Harsh breathing came across the line. Willow made a strangled sound. "I'm dead."

"We'll work it out—"

"I'm *dead*, Gia." There was a cry, then the line went dead.

Gia felt the prick of tears.

"This isn't your fault," Saxon said.

"It feels like it. She's scared."

"She brought this on herself."

"Saxon, have some compassion."

He leaned in close. "That dried up when she put you in danger."

Gia bit her lip. Emotions welled up inside, and it was all too much.

She pulled away, striding across his gorgeous living area. The lights of the city blurred, and she wondered where Willow was. Where the gems were.

She sensed Saxon behind her. "Gia."

"Don't start, Saxon. I don't have the defenses to duel with you right now."

"Then let me show you to your room. You can run a bath and relax."

"God." She faced him. "Do not be nice to me. I need asshole Saxon back."

He crossed his arms over his chest, which just drew her attention back to his muscular arms and tattoos.

"And stop looking so hot, too," she snapped.

His brows drew together. "Gia—"

"I'm used to you finding my faults and rubbing them in my face. So, fire away. Tell me this is my fault."

58

"I don't enjoy rubbing your face in your faults. And this is *not* your fault."

"You do. You've always picked on me and made me lose my temper. Ever since I was young."

"So I'd quit noticing you when I shouldn't," he bit out.

Gia blinked. "What?"

He smiled. "And I like riling you because it's so easy to do. You get so fired up and passionate."

She scowled. "Saxon—"

"You need to stop moping about Willow and what happened at your place. Deal with it."

Ah, there was the Saxon she knew. "God, you can be cold."

"You need to—"

Gia's temper flared. It was easier to be angry than sad and upset. "Stop telling me what to do!"

He grabbed her arms.

"And hands off," she snapped.

"That's not what you wanted earlier."

She glared at him. "We aren't talking about that kiss...*ever*."

"We'll be doing more than kissing soon."

His words sent her pulse haywire. "I hate you."

"I'm trying to help you," he said.

"I don't need your help. What do you know about suffering? About being stuck in a bad situation? You were born into money and had everything—"

"Not everything."

The cold tone of his voice made Gia freeze.

He stepped closer. "You don't know everything about me, Gia."

She stared at him, wondering at the shadows moving through his eyes. "Saxon..."

"No. I think we've reached our limits on deep and meaningful tonight. Come on, I'll show you to your room."

Gia pushed her hair back. She was running on fumes, exhausted. She just wanted to curl up and pretend the world didn't exist for a while. She was usually take-charge, a problem solver. She liked to grab a problem by the horns and face it down, but right now, she didn't have the energy to do that. She wished she could lean on someone and know that they would catch her.

She drew herself up. "Okay."

He led her downstairs. Then he paused, several steps down so that they were eye level.

"You don't have to worry tonight, Gia. I'll keep you safe."

The tight knot in her chest eased a little. "I told you to stop being nice to me."

Instead, he just tucked a curl back behind her ear.

SAXON WOKE to the smell of coffee. He blinked at the ceiling above his bed.

It was rare that he brought anyone back to his place, and if he did bring a woman back, they never stayed for a cozy breakfast.

Rising, he pulled on a pair of loose, black pajama pants, and went to wash his face and brush his teeth.

He went upstairs to the kitchen and his chest tightened.

Gia stood at his huge island, one hip pressed against it. She was wearing a tiny, silky robe in a dusty pink that left her slender legs bare. And her hair... *Jesus*. It was all piled up on her head, dark curls everywhere. She sipped her coffee, then glanced his way.

Her eyes were still heavy with sleep, her brow creased. She made a small, feminine grunt.

Saxon grinned. So, Gia wasn't a morning person.

He walked over. "Morning."

That got him another grunt. God, she was as cute as fuck.

He poured himself a coffee, and saw her eyeing his bare chest. She looked at his tattoos very differently than his mother had, and she wasn't hiding that she liked them.

His cock twitched.

Fuck. He turned and drank more coffee. These pants wouldn't hide a hard-on.

"You need to call your insurance today," he reminded her.

She nodded.

"And you're coming to the Norcross office." He wasn't letting her out of his sight until Dennett called off his dogs.

Gia stiffened. "I have work—"

"You have staff. They can handle things. And we

have phones and computers at the office that you can use."

"Saxon, no. I have meetings, responsibilities—"

"You're in danger. Remember the state of your apartment?" Pain flickered through her eyes, and he hated that he'd made her remember. "You can't be reckless and endanger your staff or clients."

Her eyes fired. "Despite what you think, I'm not stupid or reckless."

"I never said *you* were stupid."

Her grumpy gaze narrowed. "Just reckless."

"You can be."

"And you're arrogant."

He shifted his shoulder. "Sometimes."

"And a snob. A know-it-all. And you're bossy."

He grinned, and took another sip of his coffee. "Anything else, Contessa?"

She made an angry sound and stomped to the stairs. "I'm going to shower and change."

When he headed back to his room to get ready, he paused on the landing. He heard the faint sound of the shower running off her room. In his head, he imagined Gia naked in the shower. Imagined water pouring over her curves.

His cock throbbed. With a curse, he strode into his bedroom and straight into his large marble bathroom. He stripped his trousers off and stepped into the huge shower stall.

But the images of Gia wouldn't go away. What would those full breasts look like naked? What color were her nipples? His gut went tight.

Shit. What would she taste like? From the kiss yesterday, he knew she'd be wild and enthusiastic. She'd demand everything, deny him nothing.

With a groan, Saxon circled his hard cock. He imagined her there, her hands on him, her lips...

With another groan, he stroked faster.

"*Gia.*" Her name echoed off the tiles. His release hit and his muscles locked. He slapped a hand to the tiles as he spurted into the shower. Shit, he'd just come hard at the mere thought of her. He flicked the shower to cold and let the water pound over him.

She was his best friend's sister. Vander was going to be pissed, but Saxon was done fighting the pull of Gia Norcross. She was *his.*

After drying off, he dressed, exiting his bedroom as he fastened his cufflinks at his wrists.

Gia was waiting on the landing, dressed in dark jeans and a red, knit top that draped over her breasts.

And he was hard again.

"Come on," he growled as he stomped down the stairs.

"God, you're in a bad mood suddenly."

He wound down the staircase. "Don't start."

They passed the glassed-in wine cellar and went down into the garage.

"But making you mad always makes me feel better," she said sweetly.

He opened the door of the X6 and she climbed in with a smile.

When they arrived at the Norcross office, Vander met them and waved them into the conference room.

Rhys was already sitting at the table, along with Ace, who was biting into a donut. Another Norcross employee, Rome Nash, sat on the other side of the table.

"Hey, Rome," Gia said.

"Gia." Big and muscular, the dark-skinned man was a former Ghost Ops team member. Rome was Norcross' top bodyguard. They all had their specialties. Rhys was their best investigator. Ace was their guru on all things tech. Saxon was their troubleshooter, a jack-of-all-trades, who Vander sent into shitty situations to troubleshoot and get the job done.

Gia went over to Rhys and her youngest brother gave her a hug. As usual, his overlong hair was a shaggy mess, and he wrapped his tattooed arms around his sister and held her tight.

Once Gia sat, Vander stood at the head of the table and pressed his palms to the glossy surface.

"Dennett's not happy." Vander didn't look happy, either. "Another player has taken the gems. He's blaming Willow, and by default, Gia."

Gia rolled her eyes. "Typical man. Blame everybody else."

"Dennett wants the stones back badly." Rhys leaned forward. "He's put a bounty on Willow and the gems."

"Fuck," Saxon muttered.

"What does that mean?" Gia asked.

"It means that every asshole scumbag will be out to find her," Vander explained.

Saxon crossed his arms over his chest. "Which means someone might target Gia as a way to get to Willow."

Gia blew out a breath. "Well, this day keeps getting better and better."

Saxon shook his head. "There's something else going on here. Dennett's expending a lot of time, energy, and money on this. He's not hurting for money, so what's so special about these gems?"

Vander nodded. "Rhys?"

The youngest Norcross brother nodded. "I'm on it."

"I want to know who broke into Gia's place," Vander said. "Who took the stones."

Yeah, Saxon would like to know that, too. He wanted to make the asshole pay for the pain he'd put on Gia's face.

"Gia, if Willow contacts you again, you let us know," Vander ordered.

Gia gave a tired-looking nod.

"Come on," Saxon said. "I'll show you where you can work."

He put her in the office next to his.

"Any idea where Willow would go?" he asked.

She shook her head. "She's burned too many bridges. I don't know anyone who'd take her in."

He grunted.

"She... Once upon a time, she was a good friend."

Saxon didn't believe that. "The best way to help her might be to cut her loose. Not keep helping her enough that she stays on this path."

Sadness clouded Gia's eyes. "I can't give up on her."

He crouched, and tucked a curl back behind her ear. "You're a good friend, but I'm not going to let her drag you down." He stroked her cheekbone.

"Saxon," she murmured.

Damn, when she said his name like that, it was easy to forget everything. He rose. "You need to call your insurance company."

She nodded. "And my office. I need to get Ashley to reschedule my meetings, and go over what's on the agenda for the next couple of days."

And Saxon needed to find Willow and the gems.

CHAPTER FIVE

G ia leaned back in her chair at the end of the day and let out a long breath. She'd popped in and out of the Norcross office to visit her brothers before, but she'd never really seen the guys doing their thing. They were clearly out a lot. They all preferred action to desk work.

But today, Saxon and Rhys stayed in, working the phones and laptops hard. She wouldn't lie—watching Saxon work was sexy.

Gia licked her lips. She glanced through the glass wall and saw that his office was empty right now, but he was around somewhere.

He'd vowed to keep her safe.

He'd vowed that he was claiming her as his.

Her belly jittered and she pressed a hand to it. *God.* She was attracted to him. Insanely attracted. Any woman between the ages of five and ninety-five would be. But she'd seen him and her brothers blow through women.

They attracted women like bees to honey, but they never kept them long.

Saxon Buchanan was a risk. Gia liked to calculate risks in everything she did—her work, her personal relationships. The odds didn't stack up here.

She shook her head and looked back at her desk. *Work.* She needed to focus on her work.

She thought of Willow and the gems, but shoved that thought away. There was nothing she could do to help right now.

Surprisingly, even though she was running on low-level anxiety, she'd gotten a lot of work done. Without endless meetings, or people needing her help, she'd powered through some projects. She'd also called her insurance, and gotten a cleaning company in to fix her apartment.

Her cell phone rang. "Gia Norcross."

"Ms. Norcross, it's Diamond Fresh Cleaning. I'm just letting you know that we finished your apartment. It's clean, and the basic furniture has been replaced as you requested."

"Oh, thank you."

"You're welcome. I'm sorry you needed us in the first place, but I hope you're happy with our work."

After she ended the call, Gia stood. The sun was setting, the water of the bay darkening and the lights on the Bay Bridge twinkling like stars.

She headed out to find Vander and Saxon. Vander's office was at the end of the warehouse. Unlike everyone else, his office had real walls.

As she approached, she saw the door was open and

she heard Saxon's voice. The deep tone sent a shiver through her.

What would it be like to have all Saxon's focus on her, her pleasure? To strip those custom suits off his hard, muscular body? A rush of desire arrowed between her legs and her nipples went hard.

She realized now how many times, when she'd been busy with her vibrator, that it had been Saxon's face and body she'd imagined. Saxon's cock she'd pictured filling her.

She paused and pulled in a deep breath. She hadn't acknowledged the depth of her hunger for Saxon consciously before. But his kiss had ripped those blinders off.

She walked toward Vander's office.

"Keeping Gia safe is our top priority," Saxon said.

"Agreed," Vander replied.

Warmth bloomed in her chest.

"The biggest obstacle to that is Gia." Saxon sounded annoyed. "She'll risk herself for Willow. We need to keep her from doing anything stupid."

Her steps faltered, the warmth turning to molten anger. But under it was pain. Clearly, Saxon might be attracted to her, but he still saw her as stupid and reckless.

So, he'd been charming her, lulling her. Telling her he liked her just as a big fucking ploy to keep her in line. *Manipulative bastard.*

She stormed into the office. "How dare you?"

Saxon turned, his face hardening. "Gia—"

"Poor, stupid Gia. We need to babysit her. Make sure she doesn't make dumb decisions."

"I want to keep you breathing," Saxon snapped.

"I've done just fine for thirty years, Saxon Buchanan. I don't need you running roughshod over my life and treating me like a child."

"Gia—" Vander started.

"Stay out of this, Vander." She glared at Saxon. "You're off the hook, Saxon. I'll take care of myself, somehow, despite being so stupid."

"I *don't* think you're stupid." He sounded like he was talking between gritted teeth. "You're the sharpest woman I know."

She made an angry sound. More placation and manipulation.

Saxon strode up to her and grabbed her arms. "I do."

"As if I'd believe anything that comes out of your mouth."

He gave her a small shake. "You care too much. You make these poor decisions not because you're not intelligent, but because you put the people you care about before yourself."

Oh. Well, that was actually a nice observation. Still...

"I'm an adult. I won't let you alpha males with an overabundance of testosterone make all the decisions for me, or boss me around." She took a deep breath and stepped back. Saxon's hands fell away. "I've no plans to run into danger. I will take security advice from you both, since you're the experts. Now, I need to be at my office tomorrow—"

"No."

She glared at Saxon. "Security measures can be taken. I'll allow a bodyguard to keep me and my staff safe."

Saxon shoved a hand through his hair.

"My apartment's been cleaned and—"

Saxon shook his head. "You're staying with me."

Oh no, she wasn't. "No. I'm going home. I won't let these assholes chase me out of my own home."

Saxon's jaw hardened and a muscle ticked beside his eye. "Then I'll stay at your place."

She put her hands on her hips. "I have security—"

"Someone stays with you," Vander interjected.

Gia knew the hard stare. Vander wouldn't budge on this. *Dammit.*

"Fine. I take it you haven't found the gems."

"We're following some leads," Saxon said.

Vander rose. "I did get some intel. Nothing definite yet."

"What?" Her pulse skittered.

Saxon stepped closer, the heat of him washing over her. All the thoughts flew out of her head.

"Dennett's after a particular stone," Vander said. "It seems something very valuable ended up in that bag."

Gia gasped.

Saxon's brow creased. "Something worth more than two hundred and fifty grand?"

"Yeah," Vander said.

"What?" Gia asked.

"I don't know yet. But Dennett will kill to get it back."

God, Willow, what have you done? Surely, she hadn't

known this. A wave of exhaustion hit Gia. "I want to go home."

"I'll get your things," Saxon said.

"I can get them myself. I'm more than capable. I don't need a man to do everything for me. I can even take care of my own orgasms."

Vander made a strangled noise. "Out."

Gia turned, tossed her head back and strode out.

Take that, Saxon Bossy-as-hell Buchanan.

SAXON WOKE in Gia's guest room, in a bed with a white, feminine cover and about a thousand pillows on it.

He shoved one of them under his head and scraped a hand over his stubbled chin.

He'd brought her home the night before, and she'd given him the silent treatment. Nobody did the silent treatment like Gia Norcross. The only thing she did better was losing her temper.

As they'd eaten some dinner, she'd ignored him. But he'd watched as she'd wandered her now clean, but very bare, apartment. She'd grieved for what had been destroyed, and seeing her pain had gutted him.

She had very few ornaments and decorations left. He knew that Gia loved art and pretty things, and had collected each one lovingly.

Saxon shoved the sheets back. Well, she hadn't let him comfort her last night, clearly still pissed at what had been said in Vander's office. He didn't care if she was angry, as long as she was unhurt and alive.

Gia had always been so independent, forging her own way. Saxon didn't get it. She had a supportive family to lean on, and yet she tried her hardest not to.

Naked, he rose and headed into the adjoining guest bathroom. After pulling on some suit pants and a clean, pale-blue shirt that he'd brought with him, he headed into the hallway, hands going up to fasten the buttons.

Then his fingers froze. He heard a buzzing sound. *What the hell?*

A deep, throaty female moan came from Gia's room.

His cock rose, pressing hard against his zipper. *You've got to be kidding me.* He walked closer to her door, and heard more moans and that incessant buzzing.

The little minx was lying in there, pleasuring herself. Images filled his head like a damn sexy movie. Gia, naked, sprawled on her bed, all that hair spread everywhere, working her vibrator between her legs.

His cock throbbed, and he swallowed a groan.

Then he heard her cry out, followed by her gasping a name.

"*Saxon.*"

Fuck. His hands balled into fists and he strode back to the guest room. He closed the door and leaned back against it. Then quickly, with desperate moves, he flicked open his pants and shoved his boxers down. His swollen cock sprang free and he fisted it, and started working himself with long, rough strokes.

Fuck. *Fuck.* Far too fast, his orgasm rose, his mind full of Gia and what she was doing next door.

With a groan, sensation like lightning ran down his spine. Saxon came, spilling on the floor.

Damn. He stayed slumped against the door, panting. He had to have her soon or he'd lose his mind.

Saxon quickly cleaned up. When he strode into the kitchen, she was dressed in a sleek dress of stone gray—sleeveless and fitted—that hugged those sensational curves.

She looked at him, but stayed silent.

Oh no, Contessa, we're not doing any more silent treatment. He circled the island. "Good morning."

She turned to the coffee machine.

Saxon came right up behind her, smelled her floral shampoo and her perfume—something rich, sexy, and spicy with vanilla undertones.

"Did you enjoy coming with your toy this morning?" he murmured.

She stiffened.

"Did you enjoy imagining it was me touching you?"

She whirled. "I did *not* imagine you."

"Heard you say my name."

She made a strangled sound, red color streaking her cheekbones.

Grinning, Saxon headed to the island and sat on a stool. She'd already cut up some fruit and he popped a piece of orange in his mouth. At least he wasn't getting the silent treatment, anymore.

"I do not fantasize about you, Saxon Buchanan. Henry Cavill is my choice of fantasy material."

"Right, but I heard 'Saxon,' not 'Henry.'"

She shot him one of her trademark, scorching-hot glares.

Was it wrong that he felt this woman's glares in his

cock? All that passion inside that gorgeous body. He wanted to taste it, set it free.

"I can't believe you..." She blew out a breath, the color still in her cheeks.

"That I listened to you getting off?"

"Be quiet."

"You're awfully tense for someone who just had an orgasm. Must not have been a good one."

That earned him another glare. "Just stop talking."

"I went straight back to my room and stroked my cock until I blew. It was hot, Gia."

She stilled, her lips parting.

Saxon nabbed a bit of pineapple. As he chewed it, she was still staring at him, and he knew she was running some X-rated images through her head.

He picked up a piece of cantaloupe. He knew she loved it.

"Come here, Gia."

She hesitated.

"You know you want to. I know you're pissed at what I said yesterday, but nothing I said was bad. You put yourself out there for the people you care about. It's fucking admirable, even when I want to shake you for putting yourself at risk. Hell, Vander's the same. I've watched him risk himself for strangers, over and over. I never knew people cared like that until I met your family."

Something moved over her beautiful face. "Saxon..."

"Come here, Contessa."

She moved. On the stool, he shifted his legs and pulled her between them. He rubbed the cantaloupe over her lips and her chest hitched.

"You need to get over what I said and quit the silent treatment."

She sighed.

He pushed the fruit into her mouth, and she chewed and swallowed.

"I'm over it. You know I have a temper."

He raised a brow.

Her mouth quirked. "Don't make me mad again."

He rubbed his thumb over her lips and she grabbed his wrist, then sucked his juice-covered thumb into her mouth.

Damn. His cock was hard in an instant. "Wish I could have watched you come earlier." His voice was guttural

"Saxon," she moaned.

"Can I watch you come, Contessa?"

His hand gripped her leg, sliding up her thigh, dragging her dress up with it.

Her brown eyes widened, her breathing choppy.

"I bet I can do a better job than your toy."

Desire glazed her eyes. "We shouldn't do this..."

He paused. "You want me to stop?"

"No," she breathed.

Saxon slid a hand inside the tiny scrap of lace she called panties. He found her clit—still swollen—and stroked.

She jolted against him, air rushing out of her.

"You like that?" He started working at that little nub, pulling her closer, spinning her around so her back pressed against his chest.

She tilted her head so her face was in profile, her lips parted. "*Oh.*"

He watched her, reading every little flicker on her face. He found exactly what pressure she liked, then stroked his fingers through her folds. He felt how wet she was, loved every little cry she made.

"Saxon!"

"Ride my hand, gorgeous."

She obeyed, her hips weaving wildly. She grabbed the edge of the island in front of her. She was close.

"Look at me, Gia."

She tilted her head back, desire on her features, her eyes fever bright.

"Come, Contessa."

He pinched her clit and her body arched. She cried out.

"Say my name," he growled.

Her gaze locked with his. "*Saxon.*"

Fuck. He was close to coming in his boxers.

He held her as she shuddered through her release, and then still held her as she came down. He pulled her more tightly into his arms, her head resting on his shoulder.

After a while, she finally pulled back, and her gaze dropped to his rock-hard cock tenting his pants.

She licked her lips. "Um, can I—?"

Saxon groaned. "Baby, you're due at work in fifteen minutes. Unfortunately, I think we need to go."

She squeaked and looked at her watch. Then she yanked her dress back down into place. "Dammit, I have a meeting—"

"Go. Clean up and we'll head off."

She paused, her gaze running over his face.

He couldn't stop himself from reaching out and stroking her jaw. "Get moving, Contessa."

Or he'd drag her into her bed, and they wouldn't leave all day. Maybe all week.

With a nod, she flew into her bedroom, no doubt to change her soaked panties.

Saxon blew out a breath. It was going to be a long day.

CHAPTER SIX

Gia strode into the Firelight PR offices, trying to pretend Saxon—sauntering one step behind her—didn't exist.

Yeah, right. Ever since she'd met him, it was as if her body was designed to notice Saxon Buchanan.

At the front reception desk, Janine's eyes popped wide.

"Morning," Gia said.

"Hi," Janine breathed.

"Ignore him, he's my bodyguard."

Janine eyed Saxon. "Gia, that is impossible."

Saxon chuckled, but Gia kept walking. "Ashley, tell me you have a latte for me."

Ashley held out a cup, but her gaze was on Saxon.

"Ashley, this is Saxon, my bodyguard. Saxon, Ashley is my bossy, over-organized assistant."

Gia sipped the coffee. It was hot. Not for the first time, she wondered how her assistant managed that, especially when Gia was a fraction late today. Late because she'd been busy letting Saxon give her a delicious, breath-stealing orgasm in her kitchen.

No. Don't go there.

"A pleasure, Ashley," Saxon drawled.

"Wait, Saxon. Saxon Buchanan?" Ashley glanced at Gia. "The same Saxon you said was—" Ashley clamped her mouth shut.

Saxon laughed. A deep, sexy sound that skated through Gia.

"Don't worry, Ashley, I'm well aware of everything Gia says about me. She's never been afraid to say it to my face." He glanced sideways and smiled at Gia.

"Well, when you're as arrogant, bossy, and annoying as you are, you must be used to it."

"Ah, there's that sweet tongue of yours, Contessa."

She poked it out at him. "Enough. My staff know me as levelheaded, professional Gia."

"So, you've been lying to them?"

"Enough." She sailed into her office. She set her belongings down and Saxon followed.

She straightened. "Ashley will find you a place to sit."

He shook his head. "I'm staying close to you."

"No, I can't concentrate with you looming." Because she'd stare at him and be highly aware of him, and wouldn't get any work done.

He grinned, and it lit up his handsome, aristocratic face. He scanned her office. "I like your desk."

It was gorgeous and she loved it. Saxon managed to convey "I'd like to strip you naked on it" with just one look.

"Shoo." She waved her hand at him.

He crossed her office, sat on her couch, and pulled out his phone. He should have looked silly on the feminine piece of furniture. Instead, it just made him look more masculine.

Gia's desk phone rang. *Right, work.* She quickly got absorbed in calls, emails, and files that required her attention.

She was on her way to a meeting in the conference room, when Ashley caught her arm. Saxon had gone on ahead to clear the room before the meeting. Gia rolled her eyes. Just in case Dennett's goons could scale buildings.

"Tell me you're banging him," Ashley said.

"What? No! He's my brother's best friend. The man works my last nerve."

"Mmm-hmm." Ashley didn't sound convinced.

"It's true."

"The way you two look at each other..." Ashley fanned her face with a file.

"There's *nothing* going on."

Saxon appeared in the doorway. "Then what do you call that orgasm I gave you this morning, Contessa?"

Ashley choked on a laugh.

Incensed, Gia spun. "This is my place of *work*, Buchanan."

"The conference room is clear."

Stifling the need to scream, she brushed past him.

"Contessa," Ashley said. "He even has a cute Italian nickname for you." Her assistant sighed, taking her usual seat at the table.

Gia moved to the head. "Shut it, or you're fired."

Ashley just hummed, clearly not fearing for her employment.

Saxon leaned against the wall. Gia's team started filing in, all eyeing him with interest. He was a big distraction.

"Saxon is my bodyguard," she announced. "I'm peripherally linked to a friend's troubles. It should all be cleaned up soon." *Please, God.* "Now, let's get to work."

The rest of the day was busy. Saxon stayed close, but out of her way. She was aware of him every second, her body filled with a low-level hum.

Her traitorous hussy of a body wanted more orgasms. She glanced his way, and noted the way his pants clung to his fine, muscled ass. She wanted to bite him.

His cell phone rang, jolting her out of her about-to-turn-X-rated day dream. She tuned out his conversation and focused on her client's brand update.

"Gia?"

She looked up. Saxon stood at her desk, watching her with a smile.

"What?"

"Fuck, it is so sexy watching you work. All confidence and in command. It's hot."

She felt heat in her cheeks. Not every guy found a smart, accomplished woman a turn on. The look in Saxon's eyes said he liked it. Big time.

"Vander called," Saxon said. "We've got a lead on the gems."

She straightened in her chair. "Really?"

"Yeah. I'm going to follow it up. Rome's on his way here to take over watching you."

Gia had a second to be annoyed that she needed a bodyguard in the first place, but she nodded.

Saxon leaned down, dropped a quick kiss to her lips. "Stay out of trouble."

She glared. "I'm working, Saxon, and I'm not responsible for everything that's happened."

He ran a finger down her nose and strode out.

And dammit, she watched his fine ass until he disappeared from view.

She finished her notes and went out to Ashley's desk. "Ash, can you please—?"

"Oh, my God, I think I just had a mini orgasm," Ashley drawled.

Gia frowned. "Can you quit talking about orgasms?"

"Says the woman who got one from a hot guy today."

"You're fired."

"Whatever. The man headed this way is *divine*."

Gia looked up and saw Rome striding across the open-concept office area. Everyone stopped work and was blatantly watching him.

He did look good. His big, muscular body caught the attention, as did his brown skin and his way of moving that made her think of a big cat. He had a strong jaw, bold masculine features, and amazing pale-green eyes.

He scanned the office, and she knew he would have absorbed every entry, exit, and every person in an instant. Vander had told her that Rome made the best bodyguard because of his exceptional situational awareness.

"Gia." His voice was a deep rumble.

"Hi, Rome. Thanks for coming."

Ashley rolled her eyes back in her head.

"This is my assistant, who I just fired, so I won't introduce her."

"I'm Ashley." She smiled. "Gia fires me a few times every week."

Rome didn't smile. He rarely did. "Rome Nash. Nice to meet you."

"I need coffee," Gia announced. "Is it okay if we head downstairs to the coffee shop?"

Rome frowned. "Is it in this building?"

Gia nodded.

"Something you usually do?"

"It's not uncommon, but I don't always go at the same time."

"Okay, but stick by my side."

Ashley made a sound that said she'd like to stick by Rome's side and Gia raised a brow.

"Sorry." Ashley cleared her throat. "I'll have a skinny white chocolate mocha with extra whip."

"I think I'll get you a decaf tea."

Ashley blew Gia a kiss.

Shaking her head, Gia headed out with Rome.

The coffee shop was busy. There were several mothers there with strollers and babies, and noisy, fussy toddlers.

"You want anything?" she asked Rome.

"Americano. Black."

Apparently badasses didn't drink frothy, coffee-flavored drinks.

Gia ordered and then stood to the side with Rome, waiting. An older man in a suit with a loosened tie was waiting, too. He was hunched over his phone.

"Hey!" one mother screamed. "Get away from my baby!"

Gia spun around and saw a young, skinny guy snatch a baby out of a stroller. The mother sprang up, kids screamed.

Gia took a step forward, but Rome grabbed her arm.

"We have to help!" she cried.

Rome didn't look happy. They watched as the man started shoving his way toward the door, the baby in his arms wailing.

"You're my priority," Rome bit out.

"Rome, I don't think the barista or that guy in the suit are going to attack me. We have to save that baby."

His rock-hard body didn't move, but she saw the indecision on his face.

"Fine, I'll stop him." Gia charged forward.

With a curse, Rome shoved her back and strode ahead. He reached the man and, with a quick, practiced move, hit him in the lower back. Deftly, Rome snatched the baby before the man dropped the crying child.

The guy looked terrified and Rome quickly shoved the baby at its mother. Then he turned around and punched the guy in the face.

Suddenly, something shoved into Gia's lower back. She sensed someone move up behind her.

What the hell?

She looked back. It was the older guy in the suit, but now that she looked closely at him, she saw that it was the guy who'd attacked her at the museum.

"You!"

He was wearing some sort of makeup that altered his appearance.

"Come quietly. Mr. Dennett wants to talk with you."

"Are you insane? My brothers are going to stomp you to dust."

There was a flicker of something in his eyes. "Dennett pays well, and I have a reputation to keep clean. You muddied it at the museum."

She snorted. "None of that's any good if you're dead."

He jammed what she guessed was a gun into her back even harder. "Quit talking and move."

"What are you going to do if I don't? Shoot me?"

The man's face hardened. "A bullet hole in your leg won't stop you from talking." He pressed the gun to her thigh.

A thousand knots tangled in Gia's belly, but she grasped onto her anger. She swiveled, grabbed a teapot off a nearby table, and smashed it over the man's head.

"Fuck!" the man cried.

The ceramic pot broke, and hot tea poured over his face.

Gia shoved him and, as he fell, he grabbed her dress. They both went down in a tangle, more cups of tea and coffee falling off the table.

The gun went off, the bullet hitting the ceiling. Gia grabbed a nearby chair and tipped it over on her attacker's face. He cursed.

Then Rome was there. He lifted her off the man, and drew a gun, aiming it at the man's chest.

"Don't move," Rome growled.

Rome's face didn't change expression, but Gia knew he was pissed. Anger pumped off him in waves.

She straightened her dress. Coffee had spilled on it. *Ugh.* "It's all okay, Rome."

Angry, pale-green eyes hit hers. "Gia, I'm pissed, but I guarantee you that your brother and Saxon will be even more pissed."

Her stomach dropped. *Oh, great.*

SAXON SCREECHED to a halt in front of Gia's office building, pulling in behind a police cruiser.

He slammed out of the X6 and strode toward the coffee shop. A small crowd of onlookers had gathered out front, but when they saw his face, they parted quickly.

When he stepped inside, he saw Gia with Rome.

She was unharmed.

Saxon blew out a breath. Rome had called and told him what had happened, and assured him that she wasn't hurt, but he had to see for himself.

She had a coffee stain on her dress, and her hair was now free and a mess of curls around her shoulders, but otherwise she was fine. She was talking to a police officer and gesturing wildly before glaring at the two cuffed men kneeling on the floor.

"Buchanan."

Saxon turned to see Detective Hunter Morgan. "Hey, Hunt."

The former Delta Force soldier had his light-brown hair cut short, and kept his body military fit. He had a gun strapped to his hip, and a badge clipped to his belt. After an injury had ended his military career, he'd joined the SFPD and worked his way up the ranks. He was a good man, and shared beers with Vander, Saxon, and the rest of the team when he could.

"What the fuck is going on?" Hunt pointed to the ceiling. "Someone tried to abduct Gia at gunpoint."

Saxon saw the bullet hole and his gut cramped.

"It was lucky no one was shot," Hunt said.

Saxon grunted. "We'll take care of it."

Hunt shook his head. "You wanna tell me what this is about?"

"Trust me, you don't want to know."

"Well, I'm charging these two with attempted kidnap. One snatched a baby, likely to distract Gia and Nash."

Fuck, of course Gia would fly in to rescue a baby. And drag Rome with her.

Saxon studied the other man on the ground and instantly recognized him through his disguise. It was the guy from the museum. Dennett's man.

That fucker hadn't listened. Saxon took a step forward but Hunt threw an arm out to block him.

"You can't have him, so get that murderous look off your face."

Fuck. They'd kept the fucker in a holding room at the Norcross office after the museum. Saxon had been sure that he'd gotten the message to leave Gia alone.

"This have anything to do with the disturbance at Easton's museum?"

Saxon just looked at Hunt.

His friend sighed. "I'd like to help."

"I'll let you know if you can. My priority is keeping Gia safe."

A flicker of a smile crossed Hunt's face. "You finally went there. What's Vander think of you and the gorgeous Ms. Norcross?"

Saxon remained silent.

"Oh shit, you haven't told him yet." Hunt shook his head. "You're taking your life into your own hands, my friend."

Saxon turned his focus on Dennett's man. He was bleeding from the side of the head, and his hair was wet. "What happened to our would-be abductor?"

Hunt grinned. "Gia beaned him with a teapot."

Saxon sucked back a laugh. Of course, she did.

"You'd better not piss her off, Buchanan."

Saxon swallowed a snort. He pissed Gia off multiple times a day. He headed in her direction and when she saw him, a dozen emotions flitted across her face. He focused on the relief he saw echoed in her eyes.

"You okay?" He cupped her cheek.

"I'm fine."

"Assault with a deadly teapot?"

Her lips twitched. "He had it coming."

Saxon looked at Rome. The man's face was impassive, but Saxon knew him well enough to know he was pissed.

"Guy was standing right fucking beside us, and I didn't make him," Rome growled.

"He blends," Saxon said.

"I can't believe he tried again, knowing Norcross is involved," Rome added.

"He told me Dennett pays well," Gia said. "And that I'm messing up his precious reputation."

Fucker. "I'll get Rhys to run down who he is."

Rome frowned. "You don't think he'll come after her again, do you?"

"I'm not taking any chances."

"Hello, standing right here, getting ignored," Gia bit out.

Because he needed it, Saxon spun, grabbed her and dragged her up on her toes. He closed his mouth over hers.

She fought him...for two seconds, then she threw her arms around his neck and kissed him back. She pressed every inch of her curvy, little body against his.

When he lifted his head, she had a dreamy look on her face.

"Oh, fuck," Rome muttered.

Saxon tightened his hold on Gia. "I haven't told Vander yet, so keep this to yourself."

"Vander?" Gia squeaked. "Why do you have to talk to Vander?" Her eyes sparked. "I'm an adult, and don't need my brother's permission to do anything."

Rome coughed and looked away.

"There's a code," Saxon said.

"A code? I don't—" She shook her head. "It doesn't matter, because this—" she waved a hand between her and Saxon "—is not happening."

He scowled. "It's happening."

"No, I—"

He dragged her back and kissed her again. Soon she was clinging to him, and biting his bottom lip.

"I hate you," she muttered.

"No, you don't."

"Well, if you've got her, I'm out of here," Rome said.

"Thanks, Rome," Gia said.

He flicked his fingers at her, and then was gone.

"I think it's best I get you home," Saxon said.

"And locked up safe?" she said archly.

He pressed a hand to her lower back, leading her out of the coffee shop. "Locked up where you can't get into any trouble."

She gasped. "This *wasn't* my fault."

"Let's get your things."

Saxon waited while Gia got her bag and said goodbye to Ashley. She was quiet on the quick drive back to her place.

She was still quiet when they walked inside.

With a sigh, she set her bag down on the table. "I just want all of this done and over. I want Dennett to be a bad memory. I want Willow safe."

Saxon bit his tongue.

She turned, temper working behind her eyes. "I want innocent bystanders safe. That asshole used a *baby* today. That child could've been hurt."

Gia could've been hurt too, but he saw that she wasn't even thinking of that.

Typical Gia.

She stomped around her living room, muttering curses.

"Argh, I want to throw something, but all my stuff's been broken already."

Under the anger, she was afraid, anxious. Saxon

wanted her to relax. "Why don't I cook you some dinner, and pour you a glass of wine?"

Her eyebrows shot up. "You can cook?"

"Yep. Go and change, and I'll get that wine ready."

She stared at him for a beat, then headed to her bedroom.

He checked her fridge and pantry. Hmm, some pork medallions, with a balsamic sauce and some asparagus. Should do the trick.

Saxon rolled his sleeves up, found a bottle of Gia's favorite Syrah, and poured a glass for both of them.

He'd just gotten the meat frying when his phone rang. He picked it up, saw it was his mother, and closed his eyes for a second. *Damn*. He put it on speaker.

"Hello, Mother."

"Saxon. I heard some unpleasant news today." Her tone sounded like she'd sucked a lemon.

He waited for her to say more. "So, you going to tell me, or are we just going to wait here in silence?"

She huffed out a breath. "No manners. Missy Stevens told me she heard something unpleasant...about a situation in a coffee shop downtown. And you were involved."

"Not involved, Mother. I got there afterward. A woman who means a lot to me was attacked."

"I fail to see why you had to get involved. Dragging the Buchanan name into sordid issues."

He rolled his eyes. "Because I take care of my friends, and because it's my job."

There was a long pause and Saxon mixed the sauce in the pan.

"I wish you would stop acting out," his mother said.

Like his ten-year military career, that she knew practically nothing about, and his last few years working at Norcross were all just a tantrum to make her life difficult. When it came to Rupert and Vanessa Buchanan, they only thought of themselves. Saxon felt a familiar hollowness in his chest, but just shook his head.

"Come for dinner," his mother said. "I want you to meet the daughter of our friends, the Fishers."

Gia walked in, her gaze on him before it shifted to the phone.

"She's just lovely," his mother said. "She just attended the Cotillion Debutante Ball."

So, she'd be eighteen or nineteen. Saxon was thirty-four. He had no interest in a girl. "No thanks, Mother."

"Really, Saxon. I wish you'd stop being selfish. You have a family name to uphold—"

"Like you and Father do?"

"Yes," she said loftily.

"Dad golfs, you lunch, and you both have affairs when it suits you. How is that upholding the Buchanan name?"

His gut churned and he looked at Gia. She had a strange look on her face.

"You are so vulgar and vile, Saxon Buchanan. I have no idea how I created you—"

"Stop right there." Gia strode forward. "You do *not* get to talk to him like that."

"Who is this?" his mother cried.

Saxon blinked. He recognized when Gia was losing her temper.

"Saxon is a good man," Gia said. "He served his country, and now he helps people."

His mother spluttered. "Well, really—"

"You sound like a selfish bitch. Do you even know your son? Do you?"

Saxon's mother tried to talk, but Gia cut her off.

"He's protecting me, keeping me safe. I won't listen to your filth anymore. Saxon is—" her brown eyes met his "—well, he can be bossy, and a bit of a snob, but he's a good, honorable man. You don't deserve him."

Fire ignited in Saxon's gut. No one had ever jumped to his defense like that.

In Ghost Ops, Vander and his fellow soldiers had always had his back. But against his family, no one had defended him before. No one.

"How dare you—"

"No. That's enough." Gia stabbed at Saxon's phone and ended the call.

She snatched a glass of wine off the island and gulped some down. "Saxon, your mom is a bitch."

He smiled. "I know."

Gia sucked in a big breath. "I don't like her."

"I'm pretty sure the feeling is mutual."

She smiled at him over her glass.

He smiled back. "Thanks, Contessa."

CHAPTER SEVEN

Gia ate the delicious meal, savoring each bite. Saxon Buchanan could cook. Who knew?

He sat on the other side of the table, sprawled in his chair.

Licks of heat filled her belly. His shirt was open at the neck, and his sleeves were rolled up. Light glinted off the gold in his hair.

How was she supposed to keep him at arm's length when she wanted to leap the table and straddle him?

Down, hussy Gia. She grabbed her wine and took a sip.

"Well, at least Dennett's goon should leave me alone now," she said.

Saxon grunted. "He was released on bail."

"What? Already?"

"Hunt texted me. Apparently, he had no priors."

"How is that possible? He's a henchman for a bad guy."

Saxon leaned back. "He's good at what he does, so he

doesn't leave a trail. And it's clear that he likes to keep his reputation intact."

She stilled. "You think he'll come after me again?"

"No idea, but I'll be prepared if he does."

Great. Gia would keep her Ruger in her handbag from now on. "Dinner was great."

"Thanks. I like the way you say that with a thread of disbelief in your voice."

She grinned at him.

But in her head, her thoughts turned back to his mother. *God.* What a cow. Gia shifted in her seat. All these years she'd thought that Saxon had a golden, spoiled upbringing.

She realized now just how often he'd been at the Norcross home, eating her mama's cooking. How many times he'd slept over, crashing in Vander's room.

She eyed his handsome face.

"And now I feel like a lab experiment under the microscope," he said.

She shook her head and sipped her wine. "Your mom..."

He shrugged a shoulder. "I'm used to my parents. My father's the same. They're both snobs, lazy, and selfish. I don't know why they bothered to have a child. I was raised by nannies and housekeepers."

His tone was so...bland. Empty.

Gia reached across the table and grabbed his hand. She didn't know what to say to make him feel better, and usually she always had plenty of words.

He shot her a slow smile. "You going to comfort the poor little rich boy, Gia?"

She rolled her eyes at him.

His smile widened, his gaze tracing her face.

The air changed, charging with heat. Her belly did a crazy little dance, and he slid a long leg against hers beneath the table.

"Saxon." She tried to tug her hand away, but he held on tight.

"No more avoiding or dancing around this. You know what's between us. It's been there a long time."

She swallowed and shook her head.

"You aren't a coward, Gia Gabriella."

"Saxon, no. You're my brother's best friend, and I'm focused on my company. I don't have time for a man, especially one who, while insanely attractive, makes me want to strangle him most of the time."

Saxon's grin made her panties catch fire.

"Insanely attractive?"

She raised a brow. "You missed the strangle bit."

He leaned forward, tangling their fingers together. "We have heat. You're smart, gorgeous, and sassy. Sometimes I want to strangle you, too, but that just adds some spice."

"No." Dammit, even she could hear the waver in her voice.

"Yes." He slid his finger between two of hers, into the sensitive webbing.

A jolt of sensation rocked her and desire coiled in her belly. *Oh, God.* She felt her resolve wavering.

"You want me, Gia," he said in a low, sexy voice.

"Wanting isn't the problem." It was the fact that she'd tumble head over heels in love with him. She knew it, deep in her heart. And when he didn't love her back...

No.

She shook her head.

"You're mine, Contessa. I'm not giving up."

There was a knock at the door, and she yanked her hand out of his and leaped to her feet.

Saved by the proverbial bell.

Saxon rose, his expression turning serious. "Sit, I'll get it."

She watched him check the peephole, then relax. He opened the door, and Haven and Rhys walked in.

"Gia." Her friend rushed to her.

Gia hugged her fiercely.

"You're all right?" There was concern on Haven's pretty face. Her brown hair was pulled back in a pony-tail, and she'd clearly changed after work—she wore jeans and a knit top.

Gia nodded. "I'm okay."

Haven looked around. "Oh, your place."

Gia swallowed. "It's just things."

Haven pulled her close.

"My turn." Next, Rhys pulled Gia in for a hug. He smelled of his usual cologne. His dark, shaggy hair was messier than usual. No doubt Haven's fault. Gia's friend had confessed to loving running her hands through it... usually when Rhys was kissing her senseless.

Ew. Too much information.

Haven glanced at the table and the dinner resting on it. She raised an eyebrow and when Gia looked at it, she guessed it did look a little romantic. Haven eyed Gia, then Saxon speculatively.

Gia cleared her throat. "Saxon cooked. He's not bad at it."

"Rhys can make toast and scramble an egg. And apparently grill...although I've yet to see that."

Rhys slid an arm across Haven's shoulders. "You'll be amazed, babe."

Haven nestled into him with a smile.

"So," Rhys said. "I tracked down Dennett's man. His name is Conrad Lex."

Saxon frowned. "Yeah, Hunt texted me earlier. He got out on bail. Name doesn't ring any bells."

"He lays low. He's got a rep for blending in and getting the job done." Rhys glanced at Gia. "Word is Dennett is displeased that he has no gems and no Willow. And Lex is displeased that Gia's made a fool out of him twice."

Gia huffed out a breath. "Oh, so I'm to blame."

"Lex gets a dent in his reputation by letting a woman make him look like an idiot, it means less work for him. He'll likely retaliate."

Great. Gia shook her head. "Men are assholes. *Cazzo!*"

"Hey, not all of us." Rhys tugged on one of Gia's curls.

Saxon grabbed her hand. "Don't worry. Lex won't touch you. I promise."

She met his green gaze and nodded. She knew he'd protect her.

"Um, we'll be in Gia's bedroom." Haven took Gia's hand and towed her across the living room. "Girl talk."

In the bedroom, Haven closed the door. "You're sleeping with Saxon!"

"No! I've never slept with him. And I never will." *Wow, that lacked conviction.*

"Girlfriend." Haven cocked a hip. "He was out there eyeing you like he's a starving lion and you're a thick, juicy steak."

"Wow, and you told me my analogies were gross."

"Gia!"

"We kissed..."

"And?"

"Um, he gave me a stunning orgasm in my kitchen this morning."

Haven's eyes popped wide. "Oh."

"And he says I'm his and he's claiming me."

"That's a bit hot. I'm a little turned on."

"It's *not* happening, Haven. This is Saxon Buchanan. My arch nemesis. He's...the Alien to my Ripley. Kanye to my Taylor."

Haven snorted. "Romeo to your Juliet?"

"Half the time I want to hit him, and the rest of the time I want to..."

"Screw his brains out?"

Gia moaned and dropped to her bed. "Yes. But I can't go there, Haven. Saxon is...he's a risk I can't take."

"I understand." Haven sat beside her. "I felt the same about Rhys." She took Gia's hand. "But now I'm in love and the happiest I've ever been in my entire life. Love is a risk, Gia."

Gia shook her head. "Saxon and I, it's just lust." Out of this world, panty-melting lust. "It'll burn out."

"Mmm-hmm."

"I hate when you make that sound."

Haven pressed her tongue to her teeth.

Gia sighed. "He could really hurt me, Haven. I'm scared, and I hate being scared."

Her friend hugged her. "How about Rhys and I stay with you tonight?"

"Yes!" That meant Saxon would have to go. She could get some distance, clear her head. "I love you."

Haven rolled her eyes. "I love you, too."

Together, they headed back into the living room. The men were talking in low serious tones.

"Haven and Rhys are staying with me tonight," Gia announced.

Saxon's head snapped up and he scowled at her.

Gia grabbed Haven's hand. "I need my girlfriend with me."

Frowning, Rhys nodded. "Sure thing."

Several emotions crossed Saxon's face at lightning speed—annoyance, anger, resignation, amusement. He couldn't make a fuss about this, or Rhys would get suspicious.

"Okay, Contessa," Saxon said. "But I'll pick you up for work in the morning." His gaze bored into hers. *You can't get rid of me that easily.*

She tossed her head back. *I can try.*

Saxon smiled, slow and sexy. *You can run, but I'll catch you.*

Gia swallowed. *Crap.*

THE NEXT MORNING, Saxon waited at the curb outside Gia's building, his Bentley idling.

She'd skillfully avoided him last night. He smiled, admiring her skills. *Sneaky minx.*

His house had seemed strangely empty without her there. It was weird, because she'd only spent one night.

But she'd spend more. And not in his guest room.

He saw her exit her building and his gut went tight.

Damn, she was gorgeous. She wore a fitted, black skirt with an emerald-green shirt. She also wore heels that were high and sexy. Today, she'd left her hair down, and there were curls everywhere.

Shit, he was getting hard.

She opened the door and slid in. "Morning." She flashed plenty of leg, totally deliberately. "Sleep well?"

"Yeah, after I jacked off imagining you sucking my cock."

She sucked in a breath.

"You?" he asked.

"Yes, after I spent some time with my vibrator imagining Henry as the Witcher."

Saxon grinned. "Liar."

She sniffed and looked forward through the windshield.

They headed toward her office. She did look well rested, and her face was healed now.

"Another busy day?" he asked.

She nodded, and just then, her cell phone rang. She fished it out of her giant handbag. "It's Easton."

"Put it on speaker."

"Hi, Easton," she said.

"G, you doing all right?"

"Fine, big brother. Are you busy wheeling and dealing? Making a few extra millions?"

"Always." Amusement laced her brother's voice. "Rhys said he and Haven stayed with you last night."

"Yes, and Saxon's my babysitter again today."

"Hey, Sax," Easton said.

"Hey."

There was a pause. "You guys haven't shed any blood yet?"

Gia snorted. "When I finally take Saxon out, you won't find any blood, or the body."

Easton laughed, and Saxon just shook his head.

"Look, a business colleague of mine got in touch," Easton said. "He passed on some information that might be relevant to Dennett, and whatever was in that bag. But I don't want to talk about it over the phone."

Saxon's hands flexed on the wheel. "We can come to you."

"Great. I'll have my assistant clear my schedule."

"Gia?" Saxon said.

"I'll message Ashley and have her cancel my early calls."

Not long afterward, they pulled up in front of the tall tower downtown that housed the offices of Norcross Inc. Easton had the top two floors. They passed through security and headed up in the elevator.

Saxon followed Gia toward Easton's office. While

Gia's offices were feminine, bright, and funky, Easton's were modern, slick, and expensive.

An attractive blonde rose from the desk in front of two glossy, wooden, double doors. She wore a crisp, white shirt tucked into a tight, gray skirt, and was tall and curvy.

"Hello. You must be Gia, Mr. Norcross' sister. You have my condolences."

Gia blinked and Saxon raised a brow.

"Ah, where's Mrs. Skilton?" Gia asked.

Saxon had met Easton's fierce assistant once. From memory, she was in her sixties, with gray-streaked black hair, and possessed an iron personality. She ran Easton's calendar with military precision, and no one got past her.

This gorgeous woman was not Mrs. Skilton.

"I'm Harlow Carlson. Mrs. Skilton took leave. She has a new grandchild. She picked me to deal with Mr. Arrogant, Bossy, and Self-Important."

Gia broke into laughter, and Saxon grinned.

Easton's new assistant continued. "Mrs. Skilton said he needed someone competent. Who wouldn't cower before him, or strip naked on his desk."

Gia's laughter increased.

Easton strode out of his office and shot a hot glare at his assistant. "What did you do now?"

The woman smiled sweetly. "Just meeting your lovely sister."

Gia touched the woman's arm. "Get my number from Easton. Let's have coffee sometime. Or cosmos."

Harlow smiled. "A pleasure to meet you. And your man."

Easton scowled. "Saxon isn't her man, he's her bodyguard."

Harlow turned her back to Easton and raised her brows at Gia.

"Coffee," Gia said again.

Saxon nudged Gia into Easton's plush office. He really needed to talk to Vander, Rhys, and Easton about what was going on between him and Gia.

"You are not having coffee with my sister." Easton called out as he followed them in.

"I can have coffee with whomever I want, Mr. Bossy," came the reply.

Easton slammed the door closed.

"I like her," Gia said.

"She's a menace." Easton circled his desk and sat. Behind him, the floor-to-ceiling windows framed a perfect view of the city, with the Transamerica Pyramid in the center, and the bay in the background.

"A gorgeous menace," Saxon added.

Gia swiveled and frowned at him. "You have always had a thing for leggy blondes."

"Do not hit on my assistant," Easton growled.

Saxon raised his hands. "I find myself partial to brunettes lately."

Gia looked like she was fighting a smile.

Easton waved at the guest chairs in front of his desk. "Despite her personality failings, Ms. Carlson is an excellent executive assistant. Most of the admins from the shared pool are terrified of me."

"No idea why," Gia drawled dryly. "And I guess the rest of them are trying to become Mrs. Easton Norcross."

Her brother growled. "I don't like working with fools, or people who can't keep up with me."

"Did one really strip naked on your desk?" Saxon asked.

"Ew," Gia exclaimed, eyeing the desk.

"No comment," Easton said. "Now, Dennett."

Saxon leaned back in his chair.

"I heard on the grapevine that Dennett stole an incredibly rare, valuable diamond," Easton said.

"What?" Gia breathed.

"Well, he didn't steal it, exactly. He won it in a very high-stakes poker game. The previous owner is well beyond pissed. I had a business colleague who was at the game."

"So, Dennett wants the diamond back," Saxon said. "And its previous owner does as well."

"I took a look at the stones," Gia said. "I didn't see a diamond." Her nose wrinkled. "I was busy imagining some ruby and emerald jewelry at the time."

Of course, she was. Saxon paused. She'd look beautiful in rubies or emeralds. Vibrant colors against her bronze skin and dark hair.

He might need to get her some. He'd never felt the desire to buy a woman jewelry before, but with Gia, he liked the idea of seeing something of his against her skin.

"My contact said rare," Easton said. "The diamond's probably colored. And it has some sort of history behind it."

"Wait!" Gia cried. "There was a large, pale-pink stone."

"A pink diamond." Saxon nodded. "Pinks are worth

up to twenty times more than white diamonds. And if it's old, that would make it invaluable."

"God," Gia breathed.

"Did your contact say who the previous owner was?"

Easton's jaw tightened. "Albert Sackler."

"Fuck," Saxon said.

"Who is he?" Gia demanded.

"Eccentric old guy," Saxon said. "Made his money from tech, but the rumor is he traffics women for fun behind-the-scenes."

"You can't be serious," Gia said, horror on her face.

"It's best we steer well clear of him." There was no way in hell Saxon was letting that sick fuck anywhere near Gia.

CHAPTER EIGHT

Gia was incredibly busy at work, but thoughts of the stolen diamond and gross, evil men who abused women wouldn't leave her alone.

She tried to focus on her current project for a client, but finally pushed the laptop away and sighed.

Saxon wasn't with her right now, but he wouldn't be far away.

He had her all churned up too.

Refocusing, she checked her email. There was still nothing from Willow, and her belly clenched. Was Will all right?

God, everything was going wrong.

Frustrated, she Googled Albert Sackler. Nothing shady or evil showed up. There was a spread about his big house in Palo Alto, and several pictures of a slightly overweight man in his late sixties, who clearly liked to wear vests with his suits. He didn't look like an evil asshole. But they never did.

"Contessa?"

She glanced up to see Saxon in the doorway. "Yes?"

He cocked his head and walked over. "You okay?"

Gia blew out a breath. "No. Willow is on the run, there is a stolen, giant pink diamond out there somewhere, all my things need replacing, and then there are the bad guys, Dennett and now Sackler."

Saxon moved behind her and started rubbing her shoulders. "So, you do have a breaking point?" He kneaded her tense muscles. "I always thought the intimidating Gia Norcross could handle anything."

God, he had strong hands. She dropped her head forward and bit back a moan. "I'll handle it, but I'd be happy if we could catch a break."

"You aren't alone to cope with this, Gia."

She felt a shot of warmth, but he was another thing leaving her jittery and confused. "I appreciate that, Saxon, but we still aren't doing this 'us' thing."

He leaned down. Oh, he smelled so good. He was still massaging her muscles as he nipped her earlobe. This time, she couldn't stop the small moan that escaped.

"We're doing it," he murmured. "Every time I touch you, you light up."

"So arrogant." She hated that her voice was breathy.

He nipped her ear again. "I have to run out to meet Vander to follow up on some stuff." He swiveled and pressed a hip to her desk. "Rome's busy, so I want you to stay here."

"Okay."

"Don't leave the building, Gia. Don't go near the front doors, stay in your office, if you can. No visitors. At least not anybody that you don't know."

ANNA HACKETT

"I won't leave. I don't have a death wish."

"Ace has tapped into the building's security cameras. He'll monitor them."

Gia's eyes narrowed. "By tapped in, do you mean hacked?"

Saxon just smiled. "Stay out of trouble until I get back." He reached over and tugged on one of her curls.

Then he strode out, shrugging into his jacket.

She stood and watched him cross the open-plan area. Every one of her female employees stopped to watch him as well.

"Have you slept with him yet?" Ashley asked from the doorway.

"Don't you have work to do?"

"I'm doing it. I'm just not sure those of us around you two will survive the smoldering sexual tension much longer."

Gia rolled her eyes. Her cell phone started ringing, and she moved back to her desk. "Gia Norcross."

"Third time's the charm," a low, male voice said. "I'll get you next time."

She frowned. "Excuse me? Who is this?"

"Twice you've made me look like an incompetent fool. Not again."

"Lex," she breathed.

"Yes. My reputation is everything."

"If you suck, that's not my problem."

"Dennett let me go, but I'm doing this job for free now."

His voice was so bland, unemotional. It made goose bumps rise on her skin. "What job?"

110

"Taking you down."

Gia's mouth went dry and she swallowed. "My brothers—"

"I don't care. If I do it under their noses, or take them down too, my reputation will be bulletproof."

Oh, God. "Look, asshole, if you—"

"See you soon, Gia."

The line went dead. *Fuck.* Just what she needed. An out-for-vengeance hitman, or henchman, or whatever the hell he was.

Well, there was nothing she could do right now. She rubbed her temple and made a mental note to tell Saxon when he got back.

She sat back down at her desk and her phone rang again. She eyed it like it was a snake before answering it.

"Gia Norcross."

"Hey, Contessa."

She blew out a relieved breath.

"Heard you got a call from Lex." Saxon's voice turned ice cold.

"How do you know that?"

"I told you that Ace is keeping an eye on things."

"You tapped my phone!"

"Just your cell."

"Unbelievable."

"To keep you safe."

"You could've asked first!"

"Better to beg forgiveness after the fact."

"Well, I don't hear you begging."

His voice lowered. "I don't beg, baby."

Her hand clenched on the phone. "I bet I could make you beg."

There was silence, followed by Saxon's harsh breathing across the line.

Yes! She'd gotten to the always smooth and cool Saxon Buchanan.

"Yeah, Contessa, I reckon you could."

Oh, God. A shot of heat went straight between her legs and she shifted restlessly in her seat.

"Stay inside," he warned again.

"Yes, Master Buchanan."

His deep chuckle came over the line. "I like that."

She rolled her eyes. She knew he couldn't see it, but she hoped he could sense it. "Goodbye, Saxon."

"Bye, darling."

Gia sat back in her chair. She was turned on. She wanted Saxon. It felt like he was a black hole, pulling her closer and closer.

And dammit, she wanted to dive right in.

That scared her.

When her phone rang again, she almost cursed aloud, but then she saw it was Haven. "Hey, girlfriend."

"Hey, G. How you doing?"

"Oh, well, bad guys are after me, a priceless, pink diamond is missing, an old friend is on the run, and I have no idea if she's okay. Added to that, the hottest guy I know wants to claim me and bang my brains out."

Haven made a choked sound. "A bit of a rough day, then. Although, if you let the hot guy have his way, you'd be far less stressed."

"But then I'd become addicted to him, and things will be even more out of control."

"Gia, you aren't supposed to be in control when you fall in love."

"No one said anything about love!"

"Mmm."

"I *hate* that sound." Gia closed her eyes. "I can't fall in love with Saxon Buchanan."

"Girlfriend, you're already halfway there."

God. Gia stood, then sat again. It was like a punch to the stomach.

"You probably have been for a long time," Haven added.

Shit. Gia pressed a hand to her belly. "I can't talk about this right now."

"Okay, how about we talk about diamonds?"

"Usually, it's a subject I like, but lately, not so much."

"More specifically, a large pink one."

"Easton told you guys about Sackler's stolen diamond?"

"He told Rhys. I was there. I'm at the museum now, so I decided to talk to a few of my contacts—"

"Haven..."

"I made a few phone calls, nothing dangerous. Anyway, I tracked down a friend who's an expert in old jewelry. Gia, can you describe the diamond you saw?"

"I think so. I didn't pay too much attention. It was rectangular—"

"Okay, I want you to talk with Deborah, my jewelry expert."

"Haven, I can't leave my office. Saxon had to leave to follow a lead."

"Then we'll come to you. We'll be there in half an hour."

"All right. See you then."

Gia wasn't sure if more info on the diamond would help, but the more they had, the better.

She knew Saxon had said no visitors, but this was Haven, and her expert was someone she'd vouch for. Gia reached for her coffee mug and sipped. She grimaced. Her drink was cold.

Ashley appeared in the doorway, holding out a fresh mug. "Latte?"

Gia took it. It was hot. "How do you do that?"

Her pink-haired assistant winked. "Special assistant powers. If I told you, I'd have to kill you." Ashley winced. "Sorry, now's probably not the time to make jokes about that."

Gia waved a hand. "I'd prefer to laugh than lose my shit."

"I don't think you've ever lost your shit."

"I'm on the verge, my friend."

"Luckily, there's a strong pair of arms waiting to catch you."

Gia aimed a glare Ashley's way. "Get back to work. Oh, and Haven's coming with a guest."

Gia did some more work before Ashley buzzed her to tell her that Haven was here. Gia rose.

Haven bustled in, looking gorgeous in stylish, gray slacks, and a blush-pink top. There was another woman with her. She was about Gia's mother's age, but with ash-blonde hair in a stylish bob, flawless makeup, and a sharp suit.

"Gia." Haven circled the desk and they hugged. "This is Deborah Cohen."

Gia shook the woman's hand. "Thanks for helping."

"My pleasure." The woman had a deep smoker's voice. "Haven's always fabulous to work with, so I'm happy to help."

They all sat.

"So, she told you that we're looking for info on a rare, valuable, pink diamond?" Gia rested her hands on her desk.

Deborah nodded. "Can you describe it?"

"To be honest, it didn't really make much of an impact on me. It was rectangular, not very shiny, flat on the top. It was sort of clear, more transparent than most diamonds I've seen."

The older woman's face changed and Gia's stomach dropped.

"What?" Gia prompted.

"You described a table-cut diamond. They have less facets than a modern, brilliant-cut diamond, which is the most popular style today. The table-cut gives the stone the more translucent look you saw."

"Okay. This diamond was table-cut and pale pink."

Deborah nodded. "Something like this?" She held up her phone to show an image.

A large, rectangular pink diamond in an elaborate setting of white diamonds.

Gia nodded. "Without the white diamonds, of

course, and smaller. Yes, that looks identical to the stone I saw."

"This is the largest and oldest pink diamond in the world. It's called the Daria-i-Noor, or the Sea of Light, and came from the Kollur Mine in India. It once belonged to the Shah Jahan, and legend says it may have graced his famous Peacock Throne. It changed hands several times, and is now part of the Iranian Crown Jewels and kept in the Central Bank of Iran. It's 182 carats, and it is impossible to put a price on it, but let's go with somewhere between a hundred and two hundred million."

Gia's mouth dropped open.

"Wow," Haven breathed.

"The one I saw wasn't that big," Gia said. "It can't possibly be that diamond."

"No," Deborah agreed. "But there are rumors and legends that say the Daria-i-Noor came from a larger diamond."

"Larger?" Gia said weakly.

"In 1642, a French jeweler by the name of Jean-Baptiste Tavernier described a large pink diamond that was studded in the Shah's throne. He called it Diamanta Grande Table, or the Great Table diamond. It was estimated to be 400 carats. Some people believe that the Daria-i-Noor, and another oval pink diamond that is also part of the Iranian Crown Jewels called the Noor-ul-Ain or the Light of the Eye, were both cut from the Great Table diamond."

"So, the Daria-i-Noor is 182 carats," Gia said.

"And the Noor-ul-Ain is 60 carats," Deborah added.

"That leaves approximately 150 carats," Gia said.

The older woman nodded. "Obviously some gets lost during the cutting process, but there could have been other diamonds that came from the Great Table pink diamond."

"There are no other leads or stories?" Haven asked.

"No," Deborah said. "There are always plenty of myths and legends, though. Pink diamonds are said to increase creativity and intuitiveness. And many of the diamonds that came from the Kollur Mine are said to be cursed."

Gia remembered a cursed diamond exhibit held at a museum in Washington DC not too long ago. There was a dangerous attack that made the headlines across the country. The press gloried in diving into all the gory details on the curses.

"If this diamond was part of the Great Table, it would be very valuable," Gia said.

The woman nodded. "Quality and size aside, it's steeped in history, once owned by emperors. That adds to its value."

"God." *Who the hell had the diamond?*

Suddenly, her door flew open and Saxon strode in, unhappiness blasting off him. "What the fuck is going on?" He pressed his hands to his lean hips.

Gia rose. "Saxon—"

"I told you to stay here, and no visitors. Explain."

SAXON STARED AT GIA, waiting. He'd been mad

from the moment that Ace had called him to tell him that Haven and her friend were on the way.

Fire ignited in Gia's eyes. "Don't take that tone with me."

"I'm trying to keep you safe."

She moved toward him. "I didn't leave. I hardly think Haven is going to attack me."

"And do you know your other guest?"

Both Haven and the other woman watched them with rapt attention.

"No," Gia said. "But Haven does. And I don't think even Lex can pull off masquerading as a woman."

Her perfume hit Saxon and that chin jutted at him. Damn, he loved it when she was mad. He tried to keep a hold on his anger.

"Instead of coming in here, growling like an enraged alpha male—"

Saxon growled and gripped her arm.

"Saxon!"

He dragged her close and kissed her. It was the best way to shut her up. The kiss was hard, deep, and wet. Then he set her back down on her heels.

She blinked. "Damn you, Saxon Buchanan! You can't just end an argument by kissing me."

"Darling," Deborah drawled. "I'd let him."

Haven grinned at them.

"Saxon, this is Deborah Cohen," Gia said. "A jewelry expert Haven knows."

Saxon nodded at the woman.

"She's an expert in old, historic jewelry."

He straightened. "The diamond?"

Gia nodded and shared what they'd learned.

He scowled. "Shit, I hope what we're looking for isn't part of that diamond."

"Thank you for your help, Deborah," Gia said.

The woman rose and shook Gia's hand. "Good luck. I hope you get your situation resolved soon. Let me know if you do find the diamond. I'd love to see a picture of it."

After Deborah left, Haven grinned at them. "So?"

"We aren't together," Gia said.

"We are," Saxon said.

"God, you guys generate so much steam." Haven stood and shivered. "I might have to jump Rhys for a quickie before the get-together tonight."

"Ew. TMI." Gia held up a hand. "Wait, what get-together?"

"The guys decided on dinner and drinks tonight at some new sports bar," Haven said.

Gia pinned Saxon with a look. "Can I go?"

"Well—"

"Were you going to tell me, or—"

He pressed a hand over her mouth. "I was going to tell you. I haven't had a chance, and you gearing up to rant will delay it even more."

Chocolate-brown eyes fumed, then she bit his palm.

He yanked his hand back and shook his head. "You can bite me later, Contessa."

She sniffed.

"And yes, we can go. All the guys will be there."

"Yay." Haven hugged Gia. "I need to get back to the museum to finish a few things. I'll see you there."

Gia walked back to her desk.

"Are you almost done?" he asked.

"I have a couple of more things I want to finish—"

He pressed up against her, trapping her against her desk. "Did I tell you that I like your shirt? And your shoes?"

"No," she breathed.

"I like what's under that shirt even more." He slid a hand around her waist, then leaned down and nipped the side of her neck.

A small moan escaped her, and he felt it in his gut, his cock.

"I need you soon, Gia Gabriella. I'm burning up for you."

She pressed her ass back against him. "We shouldn't do this."

"You want it. Where's that courageous, fearless Gia I know?"

"Don't you mean reckless?"

He nipped her neck again and she turned her head. He took her mouth. The taste of her, the scent of her, the feel of her. Saxon felt like Gia Norcross was in his pores. "You be reckless, I'm here to catch you, baby."

"Gia, I... Oops, sorry." A grinning Ashley whirled away from the door.

Gia shoved Saxon back a step. "God, you short-circuit my brain."

He smiled at her. He liked knowing he got to smart, sexy Gia.

"Go." She pointed to the couch. "Sit. Let me finish without any distractions. Don't look sexy. Don't sound sexy."

His smile widened.

"No," she cried. "*Go*. I'm not looking at you."

He sat on the couch, waiting and watching as she worked. He didn't disturb her. He sent a text to Vander with info on the Daria-i-Noor and the Great Table diamond.

Shit, Saxon hoped this diamond they were looking for was just an ordinary hunk of carbon.

Once Gia was finished and had freshened up—which included a fresh coat of red, kiss-me-now lipstick—he led her out to his Bentley.

He zoomed down the street and found a parking space near the sports bar Vander had picked. When they walked in, they found the Locker Room packed. He moved in close behind her.

It was a big, open space with lots of wood and a friendly vibe. Screens lined one wall, showing lots of games. A row of pool tables was situated at the back. A sleek bar was packed with people, the bartenders hopping. The rest of the space was filled with comfy chairs grouped around low tables, or high tables with stools. One wall was decorated to look like a locker room, and covered in signed sports memorabilia.

"Nice place," he said.

"I know. My firm's doing PR for the place, and the owner's planning to open more. The End Zone, the Press Box, and the Dugout."

"Catchy." They spotted Vander, Rome, Ace, Rhys, and Haven by some high tables not far from the pool tables. The men were all nursing beers. Haven waved.

Haven and Gia both claimed stools, heads together. Saxon ordered a beer, and a glass of wine for Gia.

Vander scowled. "I hope to hell this pink diamond is not from some priceless, mythical diamond."

Saxon sipped his beer. "Me too."

"I've got a contact who might know more." Vander lifted his own beer. "I'll see if they know anything about the Great Table diamond and diamonds that came from it."

Saxon knew who Vander's contact was. A guy from a covert, black-ops team that's name was a whisper, and which completed missions that did not exist.

"I know a guy in Denver," Rome said. "He's a former SEAL, and runs security for archeological digs and expeditions. His father is a history professor."

"Treasure Hunter Security?" Vander said.

"Yeah," Rome said. "Dec's a good guy. It's a good outfit."

Vander lifted his chin. "Ask him, but tell him to keep it quiet."

A bunch of rowdy, drunk guys at the closest pool table started making a lot of noise and Saxon frowned. He saw one of them eyeing Haven and Gia. When the man took a step toward the women, Saxon shifted and shot the man a look.

The guy hastily turned away.

Satisfied, Saxon returned to his beer.

Easton arrived, yanking off his tie. "I've had back-to-back meetings, my new assistant is giving me high blood pressure, and I need a drink."

Vander raised his brows.

"Met the assistant today," Saxon said. "Firecracker."

"I'm going to fire her as soon as I find a competent replacement. One who doesn't ride me every second of the day."

Saxon pressed his tongue to his teeth. "Sure you don't want her to ride you in another way?"

Easton stiffened. "No."

"Clue me in," Vander said.

"Easton's new assistant is a curvy, opinionated blonde."

"She's my employee," Easton said stiffly. "Fuck, I need a Scotch."

Saxon smiled. Gia and Haven were still talking, and Gia was waving her hands around. Even as a kid she'd always talked with her hands.

The rowdy drunks got even louder. Trouble was brewing. One of them pushed another guy.

Fuck. A fight broke out. Sloppy punches were thrown and then a guy slammed into a chair. Wood splintered.

Pandemonium ensued, others bellowing and joining the fight.

Vander cursed and set his beer down.

A man came barreling toward Vander. One punch from Vander and the man went down.

Some of the guy's friends rushed Vander, and he calmly flexed his hands.

Then he fought.

Vander wasn't flashy, but he was fast, brutal, and effective. He bent his knees and tossed a man. Then he spun and launched a hard side kick into another man's gut.

Tables tipped over and customers screamed. Security guards pushed through the crowd.

"Oh, God, more drama for me to sort out," Gia yelled. "My client will not be happy about this."

"Incoming," Rome murmured.

Sure enough, several guys were headed in their direction.

Haven and Gia watched, wild-eyed.

"Don't move," Saxon yelled at them.

A big guy came running at Saxon. Saxon ducked, then rammed an uppercut to the guy's stomach. He groaned and doubled over.

When Saxon looked up, he saw Vander standing in the center of the room, unconscious or groaning men littered on the floor around him.

Saxon grinned and turned.

Then his stomach dropped away. Haven was on the ground, struggling onto her hands and knees.

There was no sign of Gia.

"Haven!" Saxon yelled.

She looked over her shoulder and met his gaze. "Someone knocked me over and took Gia!"

Fuck.

CHAPTER NINE

Gia tried to struggle, but the bruiser holding her was too big and strong. He held her with her back pressed to his front, one beefy arm wrapped around her as he maneuvered her out of the bar.

The place was in chaos. Lots of people were shoving to get out, so no one was paying them any attention.

She scowled. She should be afraid, but instead, she was pissed. When her brothers and Saxon found her missing...

Chaos would seem peaceful.

They exited the bar and the cool, night air hit her bare shoulders. The man dragged her down the street. For a second, his arm loosened, and she tried to shove away.

He yanked her back.

"Let me go!" she snapped.

He ignored her. He hadn't said a word since he'd grabbed her. God, Gia hoped Haven was okay.

They stopped beside a large, black limo, and her captor opened the back door, and shoved her inside.

Gia looked up. A man in a suit sat comfortably on the long seat. He wasn't much older than her. He was attractive enough, but there was nothing special about him. He had thick, brown hair, and a bland, handsome face.

"So, you're Gia Norcross," the man said.

"And you're in a lot of trouble." She pointed out the tinted window toward the bar. "My brothers and my... man are in there, and when I say they won't be happy—"

The man held up his hand. "I know. It cost me a pretty penny to organize the fight."

Her stomach dipped. To distract them.

"I just want to talk to you," the man said.

"You're Dennett."

He smiled. "Kyle." He held out a hand.

She didn't take it.

"I want my belongings back," he said, like they were friends chatting about the weather.

"And as has been communicated to you, I don't have them. I don't know who does." She avoided mentioning the pink diamond.

A frown crossed his face. "I need Willow."

"I don't know where she is."

"But she comes to you when she needs things. Willow is a user."

And he was an asshole.

He cocked his head. "You're not what I expected. I expected a strung-out junkie, with fading looks like Willow." He reached out to touch Gia's hair. "You're very attractive."

She knocked his hand away. "I don't have the gems, and I have no idea where Willow has run off to. Leave me out of this."

He smiled, but it wasn't a very nice one. "I don't like failing, Gia. I don't like losing money, or being made a fool of by a junkie whore."

Charming. "Nothing. To. Do. With. Me."

"She'll come slinking back to you at some stage. You're the only person in her life who hasn't cut her off."

Gia's belly clenched. That made her sad for both herself and Willow. She tossed her hair back. "Look, I'm done with this. My apartment was trashed. Your fucking henchman has a vendetta."

Dennett leaned back in his seat. "Lex came highly recommended, but he's been a disappointment."

"Well, he's an asshole as well. I'm getting out now—" She reached for the door handle.

Dennett grabbed her arm, quick as a snake. "I don't think so."

Suddenly, the door was yanked open. Saxon's icily enraged face appeared.

He grabbed Gia's other wrist, and she found herself caught in a tug-of-war between two very dangerous men.

She glanced past Saxon and saw Dennett's thug laid out on the pavement, unconscious.

"Let her go," Saxon said.

The lethal tone made Gia swallow.

"I want my gems, Buchanan," Dennett snapped.

"So, find them. Gia doesn't have them, and she no longer exists for you."

"She's my best lead to finding them."

"Find another way, or you will deal with me and all of Norcross Security. Vander has already warned you off. He's not a man who likes repeating himself."

Dennett just stared at Saxon, still holding Gia's wrist.

Ugh, she didn't want him touching her at all. What the hell was he waiting for?

All of a sudden, a man appeared behind Saxon, and pressed a gun to Saxon's head.

Gia gasped, fear hot and oily inside her.

Dennett smiled. He looked smug. He'd been stalling, waiting for his other goon to appear.

Saxon's face didn't change. He showed no concern or worry. "You really want to do this the hard way?"

"Saxon—" Gia's stomach contracted to a tight ball. All she could see was that gun barrel pressed to his temple. He could get hurt. That thought drove the air out of her lungs.

Saxon moved like lightning. He jabbed an elbow back, and Dennett's man grunted. The gun went off, but Saxon was a whirl of movement. Two punches and a kick, and Dennett's thug was in the fetal position on the sidewalk.

Bending down, Saxon grabbed the man's handgun.

It all happened so fast that Gia hadn't had time to move or scream.

"Oh, my God." Gia tried not to hyperventilate. "Are you okay?"

Saxon just glared at Dennett.

Then Dennett's door was yanked open, and a pissed-off Vander stood there, Glock in hand. "I told you that Gia does *not* exist for you."

Oh, hell. Gia hated when Vander entered the "scary iceman" zone. She loved him to pieces, but he still sometimes made her want to wet herself in fear.

Dennett paled, beads of sweat breaking out on his brow. "I just wanted to talk to her."

"Liar," she spat.

Saxon pulled her out of the limo. She heard sirens, and saw a police cruiser pull up in front of the Locker Room.

Well, looking on the bright side, at least her client was getting some free press.

"Go now, Dennett," Vander said. "If I see you near my sister again, I will personally make you regret it."

"Norcross—"

"*Go.* Before I change my mind."

Gia started shaking, and Saxon pulled her against his chest. She watched as the limo slid away and wrapped her arms around him, holding on tight.

"Haven?" she asked.

"She's fine. With Rhys."

Gia moved her hand up his sleeve and felt something wet and sticky. She frowned. "Saxon?" She lifted her hand.

Blood.

Every rational thought flew out of her head. "Oh, my God, you got shot!"

Vander's head snapped up.

"Creased my arm," Saxon said. "It's fine."

"You got shot!" Gia's voice raised to a shout.

"Gia, don't lose it," Saxon said.

"Too late. We need to get you to the hospital."

"I'm not fucking going to the hospital."

Her eyes narrowed. "You are."

"I am not."

She blew out a frustrated breath. "Saxon Buchanan, you stubborn, pigheaded—"

"I'll clean it up at home. I have a well-stocked first aid kit. We all do."

Vander glanced at Saxon's arm, then nodded.

Gia threw her hands in the air. "Macho badasses. *I'll* clean it up."

He'd gotten shot. For her. A confusing mix of emotions churned inside her.

Watching her, his face softened. "Okay, Contessa."

She smiled back, then saw Vander eyeing them curiously.

"Right," Gia said. "I need to check on Haven, and find my handbag. Then you can call me Nurse Norcross."

Something hot sparked in Saxon's eye.

FUCKING DENNETT HAD TAKEN GIA. Had put his hands on her.

Saxon tugged Gia out of the bar. She had her bag, and she'd said her goodbyes to Haven and her brothers. Vander was somewhere, talking to the police.

Saxon's arm stung, but he knew it wasn't bad. He'd had bad when he'd been in Ghost Ops. He'd bled all over numerous dusty deserts. Once, he almost hadn't made it home.

Rhys and Vander, and the rest of their team, had risked their asses to save him.

"Saxon, are you sure you're okay?" Gia's brown eyes were filled with worry. For him.

"I'll be happy once you're off the street."

"I meant your arm."

"I told you, it's fine."

She was surprisingly quiet for a moment.

They stopped by his Bentley. Saxon turned to look fully at her. "Are you all right?"

She gave a little nod. "I've decided to postpone losing my shit. I hated being with Dennett." She shuddered. "I don't know how many ways I can tell him I don't have his gems. Anyway, I was scared, but angry won out." Her voice lowered. "I was more scared when I realized you'd been shot."

Saxon moved close, and she pressed her hands to his chest.

"I'm okay," he reassured her. "Alive and breathing."

She moved her hand right over his heart. "I really don't like you being shot."

"I'm not a fan of it, myself."

"Can you avoid it in the future?"

He smiled. "I'll do my best."

Then he lowered his head. This kiss was slower and deeper than their previous ones. He savored the taste of her, flavored by wine. She filled him with a sharp, gnawing need for her.

"What the fuck?"

The sharp voice made them both jerk apart.

Saxon spotted Vander standing nearby, hands on his hips. He was glaring at them, furious and incredulous.

"Vander—" Gia said.

"That's my fucking sister," Vander bit out.

"I know," Saxon replied.

"You're a brother to me. I trusted you."

Gia moved, but Saxon held her in place.

He'd fucked up. He knew he should've made time to talk with Vander earlier.

"You pick up and discard women all the time," Vander said. "You put more effort into your suits than you do women."

Gia jerked.

"You never get in deep, and you never let them in," Vander continued.

Saxon stiffened, disliking the ugly feeling moving through him. "You saying I'm not good enough for her?"

"I'm saying that when you're done, you'll break her fucking heart, and then I'll have to kill you."

"Vander," Gia snapped. "We're—"

"Get in the car, Gia," Saxon said.

Her enraged gaze swung to him. "Excuse me?"

"This is between me and Vander. Get in the car." He paused. "Please."

She hesitated, then huffed out a breath. "You testosterone-addled idiots." She yanked open the passenger door of the Bentley. "Who I fuck is my concern, Vander."

Her brother gave the tiniest flinch. "You shouldn't have gone there with him. This fucks everything up for all of us."

"You don't get a vote," she said. "My love life is not a

democracy." She got in the car and slammed the door hard enough to set the Bentley rocking.

"This wasn't a snap decision." Saxon raised a hand, shoved it through his hair. "Seeing her in danger—"

"You thought you'd move in while she was vulnerable and upset?"

"No," Saxon insisted.

Vander pointed a finger right at Saxon. "I'm too fucking pissed with you right now. Fair warning, I'm going to kick your ass." He swiveled and strode off.

Saxon exhaled loudly. That didn't go well. The bad taste in his mouth intensified. Vander was his best friend. He hated this.

But Gia was his.

He wasn't letting anyone get between them. Even Vander, and especially Gia.

He slid into the driver's seat. Gia sat fuming, staring straight ahead. He put the car in gear and pulled out. He drove to his place and into his underground garage.

"I don't have any clean clothes with me," she said.

"I'll loan you a shirt to sleep in. I'll take you back to your place early tomorrow to change before work."

She nodded. "Is everything okay with Vander?"

Saxon turned the engine off. "No."

She blew out a breath. "I don't understand all this alpha-male bullshit."

"Because you don't have the right equipment."

She shot him a withering look. "Maybe because I have a brain and use it."

Saxon smiled and shifted in his seat, but that made his wound twinge and he winced.

Gia noticed. "Come on. We need to get that cleaned up."

They walked up the stairs, and in the entry, he flicked on some lights.

She sighed, looking around. "I really love your house."

They moved up the staircase, and Saxon was hit with the realization that he'd picked a lot of stuff for the house knowing that Gia would like it. He slowed his steps. *Shit.* Had he unconsciously picked and decorated this house for Gia? *Fuck.*

"Where's your first aid kit?" she asked.

She was walking a few steps ahead of him and his gaze fell to her pert ass. Suddenly, his wound wasn't feeling so bad.

Shit. No. She'd had a rough night, Vander was pissed. Saxon finally had Gia Norcross, so he was going to take his time when they got naked. It wouldn't be rushed, and not with all this shit swirling around them.

She turned and eyed his face. "You okay?"

"Yeah, baby. First aid kit is in the master bathroom."

They walked into his bedroom and he heard her sigh. She eyed his bed, then the window with its leafy view.

Then she turned and saw his walk-in closet.

"Oh. My. God."

There was pure lust in her eyes as she stalked through the huge closet. Smiling, Saxon watched her circle the island in the middle. Then she fingered his shirts hanging in a neat row.

"How many suits do you own?" she asked, one brow arched.

"How many pairs of shoes do you own?"

She grinned. "Not enough. This is totally my dream closet."

She pulled out a drawer in the island. All his cufflinks sat in neat rows. She pulled out a second drawer that contained his watch collection.

"Holy cow, Saxon." She shook her head, stroking one of his Rolexes. "You and your watches."

He cleared his throat. "Um, this is just half the closet."

She blinked. "What?"

"There are his and hers—"

She brushed past him. By the time he'd turned, she'd moved through the other door. Obviously, the "hers" closet was empty.

Fuck, he remembered that the closets had sealed the deal when he'd bought the place. He'd known Gia would covet it.

He'd bought this place for her.

She spun around in the center of the empty closet, shaking her head. "Right, I'd better not let you bleed to death because I'm busy drooling over your closet."

"I'm not going to bleed to death."

Walking briskly, she headed into the bathroom. She made another happy sigh at the huge shower, and free-standing, stone tub.

"First aid kit's on the left side of the vanity," he said.

She moved into his spacious bathroom, along the double sinks, then pulled open the cabinet below. She heaved out his giant first aid kit, and opened it. Then she frowned.

"This is well used. You're almost out of a lot of things."

"Shit happens."

Her lips tightened.

He pulled a wooden stool out from beside the vanity and sat. She helped him shrug out of his jacket, and that's when she saw the blood staining the arm of his white shirt.

She hissed. "Saxon!"

"Damn, I liked this shirt and jacket."

"Don't joke right now, Saxon Buchanan."

She started unbuttoning his shirt. Hmm, Gia Norcross standing right in front of him, unbuttoning his shirt.

She carefully pushed the ruined shirt off.

"Vander's right," Saxon said. "I'm not good enough for you."

Her hands stilled. "That's not what he said."

"I suck at relationships because I haven't had one, haven't wanted one..."

Her eyes met his. "Do you want one now?"

He saw her pulse fluttering in her neck. "I want you more than anything I've wanted in my life."

She stared at him, the connection between them pulsing.

Then she looked at his arm. "Dammit, Saxon, this must really hurt."

"I've had worse."

Those gorgeous eyes narrowed, and she set to work pulling things out of the kit. She started cleaning his wound, focused and careful. She finished with a bandage, then leaned forward and kissed it.

He grabbed her arm. "I'm trying to be a gentleman tonight. You've had a rough, emotional day. You need to rest."

"You don't need to be a gentleman."

"I'm not going to screw this up, Gia." He cupped her cheek and kissed her, but pulled back when she whimpered. "I'll find you a T-shirt to wear to bed."

"And I'll find you some painkillers."

"No." He frowned. "I hate taking them."

She cocked her hip, full of attitude. "Too bad. I'm taking care of you, Saxon Buchanan, and you're taking the pills."

His chest locked. No one had ever taken care of him. His team medic had pumped him full of meds, sure, but no one had fussed and worried. As a kid, the only people who'd looked after him were those who were paid to do it.

He lifted his chin. "All right."

"Good."

"And Gia, I'm not fucking you tonight, but you're sleeping in my bed."

She bit her lip. "Okay, Saxon."

CHAPTER TEN

She woke with her face pressed to a hard chest covered in golden skin and intriguing black ink. A strong arm was clamped around Gia, keeping her anchored to him.

Saxon.

She fought off the fog of sleep, little tingles igniting all over her. She was plastered all over him. She looked up his body and stilled.

She'd never watched him sleep before. Awake, he was always so confident, intense, but asleep, he looked more relaxed, more boyish. Or as boyish as Saxon Buchanan could ever look.

Desire—hot and overwhelming—rushed through her. She couldn't keep fighting him much longer. She wanted him. Desperately. Completely.

Gia Norcross wanted Saxon Buchanan.

Fear bubbled through her belly. He could hurt her, destroy her.

His eyes opened and she held his green gaze. She wasn't and never had been a coward.

"Morning." His voice was rough with sleep.

"Morning. How's your arm?"

His hand shifted down her body, cupping her ass which was covered only by her silk panties. The T-shirt she'd borrowed from him had ridden up.

"What arm?" he asked.

She smoothed a hand over his chest. God, he felt so good. "Saxon."

"It's fine. I don't even feel it."

"Good." They kept staring at each other.

Screw it. She leaned down and kissed him. Mmm, it was so good. His tongue stroked hers, and her moan mingled with his groan.

She moved, straddling him, cupping his cheeks. *More.* She needed more.

With a growl, he turned, half pinning her to the bed. Then he spun her so her back and butt nestled into his body.

"Saxon—"

"All mine." His big body kept her pinned in place. His hand slid over her belly, and her breath hitched.

"I can touch you how I want. Stroke you how I want." His hand slid into her panties. "Love you how I want."

She let out a small cry. His fingers found her clit and rubbed. Her hips bucked, and she jerked against him.

"Hold still," he growled.

"I want to touch you."

"Later."

He pinched her clit, rolled it. *Oh. God.* It was too much, and not enough.

He kept working her and soon she was moaning his name.

"So fucking hot. You've got me hard as steel." He ground his hard cock against her ass. "I need to taste you."

Before Gia could manage to string two words together, he moved. He pushed her onto her back and rose above her. She loved looking at that chest, those tattoos. He shoved her panties down and off her legs, then pushed her T-shirt up, and pressed a kiss to her belly. She shivered.

Then he nudged her legs apart and growled. He ran his fingers through the neat strip of hair on her mound.

"I like this." He lowered his head. "So damn pretty, Contessa."

He slid his hands under her ass, then closed his mouth on her.

Oh. Her brain stuttered. He shoved her legs up on his shoulders, then licked and sucked.

With a sharp cry, Gia's back arched. She grabbed two handfuls of his hair.

"*Saxon.*"

He sucked on her clit, and her cries turned desperate. She dug her heels into his shoulder blades. He was so good at this. So damn good. A connoisseur.

With another lick of his clever tongue, Gia imploded. She screamed, her body shaking, intense pleasure searing through her.

She slumped back on the bed, her limbs too heavy to

move. He knelt in front of her, his lips glistening, a smug look on his face. He licked his lips and her belly contracted. So sexy.

"Apparently an orgasm helps wake you up in the morning just as well as coffee."

"You're good at that," she said breathlessly.

"I'm good at a lot of things." His gaze ran over her body. "You make it easy to give you pleasure. You're so responsive." He ran a hand along her thigh and made her shiver. "You like to control everything in your life, so I wasn't sure you'd let go so easily."

She licked her lips. "I don't usually. Not unless I trust someone."

His eyes flashed. "I've also had a lot of training at reading people. I guess I use that to watch and see what you like."

He meant training from the military, and training he probably still used in his job. She already noted that Saxon Buchanan was very perceptive.

Her gaze dropped to his boxers, tented by a large, very erect cock.

"So..." she drawled.

Disappointment crossed his face. "Baby, unless you can call off work for the day..."

She shook her head. "I can't."

"Then we've got to get moving. We need to stop at your place so you can get changed."

She turned her head and glanced at the clock. Shit, they'd be pushing it already. For the first time in forever, Gia consider playing hooky.

Saxon gripped her chin. "I want time. Not a quick fuck. I want to take my time with you."

His words shivered through her. "Me too."

"All right. I'm going to take a shower. A cold one. You'd better use the guest bathroom if you want me to keep my hands off you."

He slid to the side of the bed.

That's when Gia saw the mass of ugly scarring on his side, right near his lean waist. Frowning, she crawled across the bed and touched it.

He stilled.

It was old, but bad. The thick ridges of scar tissue crisscrossed; some surgical scars, and one part of it that was circular. *A bullet wound.*

She swallowed, feeling sick to her stomach. "Saxon, what happened?"

He didn't look at her. "It was a long time ago. On a mission that's classified."

She stroked the ugly scarring and wondered why he wouldn't look at her, what he wasn't saying.

Finally, he turned his head and smiled. It wasn't quite a usual Saxon smile. He reached over and dragged her off the bed. "Get moving, Contessa."

She wanted to push him for more, but they didn't have time. Shoving her feelings aside, she gave him a saucy smile and sauntered out. She showered in the guest room that she'd used the other night, and then screwed up her nose at putting on the previous day's clothes.

By the time she was dressed, Saxon had made coffee, and she followed the smell upstairs. She made a beeline to the island, grabbed the steaming mug sitting there, and gratefully gulped it down.

"Mmm."

He smiled at her.

She ate some toast while he held a bowl of cereal, eating and reading news articles on a tablet. She glanced around his fabulous kitchen. This was very...domestic. And crap, she liked it.

Gia bit her lip, then let the worry go. It was time to pull her head out of the sand. Saxon wasn't letting her go. It looked like they were doing this.

And...she didn't want him to let her go.

She wanted him. It was time to suck it up and deal. It wasn't a hardship. She eyed him in his gorgeous Hugo Boss suit. The Patek Philippe watch on his wrist glinted as it caught the light. Hot, rich, and classy.

"Contessa, you need to quit looking at me like that."

Her gaze flicked to his face. "I can look at you however I want, Saxon Buchanan." She sipped the last of her coffee.

He shook his head. "I know you'd argue about anything, but let's get moving. And Gia, while we're at your place, pack some clothes. Whatever you need to stay at my place."

She opened her mouth.

Saxon held up a hand. "No arguing. Just do it."

She huffed out a breath. "Fine."

After a quick trip to her place, Gia changed into a black Ralph Lauren sheath dress with cap sleeves. She paired it with black Gucci pumps with a red strap. Then she tamed her hair back severely in a tight, sleek bun.

She then pulled out her vintage, Mark Cross duffel bag and packed some clothes and toiletries. She tried not to focus on what taking stuff to Saxon's place meant.

"I'm ready." With her Louis Vuitton handbag and her duffel bag, she breezed back into the living room.

The sight of her missing paintings, vases, and other things that were now all gone gave her a pang.

"You sure are."

At Saxon's drawl, she looked up. He was watching her with blatant appreciation in his eyes. He walked over and took her duffel bag.

She smiled. "Let's get moving, Buchanan."

On the drive to her office, Gia stared out the window. She bit her lip, thoughts swirling. Saxon was looking out for her. So were her brothers and Haven.

Willow was out there somewhere, and she had no one. Gia was so worried about her.

"You're thinking of Willow."

Gia jolted, and realized that he'd parked the car in front of her office and was looking at her.

"I worry about her. Dennett's really pissed off." Gia patted her hair, smoothing it down. "I just wish I knew where she was."

"I'll find her."

Gia's mouth opened. "What?"

"I'll find her."

"For me?"

"Yeah. And because I think Willow knows more than she's shared."

"You don't know that." Warring emotions knocked around inside Gia.

"Gia, I'm your brother's troubleshooter. I know where to look to ferret out info and fix problems." He leaned over and stroked her cheek. "Let's get you upstairs. I'm going to have Ace come and keep an eye on you while I track down Willow."

He walked her upstairs, and she watched him smile at Ashley. Gia's assistant sighed dramatically.

Scrounging up the courage, Gia turned, grabbed his jacket, and kissed him.

He was stiff for a second, like she'd surprised him, then he kissed her back until she was dizzy.

"I like it when you kiss me, Contessa," he murmured against her lips. "Stay inside and out of trouble. Ace will be here soon."

"Be careful, Saxon."

Ashley watched him go, then eyed Gia. "You got another morning orgasm."

"No comment."

"I'm not the paparazzi."

Gia cleared her throat. Change of topic. "Another Norcross man, Ace, is arriving—" Gia glanced up. "Oh, there he is now."

Ace sauntered in, wearing suit pants and a blue-check shirt with his sleeves rolled up. He carried a laptop backpack over one broad shoulder.

"Where does your brother find these guys?" Ashley breathed.

"Roll that tongue back into your mouth." Gia swiveled. It was time to get to work.

IN HIS OFFICE, Saxon checked a few searches he had running. Willow hadn't gone far; he was sure of it.

I will find you.

He wouldn't let anyone hurt Gia.

There was movement in the doorway, and he glanced up to see Vander. His friend's jaw was tight, his dark-blue eyes moody.

Saxon drew in a deep breath. "You're still pissed."

"Yes, I'm still pissed," Vander clipped out. "You should've fucking told me. I didn't need to find out my best friend is doing my sister by seeing your tongue down her throat."

"There's been shit happening—"

"Fuck, Saxon." Vander ran a hand through his black hair. "You're like a brother to me. We've been through so much shit together. Now this?"

"What's going on?" Rhys appeared, frowning.

Vander looked at his shoes. "Saxon and Gia."

"Saxon and Gia what?" Rhys looked confused. "Did you guys finally try and kill each other?"

Saxon looked at the ceiling. "No."

"Not yet," Vander said.

"I'm not planning to hurt her," Saxon said.

"But you will," Vander said.

"What?" Rhys looked between them like he was trying to put the pieces of a puzzle together.

"He's fucking Gia," Vander said.

"Not yet," Saxon growled. "And don't talk about her like that."

"Saxon and Gia." About a hundred emotions crossed Rhys' face in an instant.

"What is going on?" Haven appeared. "I just got here to take Rhys out for coffee, and I can hear you guys from the front door."

"Saxon and Gia..." Rhys looked like he was struggling to find the right words. "Are *together*."

Haven looked at Rhys, then Vander. "You two only just worked that out?" She shook her head. "I thought you guys were crack investigators."

Rhys shifted his feet, and Vander's scowl darkened.

Haven arched a brow. "The two of them put off enough sexual heat to power a nuclear plant."

"She's my *sister*," Vander said.

"And I'm in love with her." The words rushed out of Saxon, and he stiffened. Shit, did he just say that aloud?

Haven clapped her hands together, beaming at him.

Saxon rubbed the back of his neck. Shit. *Fuck.* He was in love with Gia.

What the hell? He didn't know the first thing about love. He looked up, and saw that Rhys had a small smile on his face, and Vander was just staring at him.

"You should've told me that," Vander said.

"Um, I'm just kind of realizing it now."

"You fuck with her..." Vander let that hang.

He met his best friend's gaze. "I'll keep her safe, and make her happy."

"Man, you are brave." Rhys grinned at him.

Haven slapped her man's chest.

Vander shook his head. "All right, let's talk work. Where are you at with Dennett and the diamond?"

"I'm tracking down Willow. Gia wants her found."

Vander's brows drew together. "Any luck?"

"I'm closing in."

"Okay, keep me briefed." With a nod, Vander strode out.

Saxon released a breath, glad that he and Vander had cleared the air a bit.

"Soooo," Haven said, with a knowing smirk.

"Mouth zipped, Haven. I haven't discussed everything with Gia. Hell, I've barely convinced her to give me a chance."

Haven nodded. "My money's on you, Saxon."

He smiled at her. "Thanks, Haven."

Rhys dragged his woman away. "Come on, angel."

At that moment, Saxon's laptop beeped. There was a message from Ace. He read it and his muscles tensed. *Shit.* They'd found Willow. He scanned the info. *That fucking bitch.*

He kept a stranglehold on his anger and called Ace. "I'm on my way. I'll pick up Gia and take her with me."

"Got it," Ace replied. "No rush. I like Gia's offices, and there's plenty of pretty scenery."

"As long as that scenery doesn't include my woman."

Ace laughed. "She knows you've claimed her?"

"Yeah. She's not quite on board yet, but I'm working on it."

Saxon drove to the Firelight offices and parked, then jogged upstairs.

He saw Ace sitting at a desk near Ashley's, bent over his fancy, high-powered laptop. Several of Gia's employees were watching him from under their eyelashes.

"Hey, Ace."

The other man lifted his chin. "You going to talk to the friend?"

"Yeah."

Ace closed his laptop. "Good luck."

"Thanks for watching Gia."

His friend winked. "No hardship." With a wave, Ace headed out.

"She free?" Saxon asked Ashley.

The woman nodded.

"Can you clear her schedule for the next hour?"

"Sure. Luckily, I can perform miracles."

He walked into Gia's office. She was at her desk, scribbling notes. The light from the windows behind her made her skin glow.

Beautiful. And all his.

"Hey," he said.

"Saxon." She smiled at him, but then it dissolved. "What's wrong? Did Dennett hurt someone?"

"I found Willow."

Gia gasped and rose. "So fast?"

He nodded. "She's holed up in a hotel in the city."

Gia walked to him. "Thank you."

"Don't thank me, yet. Let's go and have a chat with her."

"I'm not getting good vibes from you."

"Get your bag, Contessa."

In the car, he drove them toward Nob Hill. When he pulled up in front of the historic façade of the Fairmont, the swankiest hotel in San Francisco, Gia frowned.

Saxon grabbed her hand and walked straight into the old-world grandeur of the opulent lobby. It was all marble, elegant columns, and gilt touches. Near the elevators, a young man in a hotel uniform appeared, and nodded at Saxon.

They circled a large, potted plant, and the man—who worked on the hotel maintenance team and was one of Saxon's contacts—slid Saxon a key card.

"She's in a suite." The young man rattled off the floor and room number.

Saxon slipped him some money. "Thanks, Joe."

He took Gia's hand and pulled her into the elevator, then used the card and stabbed a button for one of the top floors.

"She has a suite?" Gia frowned. "How can she afford this? She doesn't have any money."

Saxon didn't answer her.

The elevator slowed and they exited. He stopped in front of the door and knocked. "Housekeeping."

"No, thanks," came the muffled reply.

Gia stiffened. It was Willow's voice.

Saxon slid the card through the lock and they walked in. They rounded a corner into the large living area.

An angry Willow stormed out of a bedroom. "I said —" She broke off, panic blossoming on her face.

"Willow." Gia pushed forward. "What the hell? I've been so worried about you."

Gia's gaze swept the room. The heavy drapes were drawn, and boutique shopping bags were strewn all over the floor. Her gaze fell on the glossy, round table. A half empty bottle of champagne sat in an ice bucket, a card and the remnants of white powder sat beside it, along with the remains of some chocolate-dipped strawberries.

There was also a black, velvet bag resting on the surface, an emerald and a ruby spilling out of it.

Saxon had guessed as much. Ace had tracked down that Willow had pawned a ruby to afford the hotel.

Rage flared in Gia's eyes. "You have the gems."

Willow held up a hand. "Gia—"

Gia exploded. "You trashed my place! You took the gems!"

CHAPTER ELEVEN

Gia couldn't *believe* this.

"You did all of this." Anger and hurt were a violent mix in Gia's gut. "You came to me for help, you used me, you put me in danger. You *wrecked* my place."

"Gia, listen—"

Gia actually saw Willow trying to look contrite, trying to find an angle to manipulate Gia. Sucking in a breath, Gia stepped forward, and Saxon shifted closer, protecting her.

"I cared about you," she said quietly.

Willow flinched.

"I tried to help you. Everyone told me you were poison, and I defended you. You were *using* me." Gia shook her head.

Saxon moved close enough for his chest to brush her back. He was right behind her. The silent support she needed.

Willow's gaze flicked to him and her face twisted.

"Oh, so now you're banging Saxon Buchanan, taking rich cock, you're dumping me like I'm crap."

"This has nothing to do with Saxon." Gia hardened her tone. "I can't believe you!"

Willow tried for wounded again. "My life's been shit, my family's shit, everyone's been against me—"

"You can't keep using that excuse. You can't keep playing the victim."

Willow's expression turned poisonous. "Oh, it's easy for you to say. Perfect Gia Norcross. Good family, hot brothers, a hot, rich guy looking out for you, your fancy PR firm."

Gia sucked in a breath. Her eyes were wide open right now. "I got lucky with my family, but everything else I worked hard for. I didn't feel entitled, like the world owed me something. Like I should be given everything. I worked hard at college. I studied and earned my degree. I didn't party constantly and then sleep with a married professor in the hope of getting a better mark."

Willow crossed her arms and glared.

"I worked my butt off, saved, started Firelight all on my own. And I'm still working my butt off to make it successful." Gia threw out an arm. "You look at the success, the good stuff, and you want it, but you fail to see the hard work behind it. The blood, the sweat, the tears, the sleepless nights. Just being given stuff is *not* how life works, Willow."

"Fuck you," Willow said.

Pain sliced through Gia. She realized her friend from high school, the girl who'd giggled with Gia over makeup and boys, who she'd whispered secrets to in the dark was gone. The goodness in Willow had dried out, or was buried deep under the waste, selfishness, and jealousy.

"I loved you." Gia's voice was a whisper.

Willow just glared.

"You're coming with us, Willow," Saxon said. "Get your shit."

"Fuck you too, Saxon Buchanan," Willow spat.

He made a scoffing noise. "I'd prefer not to be in the same room as you. You tried your hardest to fuck all of us, but we disabused you of that notion a hundred times."

What? Gia whipped her head around to look at him. *What did that mean?*

Willow stomped across the room, and shoved her feet into some running shoes. New, shiny ones. Her clothes were new too. Gia's mouth tightened. While Gia had been worried and dodging bad guys, Willow had been shopping, snorting shit up her nose, and living the high life.

Suddenly, Willow darted to the wall and flicked the lights off.

"Willow!" Gia cried.

"Fuck," Saxon bit out.

With the blackout drapes pulled, the room was pitch black. There was the thud of falling furniture, and a second later, the fire alarm started blaring.

Saxon's curses got louder and more creative.

Damn you, Willow. Gia's nails bit into her palms.

She saw a flash of light round the corner in the entry and then a door slammed. Gia took a step and almost tripped over a chair.

The lights came back on, and she spotted Saxon by

the switch, scowling. Several chairs were overturned.

Willow was gone.

So were the gems.

Gia's stomach dropped.

"Come on." He took her hand. "We don't want to get stuck here answering questions with security."

He tugged her out of the suite and into the stairwell. Voices echoed louder as other people evacuated.

Gia stewed all the way down. Saxon's jaw was tight, and he kept glancing at her.

They finally made their way out of the hotel, and to his Bentley.

"You all right?" he asked, as they got inside.

"No." She clicked her seatbelt into place.

He pulled the car out onto the street just as a fire engine roared past, lights and sirens blaring.

"What did you mean, Willow tried her hardest to fuck all of you?"

Saxon's hands tightened on the wheel.

A horrible sensation filled her belly. "Saxon, the one thing you've always been with me is brutally honest."

"She came on to all of us back in school. Me, your brothers. Anytime you weren't around, she was rubbing up against us, making offers, trying to sneak into your brothers' beds when she stayed at your place."

Gia gasped, an ugly sensation moving inside her. "You can't be serious?"

"None of us liked her, Gia. Not one of us took her up on any of that shit."

"No one told me," she whispered.

"We tried, gently, but she was your friend, and you're

loyal as hell."

God. She couldn't believe this. "She knew I had a crush on you."

His head whipped around. "You had a crush on me?"

"From the first moment I saw you."

Flames ignited in his eyes. "Gia."

"She knew. And she still tried to sleep with you."

Saxon eyed Gia carefully.

Pressure was building inside her. God, she'd been such a fool. Willow had played her. For years. "I need a drink."

"It's lunchtime."

"I don't care." She fished her phone out of her bag and stabbed the screen. "Ashley, I'm not coming back to the office."

"What?" Her assistant squawked. "You have meetings?"

"I know. I'm sorry. Cancel the Diaz call. Reschedule it for another time. Have Evan take my other meetings."

"His head will explode."

"Help him out."

Ashley let out a gusty sigh. "Will do. We'll handle it." She paused. "Are you okay?"

"No, but nothing a stiff drink won't fix." Or at least take the edge off.

"All right, Gia. See you later."

Gia looked up and realized Saxon was pulling into his garage.

"This isn't a bar."

"I have booze, and I figure a less public place will be better for you to lose that temper of yours."

She crossed her arms over her chest.

"I've known you a long time, Contessa. I know when the pressure's brewing and you're about to explode."

Her gaze narrowed.

"I'm just glad that, for once, you aren't pissed at me."

"I need tequila, Buchanan." She shoved open the door of the Bentley. "Now."

They headed upstairs, and he led her into his wine cellar room.

The wall of wine glowed gently with backlights. There was a table and four chairs in a gorgeous, glossy wood, sitting in the center of the space, and a built-in bar off to one side.

He pulled out a bottle of tequila and two shot glasses.

She eyed the expensive Gran Patrón, then the glasses.

"Those are crystal."

"Alcohol tastes better from crystal."

"Snob." It was such a Saxon thing to say.

He poured the tequila. Instantly, Gia threw back the shot. Oh, that burned. It complemented her smoldering fury.

"She played me. The entire time I was just a gullible fool."

Saxon did his shot. "She feels something for you, but she is...selfish and messed up. I don't think everything was a lie."

"But a lot of it was." Gia grabbed the bottle and took a swig directly from it. "Let's go upstairs. I want to sit on your couch and look at your kick-ass view while I down more tequila."

He lifted his chin and they went upstairs. At the top level, she kicked her heels off and took another swig from the bottle.

She set the bottle down on the kitchen island with a loud click.

Then the dam inside her burst. "I'm so fucking pissed!"

She strode across the space to his couch, then grabbed some of the cushions and threw them.

They hit the floor, but it wasn't very satisfying. She stomped on them, then let out a little scream of frustration. As she stomped around, her hair fell out of its bun, falling around her shoulders.

"She *used* me. Put me in danger without a single thought. I cared about her."

Saxon grabbed Gia's arms. "She hurt you."

Gia lifted her chin. "I'm not thinking about that. How could I have been so stupid?"

Saxon cupped her jaw. "You're not stupid. You're the smartest, wittiest, sexiest woman I've ever known."

She blinked, staring at his handsome face. Her anger morphed into pure need and her body flared to life.

All these years, she'd seen Saxon as an enemy, an annoyance, but she realized that he'd been there for her, just like her brothers.

She shoved him back several steps until he dropped to sit on the couch.

Then she hiked up the hem of her dress and straddled him.

GIA STRADDLING HIM, fire in her eyes, made Saxon's cock hard in an instant.

He gripped her chin. "You want to use me, baby? You want to fuck out all that anger?"

She undulated against him, shooting him a defiant look. There she was. His Gia wasn't broken. You couldn't keep her down for long.

"Maybe," she said finally.

"I'm not going to say no." He gripped her curvy hip and ground her down on his cock.

Her lips parted and she moaned his name.

"But it's not just that," she said. "I want you. I feel like I've wanted you forever."

With a groan, he kissed her, savoring the taste of her and tequila. "Same, Contessa. Forever."

Need gripped him. The kiss turned rough, and he thrust his tongue inside her mouth. She kissed him back, giving him everything. That curvy, little body moved on him like she couldn't stay still.

She sank her teeth into his bottom lip.

"Christ," he muttered.

She laughed and the sound hit him in his gut.

He slid his hand under her dress and between her legs. She bucked, and desire roared in his head. Clinging to the edge of his control, Saxon gripped her panties and tore them off. She gasped into his mouth.

"This pretty pussy is all mine." He stroked her, feeling how wet she was growing. Then he slid a finger inside her tight, wet warmth.

With his other hand, he slid it up into the thick mass

of her hair. He pulled, tugging her head, arching her back.

Then he set his mouth on her throat, feasting. The sounds she made drove him wild.

"All this heat under your beauty." He pressed his thumb to her clit.

She rocked, riding his hand. He slid his other hand along her back and found the zipper of her dress. He lowered it, then pushed the fabric down to her waist.

The cobweb-like black lace bra made him growl. It showed off more than it covered.

"Take the bra off," he ordered.

Her eyes were heavy, her cheeks flushed. Her lips were swollen from his kisses. She'd never looked more beautiful.

She reached behind her and a second later, her bra fell away. It left those rosy-peaked breasts bared to him.

"Gorgeous." He cupped one, then leaned forward. He pulled one nipple to his mouth.

"Yes, *oh, Saxon*."

She moved on him, her hands sinking into his hair. He licked, sucked, made her squirm and pant.

"Other one, Gia," he growled.

She arched back, offering her breasts to him.

He sucked the other nipple into his mouth, making it a hard bead. With his other hand, he sank another finger inside her. She was so wet.

"*Saxon*." A plea.

He kissed her again. "You can't know how beautiful you are." His voice was guttural. "So fucking gorgeous. So fucking mine."

She undulated. "Less talking, more fucking."

God, she was something. It took some control not to throw her down and hammer inside her. He wanted to take and possess. He had a near-naked Gia on him, while he was still fully clothed. Hot as fuck.

"You want my cock inside you, Contessa?"

Her brown gaze met his. Direct and not hiding a thing. "Yes."

"Unbuckle me, baby."

Her hands attacked his belt. She got it open, then his pants, then she shoved his boxers down. His cock was finally free.

"Saxon," she breathed.

He couldn't wait any damn longer to get inside her. He reached back and pulled out his wallet from his pocket, and found the condom inside.

While he did that, Gia wrapped her fingers around his cock and stroked.

Shit. His muscles clenched. For the first time in a long time, he worried that he'd come before he got inside her.

"Contessa, if you want me inside you, quit that." He tossed his wallet on the floor, and opened the foil packet.

Gia watched him, biting her lip as he rolled the condom on. She trembled.

Then he wrapped his fingers around his rock-hard cock while his other hand cupped her ass. She moved, lifting up, the head of his cock sliding through where she was so wet.

Her hands gripped his shoulders, and the head of his cock sank an inch inside her.

"Saxon," she breathed.

He stopped there, wanting to absorb every bit of the moment when he finally sank inside Gia Norcross.

So fucking good. His muscles trembled, his gaze met hers.

He needed to be deep inside her, nothing between them. A groan ripped out of him. Saxon thrust up at the same time she drove her sexy body down.

Connected. *Finally.*

He slid deep inside Gia and she cried out, her nails biting into his shoulders.

"Like you were made just for me, Gia."

"Saxon!"

She lifted her hips, gliding up, then down.

"So tight, baby. So wet. All mine."

"*Yes.*" She moved faster; their gazes locked.

"Ride my cock, beautiful."

"So long and hard." Her voice was a moan. "You fill me up, Saxon. The sweetest ache."

She rocked hard, hips moving fast. He clamped his hands on her sweet ass. He didn't take his eyes off hers. He moved one hand between them and found her clit.

"You ready to come on my cock, Gia?"

"God, yes. Please make me come."

"We're both going to come, baby."

Her climax broke. She screamed his name, her back arching.

So damn beautiful.

He slammed her down and heat roared through him. Saxon came, his vision blurring, and finally poured himself inside Gia.

CHAPTER TWELVE

Trying to get her breath back, Gia stayed sprawled on Saxon, her face buried in his neck.

God. She'd done the nasty with Saxon Buchanan. And it had been *amazing.* She shifted her legs, feeling the pleasant ache between her thighs.

His big hand slid from her ass, up her back. She made a little sound and his fingers slid into her hair, tugged, then he kissed her.

It was slow, deep, and he took his time.

When he pulled back, he looked at her face. She couldn't read the look on his features.

He smiled. "Didn't think you could get more beautiful, Contessa, but that body of yours—" He made a humming sound.

"Meanwhile, you have too many clothes on," she said tartly.

"I think you're right." He slid her off him and onto the couch. "Don't move."

He rose, starting toward the half bath off the living room, no doubt to take care of the condom.

Gia was feeling too good and lazy to move. She lay sprawled on the couch, half naked, enjoying her post-orgasm bliss.

Saxon returned, his hungry gaze running over her body. "Like a goddess waiting for her worshippers to do her bidding."

She smiled at him. "I like that."

He scooped her into his arms and headed for the stairs. "Well, I'm not done with you, yet," he murmured.

Ooh. She liked him carrying her. A lot.

He strode into the master bedroom and set her down on the bed. Then he stood beside it and stripped.

He tossed his suit jacket on a chair. Then he unbuttoned his shirt.

With greedy eyes, she watched as he uncovered his muscular chest, his ridged abs. Damn, he was a woman's darkest fantasy. She took a second to wriggle out of her dress.

He dropped his shirt on top of his jacket. Then he unfastened his trousers, and with one quick move, they and his boxers were gone. Saxon stood there naked in front of her.

Oh, boy. Gia's heart bumped against her ribs. Amazingly, gloriously naked. All those muscles and black ink. She shivered. She took in the tattoos on his chest and arms. They were almost elegant. He was a hot, intriguing mix of class and badass. It totally worked for her.

Desire unfurled and pulsed between her legs. She

looked at his long, hardening cock. She wanted him again. *Needed* him.

He opened the bedside table drawer and pulled out a strip of condoms. He tossed them on the bed and her belly clenched.

Then, he pressed one knee to the covers, looming over her. Her pulse sped up.

"Finally, Gia Norcross in my bed where I've fantasized about her a thousand times."

Her lips parted. "Saxon—"

"Where I've jacked my cock thinking about you. Dreamed about you."

Emotion swelled, filling her chest. "Come here, Saxon. I need you inside me." She drew in a breath. "Where I've fantasized having you a thousand times."

He made a harsh sound, dealt with the condom, and covered her body with his. He gripped her legs, urging her to wrap them around his hips.

"Ready, baby?"

"Yes."

"It's going to get rough. I need you to take me. All of me." His deep voice was strained.

"It's yours, baby." The head of his cock slid against her. *Oh.* She bucked. She needed him just as much as he needed her. "Saxon."

"Ready, Gia?"

He thrust inside her—hard and deep.

She ran her nails down his back and cried out.

"Gia?" He paused.

She clung to him. "Fuck me, Saxon."

With a growl, he did.

His thrusts were firm, powerful, relentless. She slid her hands up his back, knew she was scratching him, but didn't care. She wanted to mark him.

"Beautiful," he growled. "Christ, so beautiful."

"Faster, Saxon."

"Patience, Contessa."

Screw patience. She needed to come again.

But he did move faster, driving her up the bed with each thrust. He angled his hips, and each time he sank into her, she felt it in her clit.

He powered deep inside her and Gia felt her orgasm growing, like an impending storm. Her belly clenched.

"*Saxon,*" she breathed.

"Get there, Contessa. *Now.*"

On the next thrust, the storm broke. Gia came, the brutal pleasure dragging a hoarse scream from her. She turned her head and bit Saxon's bicep.

Her body shuddered, the pleasure almost making her black out.

Above her, he kept thrusting, his deep grunts echoing in her ears. Then he thrust deep one last time and his body locked. With a fierce growl, he threw his head back, his climax rocking through him.

Damn, he was beautiful.

Gia drank him in—the muscled throat, the high cheekbones, the face twisted with pleasure.

For her, there was only Saxon.

The scents of his cologne and sex filled the air. His big body covered hers, his cock still buried inside her. All Gia could think was *finally.*

Saxon pressed his face to her neck and collapsed on

her. She noted that he didn't give her all of his weight, careful not to crush her.

His lips moved over her skin and she trembled. His harsh breathing matched hers.

He rolled to the side and pulled her close. Gia held onto his arm. She didn't want to move from here. Ever.

She bit her lip. This was it. She knew. Maybe she'd always known that Saxon was it for her. There would be no one else. She'd never get over him.

She was stupidly, irrevocably in love with Saxon Buchanan.

Her throat tightened and she swallowed. He could break her into a million shattered shards.

Previously, sex had always been a fun interlude between two single, like-minded adults. Fun was *not* a word she'd used to describe what she and Saxon had just done. Twice.

"Babe? You okay?" He dropped a kiss to her shoulder.

"Yes."

"Have I rendered you speechless with my skills and prowess?"

She snorted. "Don't get cocky."

"I already did." He nudged her butt with said cock. "Twice."

Gia giggled and slapped a hand over her mouth. She never giggled. And especially not naked in bed with a man.

"I heard that." His hand smoothed over her hip. "How about I grab that tequila and see what I've got to eat in my fridge?"

"Sounds like a plan."

He cupped her jaw. "Then I'm gonna have you again, Contessa."

Her pulse spiked.

"I shouldn't need you this much," he muttered.

She met his turbulent gaze.

"Tell me you want me?" he demanded.

"More than anything." The words tumbled out of her. "So much it hurts." She wrapped her hands around his wrist. "Give it back to me, Saxon. Tell me."

"I can't breathe without wanting you, Gia Norcross." He lowered his mouth to hers. "Only you."

NOW, he could get used to this.

Saxon lounged in the bathtub, a naked Gia lying back against him. Her hair was all piled up on her head, a few damp strands dangling around her face and neck.

A half empty bottle of tequila rested beside a bottle of wine and the remnants of the snack he'd put together—cheese, crackers, dip, and salami—on a stool beside the tub.

He'd never used the tub much. He didn't mind a soak, but he rarely had time for it.

Something told him that Gia enjoyed regular baths. She'd rummaged around in the vanity looking for bubble bath or bath salts, then crowed triumphantly when she'd found the citrus-scented bubble bath.

Of course, she was lying back against him, holding her phone and checking her emails.

He smiled at her. Her pretty breasts were playing

peekaboo with the bubbles. He lazily reached out and tugged one nipple.

"Hey," she said.

"I'm being ignored for your phone. It's hurting my feelings."

"You mean your ego." She reached over, grabbed a piece of brie, and popped it in her mouth.

"I think after your fourth orgasm, my ego is just fine," he said.

Tequila in bed had turned into him going down on her, then fucking her again.

She sniffed, but he saw her lips curve.

Before the bath, he'd updated Vander on Willow. Vander had been unsurprisingly pissed, and said he'd put more resources on running Willow down.

The upside was that Gia had seen all sides to Willow. The downside was that Saxon hated seeing Gia hurt.

Vander had also said that he hadn't heard back from his black ops contact. That could just mean they were out in the field on a mission, but Vander didn't like it.

Gia's phone rang. "Crap, it's my mom. Don't say a word." She answered. "Hi, Ma."

Saxon heard Mrs. Norcross' voice from the phone.

"Gia Gabriella, I heard from your brother that your apartment was broken into and vandalized." Clara Norcross' voice rose to a high pitch. Just like Gia's when she got worked up.

"Mama—"

"You didn't call. Your father and I are worried."

"It's all okay, Ma. I didn't want to worry you guys."

Mrs. Norcross made an angry, tsking sound. "Not

worry us? You were always so independent, from a little girl. Had to do it yourself. Had to keep up with your brothers."

Saxon knew that story. He pinched her butt and Gia glared at him. Of course, that made his cock twitch.

"We're your family, Gia Gabriella. We're here to help."

"Thanks, Mama," Gia's voice softened. "Vander and everyone are helping me."

"Good."

"I guess Vander ratted me out."

"It was Easton," her mother said.

"I should've *known*. It's that big-brother gene. He can't help himself."

"*You* should have told me. Now, I want you over for lunch tomorrow."

"Ma—"

"It's Saturday, so no excuses."

"Well, um—"

She shifted on Saxon, which had his cock hardening even more.

"What?" Mrs. Norcross asked.

"Can I...bring someone?"

Saxon stilled. There was a long pause from the phone.

"A man?" her mother asked.

Saxon heard the hopeful edge to Mrs. Norcross' voice.

"Yes, a man," Gia said.

He reached around and cupped her breasts. She tried

to push him away, and he let one hand slide under the water and between her legs.

She gasped, the water lapping the rim of the tub. "Sorry, Ma, what did you say?"

"What's his name?" Mrs. Norcross asked.

Gia blinked. "Saxon."

There was another long pause. "Saxon isn't a common name."

"No, it isn't."

Saxon chuckled and Gia smacked his arm.

"So, it's our Saxon."

Mrs. Norcross' words made his gut tighten. He'd never really belonged to anyone before.

"Yes, Ma," Gia replied quietly.

"Well, tell him that I'm making lasagna, and I'll make my garlic bread especially for him."

He got another jolt. He loved Mrs. Norcross' garlic bread.

Suddenly, he realized that the Norcross family had claimed him. Hell, they'd claimed him a long time ago, he just hadn't realized it.

Gia was watching his face, warmth in her eyes.

Then he shifted her, so his cock was right where he wanted it. He pushed her down, his cock sliding into her.

She squeaked, her eyes going wide. "I'll tell him. Got to go, Ma."

"Love you, Gia."

She managed a strangled reply before she ended the call. Her phone clattered onto the tray with the cheese and crackers.

"You can't make love to me while I'm on the phone with my mother!"

"Why not?" He thrust his hips up.

She moaned. "Saxon, condom."

He cursed. He'd forgotten. Shit, she fried his brain. He pulled out and grabbed one from beside the tub. He'd stashed them there when they were running the bath.

He quickly rolled one on and Gia swiveled to straddle him, face-to-face.

She sank down on his cock and he groaned. Her gorgeous breasts were right in front of him and he sucked one pink nipple into his mouth.

She started riding him, water sloshing out of the tub. She gasped, but he didn't give a fuck.

"God, how can I want you this much?" she panted.

"I know." It was like he'd never get enough of her.

More water splashed.

Saxon exploded up and turned her. He pushed her against the edge of the tub, cupped her ass with one hand and fisted his cock with the other. Then he plunged back into her.

Her back arched, her husky cry bouncing off the marble tiles.

"Take it, Gia. Take it all."

"Yes!"

He reached a hand under her body and stroked. He knew just what she needed to come. "I know what you need, Contessa. I know you."

The force of her climax made her buck and cry his name.

Her body clamped down on his cock and Saxon

shoved into her again, once, twice. His release slammed into him like a speeding truck. He groaned her name, face buried in her hair.

Ruined. She turned him inside out, and he loved it.

Finally, after a while, he found the strength to lift himself off her.

"I'm not cleaning up the mess," she said lazily.

Saxon eyed the water on the floor. "Screw it." He didn't give a shit. "It'll dry." He nuzzled her neck and cheek. "Bed?"

She looked back and eyed him. "To sleep?"

"We'll do some of that too."

"Surely you can't keep this up all night?"

Saxon smiled. "Is that a challenge, darling?"

CHAPTER THIRTEEN

She rolled over in the big bed, sleep making her head fuzzy. Gia wished she was one of those people who woke energized, ready to conquer the day. But long ago, she'd accepted that she woke up like an angry bear just out of hibernation.

Sunlight streamed in through the window, and with a groan, she flopped facedown on a pillow that smelled like Saxon.

Saxon. *Oh, boy*.

She cracked open one eyelid. There was no sexy, golden-skinned man in the bed beside her. Maybe she'd dreamed the night of nonstop, incredible, toe-curling sex?

But as she shifted on the sheets, the ache between her legs said something different. She cracked open her other eyelid. She had a few interesting bruises on her naked body, and this was definitely Saxon's bed.

"Good morning, Contessa." He strolled in with a smile.

She wasn't sure where to look first—the steaming

mug of coffee he held, the tousled dark-blond hair, or the sexy, bare chest. He wore a pair of loose, black pants that rode low on his hip bones.

A little hum rippled through her body. "Coffee. Gimme." She sat up and held out her hand.

Saxon's gaze went straight to her boobs.

Gia took the mug and sipped, moaned.

He sat beside her and grinned. "That's the same sound you make when I have my mouth on you." He cupped one of her breasts and lazily stroked her nipple. Then he dropped a kiss to her shoulder.

She was shocked at the tingle of desire that flared to life in her belly. She'd been certain that the five thousand orgasms she'd had last night would have made that impossible.

"If you want sex, you'll have to do all the work." She drank some more coffee. "I'm not awake enough yet, but I'll lie back and take it like a champion."

He smiled and her gaze riveted to his handsome face.

"Baby, if we do that, we'll be late to your parents' house."

"What?" She glanced at the clock and gasped. Clearly, they'd slept in. "Crap." She slid to the edge of the bed, careful not to spill the coffee. She needed *every* drop of caffeine. She wrapped the sheet around her body.

But a strong arm curled around her.

"Saxon, there's no time. I need to shower—"

He kissed her.

Hmm. Maybe there was a little time. He tasted like coffee and yumminess.

Then he lifted his head. "Go. Get ready. I put your

bag in the bathroom. I'm already hungry for your mom's garlic bread."

Gia stood. "I can make it too, you know?"

"You going to cook for me, Contessa?"

"Maybe. If you're very lucky."

His gaze moved over her face. "I'm feeling pretty lucky today. Gia Norcross, right where I want her, after sleeping in my arms all night."

Heat bloomed in her belly. Who knew that sexy, classy Saxon could also be sweet?

"I don't recall much sleeping." She shot him a sassy smile, then hurried into his bathroom.

Gia showered, then did her hair and some light makeup. She pulled on a simple, chocolate-brown wrap dress and sandals.

Saxon was dressed in tan chinos and a white, linen shirt—sleeves rolled up—and sitting at the kitchen island. There was a bunch of brightly-colored flowers resting on the countertop—daisies of all different colors. Her mom's favorite.

"Where did you get those?" Gia asked.

"I have my ways."

Must be nice to be so rich you had people at your beck and call. "You trying to charm my mother?"

"She already loves me."

"But now you're sleeping with her daughter."

Saxon winced. "I'm more worried about your dad."

Ethan Norcross was fairly easy-going. Her former-firefighter dad had never given any of her other boyfriends a hard time, although she'd never brought many home.

"Where are my flowers?" she asked.

"These flowers are for the first Norcross woman I ever fell for, but I'll get flowers for you too."

Those words made it hard to breathe.

He rose and stroked her cheekbone. "Let's get going."

Before long, they pulled up at the Norcross home in Noe Valley.

Gia smiled. *Home.* She'd grown up here, and the neat and tidy Edwardian house was filled with so many memories. She was surprised to realize how many of them also included Saxon.

Her mother opened the front door. "*Bambinos.*"

Gia kissed her mom, and then Clara Norcross turned to kiss Saxon. He handed over the flowers and Gia watched her mother gush like a teenage girl.

"Finally, you two worked yourselves out." Her mother smiled at them smugly.

"Ma—"

"Gia, this one has watched you for a long time." Her mom's gaze narrowed on Saxon. "You were much slower to act than I guessed."

"Gia's special."

Gia's mom beamed at him. "She is. And she's had her eye on you too. Both of you, so slow." She shook her head. "Me, the first time I saw my Ethan, I knew he'd be mine."

"That's not how I remember it." Gia's dad strode up behind her mother.

He was still tall, strong, and handsome, with salt-and-pepper hair.

"Hi, Dad." Gia hugged him.

"Your mother made me work for our first date."

Clara raised a brow. "Of course, but I'd already decided you were mine."

Gia's father smiled. "I know. I remember a certain cat fight with Theresa Russo."

"That girl was moving in on *my* man." Clara's dark eyes flashed. "And you didn't seem to mind very much."

Gia's father laughed. "I only had eyes for you, beautiful. I just had to make you work for it a little."

Fighting a smile, Gia's mom slapped his arm and they shared a look.

They'd always been like this. Gia had always known that her parents' love was strong and true. And she'd always wanted that for herself.

Saxon ran a hand down her back and she looked up at him. He was watching her with a smile.

Ethan cleared his throat. "Saxon, why don't we get a drink while Gia helps her mother?" Her father looked a little uncomfortable.

Gia narrowed her gaze. "Is that code for you're going to grill him?"

Her father sniffed. "I was considering breaking out my pliers and hacksaw for some torture."

Gia's mother rolled her eyes. "Come, Gia."

Gia cocked her hip. "So, the women have to be in the kitchen, cooking and—?"

"Go." Saxon tugged on her hair. "I'll be fine. Don't throw a tantrum, and delay me getting some of your mom's garlic bread."

She glared at him. "The garlic bread might end up burned, if you aren't careful."

The annoying man just grinned at her.

Vander appeared in the hall, beer in hand. Easton was behind him.

"When are we eating?" Vander asked.

"After Dad grills Saxon," Gia snapped.

"After Rhys and Haven arrive," Clara amended.

"Three guesses why they're late," Easton muttered.

"Come on, Saxon." Her father slid his arm around Saxon's shoulders. "Let's get the torture over with."

Vander's lips twitched. "I'll help."

"Me too," Easton added.

"*Mom!*" Gia cried.

"Oh, Saxon can take care of himself." Her mother herded Gia into the kitchen Easton had renovated for her a few years back.

Gia helped her mother finish prepping lunch, trying to overhear the conversation coming from the living room. But all she heard was the low murmur of deep voices.

"He'll be fine." Her mom took the lasagna out of the oven.

Familiar, delicious scents filled the air. "I know." Gia blew out a breath. "I know this is all a bit strange. Me and Saxon together. Vander...might need a little while to adjust."

Her mother smiled. "I know you've always had feelings for Saxon."

"Mama—" Pressure built in Gia's chest, and she pressed a hand between her breasts. "I think I'm..." She couldn't say the words aloud.

Her mother smiled and cupped Gia's cheek. "I know, *cara mia*. He's worthy of your love."

"He's taking care of me. He drives me crazy sometimes, but I know I can trust him."

"He's a good man, and he made himself that way." Her mother scowled. "The Lord knows those parents of his had no hand in raising him."

"You know them?"

"I've met them a few times." Her mother met Gia's gaze. "Saxon has wounds, Gia. From long before he served his country. You take care."

The front door opened. "We're here," Rhys announced. "And we're hungry."

Haven appeared in the kitchen, smiling, her face flushed. "Hi."

Yep, she'd totally gotten laid.

"Hello, *bambina*." Clara kissed Haven's cheeks. "Let's eat."

STUFFED FULL OF MRS. NORCROSS' amazing food, Saxon sat on the back deck with the other men, drinking his coffee. The Norcross' had a small yard with a shed that housed Mr. Norcross' workshop.

Gia's dad hadn't tortured him, just made him promise to take care of Gia. The memory of her dad's words still echoed in Saxon's head. *You've had my boys' backs for years; I know you'll take care of my girl too.*

The sentiment had rocked Saxon. His parents had never had faith in him, never believed in him.

Mr. Norcross hadn't stopped there. *Besides, if you don't make her happy, Gia won't be shy to tell you off.*

Saxon smiled over the rim of his coffee mug. His feisty woman was inside with her mom and Haven, and he had no doubt she wouldn't hesitate to tell him off.

"So, you're all keeping Gia safe while you fix the situation," Mr. Norcross said.

Saxon nodded.

"I don't trust Dennett," Vander said.

Easton made a sound. "After that stunt at the sports bar, I made a few calls. Some of Dennett's prospective business deals are going to dry up."

Easton was all slick businessman on the surface, but he was a warrior at heart.

"Sackler hasn't reared his head," Saxon mused.

"He's lurking," Rhys said from where he leaned against the railing. "An informant told me that he's really pissed about losing the diamond."

"And let's not forget about Lex." Saxon scowled. He wasn't letting any of these guys near Gia.

"Any luck finding Willow?" Mr. Norcross asked.

They all shook their heads. Willow was laying very low.

The back door opened, and Gia and Haven appeared.

"Finished talking about manly-man things?" Gia asked.

Saxon snagged her and tugged her into his lap. The feel of her, the scent of her perfume, calmed something inside him. "We were going to talk about bear hunting and spear making, next."

She rolled her eyes.

He thought it would be weird to be at the Norcross'

home with everyone knowing he and Gia were together. But it wasn't. It felt right.

He looked up, and spotted Vander watching them. His best friend had an unreadable look on his face, but he didn't look angry.

He gave Saxon a slight nod.

Saxon nodded back.

"Ready to go?" Saxon asked Gia.

She nodded. She kissed her father and her brothers. She hugged Haven, then shared a long hug with her mother.

Mrs. Norcross kissed both of Saxon's cheeks. "Do right by my girl, Saxon."

He nodded.

She patted his cheek. "And by yourself. You always deserved more than you believed. You're nothing like those parents of yours."

Her words sent a hit of emotion driving into his heart.

Gia took his hand and they headed out to the Bentley.

"Can I drive?" she asked.

"No."

"Typical man." She flounced into the passenger seat.

God, no one gave off attitude like his woman.

His. He was going to keep her.

But first, he had to get her safe.

They headed back toward the city and his place.

"Well, you survived lunch with the Norcross family," she said.

"I've eaten with your family a hundred times. At school, I used to wish they were my family."

She rested her hand over his. "They are."

Yeah, they were, in all the ways that mattered.

Her nose wrinkled. "I don't relish meeting your parents."

"For your sake, I'll try to make that never."

"Your parents must not be *all* bad."

"There's my Gia, always looking for the best in people."

She scowled. "Look where that got me with Willow."

He squeezed her fingers, resting them on his thigh. When he pulled onto the freeway, he glanced in the rearview mirror and frowned.

"What?" she asked.

"We're being followed."

She was a Norcross, so she didn't turn around. "You're sure?"

He nodded and sped up. "Silver Chevy Blazer."

The SUV sped up as well, following them. Saxon thumbed a button on the steering wheel.

The call connected. "Norcross," Vander said.

"I've got a Chevy Blazer on my tail. We're on Bayshore, but I'm going to take the next exit."

"I'm on it." Vander hung up.

Saxon picked up speed and zipped between two cars. A car honked its horn, and the Blazer roared into the other lane to follow.

"Hang on." He took the exit fast, tires screeching. The Bentley was well-designed, and hugged the curve.

Gia quickly glanced back. "They're following."

Saxon took another turn. Thankfully, the traffic was

light because he didn't want to put anyone in danger. He roared through a stop sign.

He glanced in the rearview mirror. *Fuck.*

"Down!" He reached across and shoved Gia's head down.

There was a man hanging out of the SUV's passenger window. He was holding a gun.

He fired. Bullets pinged off the Bentley.

"They're shooting at us!" Gia's voice was enraged.

"Stay down."

"They're shooting at us." The rear window of the Bentley shattered, and Gia screamed.

Saxon took another turn, accelerating up a hilly street.

Leaning forward, Gia opened the glove compartment.

"Gia—"

She pulled out his HK VP9, checked it.

"Stay down," he growled.

"You just drive, Saxon." She opened her window.

He cursed. When she unclipped her belt, he cursed some more.

She stuck her head out the window and fired.

Bam. Bam. Bam.

The Blazer swerved and clipped a parked car before it righted itself. Gia fired again.

"Inside, Gia!" Saxon roared.

She slid back into her seat.

He jerked the wheel and pulled into the empty parking lot of a high school. He was pissed as hell.

He swung the Bentley into a sharp turn, tires squealing. They came to a stop facing the direction they'd came.

He grabbed the HK VP9 from Gia. "Stay in the car." He gave a quick, hard kiss, then shoved open his door.

The Blazer pulled to a stop.

"Saxon, you aren't bulletproof," she cried.

He strode toward the SUV, lifted the gun and aimed. He fired on the driver side of the windshield—once, twice, three times. The glass cracked.

The door of the vehicle opened, and the driver tumbled out.

Saxon fired, hitting him in the leg. The man cried out and dropped his handgun.

Saxon snatched it up.

The man who'd climbed out of the passenger seat took one look at Saxon and ran.

"No, you don't." Gia's voice.

Dread filling him, Saxon spun. His gut clenched. She hadn't stayed in the car.

She was aiming her Ruger at the fleeing man. She fired several shots.

The man stopped, dancing on the spot like a tap dancer.

Gun up, Saxon advanced. "On your knees."

The man dropped. A second later, a black X6 screeched into the parking lot, and Vander got out.

Saxon turned and zeroed in on Gia. "I told you to stay in the car." His voice was a roar.

She didn't even blink, just tossed her hair back. "You'd better get used to me making my own decisions and not following orders."

He wanted to either hit or kiss that stubborn chin of hers. Since he didn't hit women, and this was Gia, he suspected the kissing would win out.

Then he heard Vander's laugh.

"Don't you start," Saxon said.

"You signed up for it, brother."

"No comment."

Vander slapped some zip ties in Saxon's hand. While Saxon tied up the man on his knees, Vander knelt beside the bleeding driver. "Clear shot, didn't hit an artery. He'll live."

"Who do you work for?" Saxon demanded.

The driver just glared at them, while the second man looked at the ground.

Saxon smiled. "Oh good, I was hoping you'd pick the hard way."

The driver's defiant look wavered.

Then Gia walked up and slapped the man's cheek. "Who do you work for?"

"Jesus," Vander muttered.

She slapped the man again. "Answer. Now."

Shaking his head, Saxon stepped forward. "Gia—"

"Albert Sackler," the man mumbled.

Saxon met Vander's gaze. *Fuck.* Sackler had entered the game.

Gia nodded. "I'll wait in the car." She stalked off like she was just out enjoying a stroll.

"She's a handful," Vander said.

"I'm aware."

"Too late to back out now." Vander hauled up the

bleeding driver. "I'll get this one to the hospital, and call Hunt."

"And the other one?" Saxon glanced at the guy tied up with zip ties.

"I'll take him too. Think a visit to our holding rooms is in his future."

Saxon nodded. "Call me if you get any more information."

"Good luck with your handful."

CHAPTER FOURTEEN

They pulled in at Saxon's.

Gia was buzzing. The car chase, seeing Saxon be a complete badass, her taking that guy down. She looked at Saxon as he parked the car. Delicious, with a capital *D*.

"Sorry about the bullet holes in your Bentley," she said.

He shrugged. "I'll call someone to collect it tomorrow and get it fixed."

She crossed her legs, uncrossed them.

He glanced at her. "You're wired."

"Totally. Watching you do your thing, me doing my thing..."

"Instead of staying in the car," he said dryly.

"You had it under control. I was armed, and I know how to shoot. I wasn't letting you deal with it alone."

He got a hot look in his eyes.

Gia squirmed in her seat. She was so turned on.

A faint smile curved his mouth. "You hungry, Contessa?"

"My panties are saturated. Or they would be if I was wearing any."

He growled.

She opened her door. As she stood, she watched him get out on the other side of the car, her heart thumping like a giant drum.

"Think you can make it to the bedroom?" he asked silkily.

"I hope not," she murmured.

She ran for the stairs.

Her heels clicked as she flew upward. She heard him behind her, sensed him. She made it to the entry before he was on her.

He grabbed a handful of the back of her dress, spun her. Then Gia found herself pressed against the wall, Saxon's mouth on hers.

Yes. Yes. Yes.

When was the last time anything had felt this right? Maybe the first time she'd sat at her desk in the Firelight PR offices? Making friends with Haven?

Now Saxon.

His fingers were in her hair, his mouth hard and demanding on hers. She moaned. Waves of desire rolled through her, concentrating between her legs

She needed one thing. Him.

His mouth moved on hers and he deepened the kiss. He parted her lips wider and she gripped his firm biceps, sliding her tongue against his.

Gia was a giant mass of need. She wanted to see Mr.

Cool Saxon Buchanan there with her, as well.

She reached down cupping the bulge in the front of his trousers, squeezed. He made a hungry sound that made her belly twist. "Saxon."

"Hold on, Contessa."

She tried to climb him, wrapping a leg around his hip. She needed him so much it hurt.

He slid his hands under her ass and took a few side-steps to a hall table resting against the wall. With one arm, he swept a wooden bowl off it. It clattered to the floor.

He lifted her and set her ass on the cool metal.

Gia attacked his shirt. She gave a few desperate tugs, and buttons pinged on the tiles.

"Faster," she panted.

Then his shirt was gone, and she was distracted by his gorgeous chest and ink. She leaned forward and bit his pec.

Saxon growled, his breathing harsh pants. He yanked a condom from his pocket and tore his fly open.

Her gaze locked on his rock-hard cock. "Yes. *Now*."

He rolled the condom on, then yanked on the tie holding her dress together. With a quick tug, he unwrapped her. He jolted, his gaze crashing into hers.

"I thought you were joking about the panties. All this time, at your parents, you weren't wearing any underwear?"

"Yes."

He shuddered. "Grip the edge of the table, Gia. This is going to be hard."

Every muscle in her body tightened. She gripped the

cool metal, leaned back, her legs falling open.

The scorching-hot look in his eyes seared her. He gripped her hips, leaned forward, and with one hard thrust, he was inside her.

Gia cried out, heard his strangled groan.

Her head dropped back against the wall. She felt so full, so stretched. "Saxon—"

"Hang on, Contessa." He pulled out, thrust back in. He started a fast, brutal rhythm.

The table rattled with each thrust, each plunge of his cock filling her. A moan escaped her and she wrapped her legs around him, the heels of her sandals digging into his back.

It was a relentless assault on her senses. Pleasure drenched her and she gripped his shoulders, clawed at him.

"Saxon, *please*."

With another hard thrust, her climax hit her—wild, hot, ruthless. She screamed.

With a hoarse groan, he sank deep, one hand in her hair, tilting so her gaze met his. His eyes were intense. He watched her come, and she watched him groan through his own release.

Then there was just their harsh panting.

"I'll never look at this table the same way again," she murmured.

He made a sound that might have been a chuckle. He caught her chin. "Next time, stay in the car."

She grinned. "Hot Stuff, I might need to explain consequences and rewards to you. If this is what I get when I get *out* of the car..."

He tweaked her nipple, and her pussy rippled on his cock. He groaned.

"Don't move." He pulled out, then disappeared to the downstairs powder room.

She heard a toilet flush, then water running in the sink. He was back, wearing only his chinos. Hmm, that chest, that body.

"I have heel marks in my back." His gaze roamed over her.

She must look like a picture, dress open, splayed on the hall table.

He half turned and she bit her lip. She didn't notice the heel marks, because she was too busy taking in the scratches. She'd drawn blood.

Heat hit her cheeks.

Saxon noticed her looking and grinned. He lowered his head to nibble her lips. "Gia Norcross, hellcat. *My* hellcat." He lifted her and tossed her over his shoulder.

"Saxon!" He headed up the stairs.

"We're going to bed."

"It's the afternoon."

"So?"

"More sex will kill us."

He smacked her bottom. "We'll go out smiling."

He did a lot more than put a smile on her face, and he did it for most of the night.

When Gia awoke the next morning, she was sprawled sideways on his bed. She stretched and smiled. There were definite upsides to this "being targeted by bad guys" situation.

She turned her head. Saxon was still asleep. His cock,

for once, wasn't hard, and lay against his powerful thigh. Sunlight stroked his body like it couldn't get enough of him.

She could do this every day. Wake up beside this man.

The scars on his side caught her eye and her belly hardened. She crawled closer and kissed them, her lips moving lightly over the scarred skin. She sensed him wake.

"Contessa?"

She looked up and saw the serious glint in his eyes.

"Tell me," she said. "What you can."

He was silent for a moment. "A mission went bad. I got shot."

He sat up, and pulled her against his chest. She stroked her fingers over the scars.

"We were in the middle of a bad area. Enemy all around us."

Her heart knocked hard in her chest.

"Vander organized an evac, but it was ten miles through harsh terrain to get to the evac point. Rhys carried me."

She pressed her head to his chest, thanked God for her incredible brothers, and held on.

"Rhys talked to me to keep me conscious. Vander, and the rest of the team, kept the bogeys off us." A pause. "I told them to leave me."

She tightened her grip on him. *No.*

"I knew I was dying. I was only slowing them down."

Gia made a sound. She could have lost him, this

amazing man, before she'd ever had him. Emotion closed her throat.

"But anyone with the Norcross name is stubborn. Your brothers got me out. They didn't let go, didn't give up."

She cupped his cheeks and kissed him. A tear rolled down her cheek, and he reached up and wiped it away.

"We don't let go," she whispered fiercely. "Not of the things we care about."

He kissed her again.

At that moment, the doorbell rang.

Saxon frowned, but Gia was already moving.

"Wait," he said. "I'll answer it."

She hunted around on the floor, pulled on his discarded shirt, and did up the remaining buttons. He found his pants.

"I'm coming," she said.

He sighed. "Of course, you are."

She smacked a kiss to his mouth.

"WE'LL GET RID of whoever it is, then I'm taking you out for breakfast." Saxon ran through the safest places he could take her. "Or, at this point, it might be Sunday brunch." They'd slept late again.

"I love brunch," Gia said.

They headed down the stairs. She looked far too sexy in his shirt.

"Maybe Vander has information?" Gia said. "Maybe he found Willow?"

"If it's your brother, he probably won't appreciate an eyeful of his sister in my shirt." With several bite marks on her neck.

Although Saxon had a few marks of his own. He felt the sting of the scratches she'd left on his back and smiled.

They reached the entry and he checked through the smoked glass panels flanking the doors. He spotted a couple standing on his doorstep

When he looked through the peephole, he swallowed a curse. "Brace."

He opened the door to his parents.

Rupert and Vanessa Buchanan were both dressed, pressed, and polished.

Saxon didn't look like either one of them, but rather a blend. Saxon had inherited his father's face, but not his dark hair. That, he'd received from his blonde mother. His father had probably already played a few rounds of golf this morning, and fucked whoever was his flavor of the month.

"Saxon." His mother eyed his bare chest and tattoos, barely concealing her grimace.

His father's gaze dropped to Gia's bare legs.

Bastard. Saxon pulled her close, wrapping his arms around her. "To what do I owe this pleasure on a Sunday morning?" he asked sarcastically.

Gia pushed into him, her hand pressed to his gut. The feel of her helped ease the inevitable resignation he got from dealing with his parents.

"We want to take you to lunch," his mother said.

They never turned up on his doorstep like this.

"Why?"

His mother sniffed. "We haven't caught up for some time."

"Why?" he said again.

His mother's mouth pressed into a flat line. "We're meeting friends—"

Realization hit him. "Friends with the socialite daughter you want to marry me off to."

Gia's fingers tightened on him.

"She's a nice girl," his father said jovially.

"I'm standing here, a grown man, with my woman in my arms, and you're pulling this shit?"

"Your woman?" His mother's nose wrinkled. "Your women come and go, so I—"

"Not this one."

Gia smiled up at him and he stroked her cheek.

"Are you going to introduce us, son?"

His father's oily-salesman voice put Saxon on edge, as did him calling Saxon son.

"Mrs. Buchanan and I already talked on the phone the other day," Gia said sweetly.

Uh-oh. Saxon recognized that tone. He wrapped his arm more securely around Gia. She was glaring at his mom.

Vanessa Buchanan's lip curled.

"Gia, this is Rupert and Vanessa. Mom, Dad, this is Gia Norcross."

"Norcross?" His father frowned.

Saxon's mother stiffened. "That family. Always trying to worm their way into your life. Now this one has made her way into your bed?"

Gia jerked, and he felt her muscles tense.

"No, mother," Saxon said. "I was always trying to worm my way into their family. A real family, with people who care."

"Golddiggers," his mother spat.

Gia turned her head. "Is she serious?"

"Yes. Not to mention, my mother's family lost all their money years ago. Marrying my father was the ultimate gold-digging exercise."

His mother gasped. "I come from a *very* good family."

"You don't know the meaning of the word good, Mother."

"My brother is Easton Norcross," Gia said. "He could buy and sell you a hundred times. And I have my own successful business. God, Saxon has more going for him than money and his name."

He smiled. "Oh, yeah?"

"Quiet," she said. "I feel a rant coming on."

"Have at it, Contessa." He looked at his parents, and the poisonous feeling in his gut eased. Gia was like antivenom.

"He didn't worm his way into our family, we claimed him. First, my brother, then the rest of us, including my parents. We love him, just as he is. He's ours."

Saxon's chest locked. *Loved him?* He felt like the ground had fallen away from under him.

"So, you can't have him," Gia finished.

"I don't need to listen to some whore wearing my son's shirt," his mother spat.

"Don't you dare talk to her like that," Saxon growled.

His mother's mouth snapped shut.

"You ignore him, insult him, don't support his choices. You're terrible, selfish people. So, I think you should go." Gia made a shooing motion with her hand.

Saxon bit back a laugh. The Countess dismissing the peasants. His parents looked stunned. No one spoke to them like that.

Looking at them, he realized that Gia was right. They were just weak, selfish people. It was never anything he'd done or didn't do that had made them treat him the way they had.

His mother bristled. "We are Saxon's parents—"

Gia straightened. "Saxon made himself who he is, with no help from you, so you can fuck off."

His father's face turned red. His mother spluttered. "Well, I never—"

Gia slammed the door closed. "Are you all right?" Worry edged her gaze.

"Yeah."

"Really? I just swore at your parents."

"It was pretty fucking awesome." He swept her up in his arms and kissed her.

"Right, so brunch." She pulled in a breath. "After that, I need champagne."

"You'll have to wait, because I need to fuck you first." He carried her towards the stairs.

"Saxon, I'm starving!"

He set her down on the stairs and decided he couldn't make it to the bedroom. He swiveled her and pushed her down until her hands hit the stair above her. He slid his hands under her shirt and stroked.

She gasped. "Oh, okay, but make it quick."

By the time they made it to Nopa for a late brunch, Gia was flushed from two orgasms. She sat in a booth across from him in the open, two-story restaurant North of the Panhandle, sipping her champagne. Nopa was always busy, and touted their food as urban rustic. Saxon just called it good.

Gia looked beautiful in a pretty sundress and strappy sandals.

"Your parents don't deserve you," she said.

"I think I finally realized that." He took her hand. "I stopped trying to please them years ago."

"But it's ingrained in kids to want their parents' love and approval." She cocked her head. "You got expelled from your fancy private school so they'd notice you, didn't you?"

He nodded. "Best thing I ever did." He'd changed schools and met Vander, and his life had become infinitely better. If he hadn't decided to join the Army like Vander, he might very well be the rich, useless man his parents wanted.

She squeezed his hand. "I don't think your parents are capable of loving anyone but themselves."

Saxon looked up and saw a man moving across the restaurant toward them. He froze.

Gia frowned. "Saxon?"

"Good morning." The man was older, with gray hair and round cheeks, and even though it was Sunday, wore a three-piece suit.

When Gia stiffened, Saxon realized she knew who their visitor was.

"Mr. Buchanan, we've never had the pleasure," the man said.

"Sackler."

Gia straightened in her chair.

"I don't know your lovely companion." Sackler smiled at Gia, but it didn't reach his dark eyes.

"I think you know exactly who I am, Mr. Sackler." She smiled sharply. "I especially liked taking down the goons you sent after us yesterday."

The man's smile dimmed, his gaze boring into Saxon's. "I hear that Norcross Security has a reputation for getting things done. I suggest not sticking your nose in where it is not wanted."

Saxon kept his face impassive.

Gia scoffed. "Vander does whatever the hell he feels is right, Mr. Sackler. So, your veiled threats are wasted on us." She lifted her champagne flute and sipped.

"I want my diamond back."

"We don't have it," Saxon said. "And it sounds like you lost it fair and square. Don't go after my woman, who is also Vander's sister, or we'll stick our noses in so far, it will get pretty fucking uncomfortable for you."

Sackler glared at them. "A pleasure to meet you both."

Gia smiled. "Sorry, I can't say the same."

The man ambled off.

"Boy, you have to deal with more assholes than I do at work," she muttered.

"I need to call Vander." Sackler had well and truly entered the game, and it wasn't giving Saxon a very good feeling.

CHAPTER FIFTEEN

Albert Sackler had really put a dampener on their Sunday.

"We need to find Willow and those damn gems," Saxon ground out. He was driving the X6 with ruthlessly leashed anger.

Gia leaned back in her seat. "I take it that Ace hasn't tracked her down?"

"She's not staying at any other fancy hotels. And he's checked high-end Airbnbs and other rentals, as well."

"She won't stay somewhere like that again. I know you don't like her, but she isn't dumb."

A muscle in his jaw ticked. "I'll have Ace widen the search."

"I know a few of her old hangouts. We could check them out."

Saxon glanced at her, thought it over, then nodded. "Not exactly what I had planned for today. We need to change clothes."

Back at Saxon's, Gia changed into her favorite J

Brand jeans, a pair of boots, and an olive-green tank with a lightweight, gray cardigan.

She met him in the kitchen.

He looked up and shook his head. "You still look like you should be at a fashion show."

"I don't do scruffy, Saxon." She eyed him, her heart doing a little dance in her chest. "You should wear jeans more often."

His jeans were faded in all the right places, and fit him in a way that made her mouth go dry. A navy-blue T-shirt stretched over his chest, the bands on the sleeves cutting into his muscled biceps. Sunglasses were hooked over the neckline.

Saxon Buchanan in casual mode. Yum.

"I spoke with Ace," he said. "He's running more searches."

Gia swung her leather DKNY tote over her shoulder. "Let's go."

"You got your Ruger in there?"

"Yes, Mr. Overprotective."

They headed out, the X6's engine growling as Saxon drove them down the street. "Where to first?"

"A bar that Willow spends a lot of time at in the Mission District."

When they pulled up at the bar, Saxon didn't look happy. The place was worn, and more than a little seedy.

They walked inside and Gia headed for the bar. An older lady, with wrinkles around her eyes and gray-streaked hair in a ponytail, was wiping down the bar's scarred, wooden surface.

"What can I get you?" she asked with a deep voice.

"Just a Diet Coke, please." Gia sat on a stool. Saxon was pressed right up against her, scanning the bar.

The woman brought Gia her drink.

"I'm a friend of Willow Richards. Have you seen her?"

The woman's eyes narrowed. "Not for a week or two."

Bummer. Gia let out a sigh.

"Last time she was here she didn't pay her tab."

"Sounds like Willow," Gia said.

The bartender scowled. "She in trouble?"

"No," Gia answered.

"Yes," Saxon said.

Gia shot him a glare. The bartender just raised a brow.

"Yes." Gia blew out a breath. "I'm trying to help her, but she doesn't make it easy."

The woman's face softened minutely. "I've got a daughter like that. Been a few people in looking for Willow."

Gia nodded. "That's why I need to find her first."

"Heard she's been playing pool at Roll lately," the woman said.

Gia smiled. "Thank you." She took a long swallow of her drink and set some money on the bar. "How much was Willow's tab?"

"No." The woman shook her head. "Honey, take it from me, if you keep bailing them out, they never learn."

The words reverberated around in Gia's head, but she still felt a lick of guilt. When they walked outside, Saxon took Gia's arm.

"Baby, Willow could've grabbed onto the hand you've held out to her numerous times. She's had every chance to make different choices."

Like he had. Vander's friendship had helped Saxon make good choices in his life.

Gia blew out a breath. "I guess like your parents, she's weak and selfish."

Saxon ran a hand down Gia's hair.

They got in the X6 and drove to Roll—a pool hall not far away.

"This place is owned by the local mafia," Saxon said.

Gia groaned and opened her door. "Great." Just what they needed, the mafia involved. "Same ones that were involved with Haven's ex and the Monet theft?"

"These ones are the Italian version, not Russian. We'll go in, look for Willow, then get out."

They walked inside. It was well-lit and nicely decorated. Gia had been picturing smoke hanging in the air and dangerous-looking people everywhere. It looked normal.

They did a quick lap of the interior, but there was no sign of Willow.

When they got back in the SUV, Gia huffed out a breath.

"Contessa, don't go into private investigations. Most of it is like this. Following leads, talking to people, and not getting what you need as fast as you want it."

Together, they checked out a few more places, including an ex of Willow's. The guy didn't have nice things to say about her, and he hadn't seen her in months.

With a sigh, Gia leaned back against the side of

the SUV.

"Patience, Contessa. It'll be over soon." Saxon pulled her in for a hug.

Then what? What was next for them? She leaned into him, breathing in his scent. She couldn't think about that right now. She needed to fix this Willow situation, and then she could deal with the fact that she was in love with Saxon.

The peal of Saxon's cell phone cut through the air.

"Ace, talk to me." Saxon scanned the sidewalk. "Uh-huh. Address?"

Gia straightened.

"We'll head there now." Saxon turned to Gia. "Ace found Willow. Shady Rest Motel near the airport."

Gia's eyes widened. "How did he find her?"

"He hacked some security cameras. She hadn't used any ID, just paid cash, so we got lucky."

Gia's eyes popped wide. "He hacked some security cameras?"

Saxon grinned. "With Ace, it's best not to ask for the details."

They drove south toward the airport. As they got closer, a plane flew in low overhead. Gia watched the huge jet descend toward the runway, suddenly trying to remember when the last time was that she had a vacation. Maybe after this, she could convince Saxon to go away for a trip. Preferably somewhere warm and balmy, with a pool bar.

They left the freeway and drove down a street lined with low-end motels. Most looked like they could be improved by a match and a can of gasoline. Saxon pulled into the Shady Rest. Gia grimaced. It had needed an update about two decades ago.

A couple of guys were having a cigarette under an awning, watching them with suspicious eyes.

"Do we need to rough up the hotel receptionist?" Gia asked.

Saxon raised a brow. "No. Usually some cash greases the wheels."

"Oh."

"Try not to sound so disappointed, Contessa." He shook his head. "Besides, Ace gave me her room number."

It was on the lower level, and they walked along the row of doors, then stopped. Saxon knocked, but there was no answer.

A second later, he angled his body and pulled out some lock picks. It took him literally two seconds to open the door.

As Gia looked inside, she grimaced again. It was a real step down from the Fairmont. Maybe a whole flight of steps down. An ugly, multicolored bedspread was draped over a sagging double bed. The carpet was stained, and an ancient TV rested on a rickety table. The smell of stale smoke hung in the air.

There were some clothes scattered around on the bed and the back of a chair.

Gia checked them out. "Female. Willow's size." She saw a pack of gum and coins resting on the table. "Big Red gum. Her favorite."

"She can't be far." Saxon quickly and expertly searched the room and adjoining bathroom. "Must have the gems on her. Let's wait in the car."

They slipped out. As they crossed the parking lot, the two men stubbed out their cigarettes and approached.

"What do you two want?" one demanded.

"You don't belong around here." The other one eyed Saxon's Rolex. "Nice watch."

Gia shook her head. "You need an undercover watch. A Casio or something."

Saxon looked at her, aghast. "I'm not wearing a Casio."

She snickered.

"Hey," one of the men barked.

Gia studied the pair carefully. They were both solid, not ripped, but had bulk. One had a tattoo of a skull on his neck, and the other one was bald, with a thick beard.

"We were just leaving," Gia said cheerfully.

"I want the watch," the bald one snapped at Saxon.

"And I want your earrings, Princess," Skull Tat said to Gia.

She smiled. "No, I like these."

The men both blinked, then scowled. "You want us to fuck you up?"

She sighed. "See my man?" She jerked a thumb at Saxon.

Both men glanced at him.

"He's a badass. He can fuck you both up without even trying."

"He's a pretty boy." Skull Tat sneered, then spat on the asphalt.

Gia opened her tote and pulled out her Ruger. She aimed it at Skull Tat's chest. "I could do it myself."

Saxon cursed, then moved. He shoved the bearded man into a nearby parked car.

Skull Tat roared and Saxon swiveled. He lunged and punched the man in the face. When the man staggered, Saxon followed with a hit to the gut and a hard chop to the back.

With a long groan, Skull Tat went down.

The bald, bearded man moved, bracing to attack Saxon. Gia swiveled around and slammed the butt of her gun into the back of his neck.

With a garbled cry, he collapsed.

"Buy a Casio." Saxon straightened with a sniff. "I don't want to hear that again."

They turned to head to the SUV, and Saxon cursed.

Willow stood across the parking lot, staring at them.

Then she bolted.

A millisecond later, Saxon took off after her.

Gia followed. She tried to keep up, but one, her boots weren't made for running, and two, she hated running. She lost sight of Saxon as he gave chase.

Moments, later she stopped, and bent over to suck in some air.

It wasn't long before Saxon reappeared, a dark look on his face. "Lost her."

"Damn." Gia gave herself a second to absorb her disappointment. At least Willow was still alive.

Saxon's lips twitched. "You need to work out more, Contessa."

"Oh, no thanks." She tilted her head. "Unless sex counts."

He smiled. "It counts."

IT WAS MONDAY MORNING, and the results of taking Friday afternoon off meant Gia was extra busy.

Saxon was busy too. He sat at a desk by Ashley, busy on his laptop and phone. Gia craned her head and looked out her office door at him. Today, he wore a charcoal-gray suit and white shirt. So hot.

And despite a lot of great sex, she was still hungry for him.

Ashley appeared, slapping some files on Gia's desk. "Your guy is hot."

"I know."

Her assistant smiled. "You're claiming him now?"

"Yes."

"Tell me you spent the entire weekend having hot-guy monkey sex."

"I spent the entire weekend having hot-guy monkey sex."

Ashley's mouth dropped open. She held up a hand. "Give me a moment."

Gia shook her head as her assistant wandered back to her desk, fanning her face.

Gia's phone rang. "Gia Norcross."

"Gia."

Stiffening, she clutched her phone. "Willow. Where are you?" Gia waved at Saxon and he strode in.

"Gigi, Dennett found me." Willow's harsh breathing cut across the line. "God, Gia, he's going to kill me."

Sludge coated Gia's stomach. Despite everything, she didn't want her friend dead. "Where are you?"

"Golden Gate Park. I've no idea how he found me."

Gia met Saxon's gaze. "She's at Golden Gate Park. Dennett found her."

Saxon cursed. "Tell her I'm coming."

Relief flooded Gia. "Willow, Saxon's coming to get you."

Willow sobbed. "Okay. Okay."

"Hide," Gia said. "And hold on."

"I'm near the Rideout Fountain."

The line went dead.

"Golden Gate Park, by the Rideout Fountain. Saxon—"

He gave Gia a quick kiss. "I'll find her. For you, not for her."

"You're a good man, Saxon."

"I'm calling Ace. Don't leave the office."

She nodded, then watched him stride out, his phone to his ear. She sat back in her chair, clenching her fingers and biting her lip. Great, now she had to worry about Saxon *and* Willow.

Jumping up, she paced across the office, unable to sit still. *Please be okay. Please be okay*.

She now knew why Vander and his guys were never in the office. Waiting and sitting around was excruciating.

"Gia?"

Ace stood in her doorway. As always, he looked hot, but his face was serious.

"Any news?" she asked.

"Nothing yet."

Ace claimed the desk he'd used last time, opening his

fancy laptop, his fingers moving fast over the keyboard. He clipped a Bluetooth earpiece on.

Gia kept pacing, and then she saw Ace stiffen.

She hurried out and pressed her hands to his desk. "What?"

Ashley was watching from her desk, face concerned.

"Nothing yet. Just heard a 9-1-1 call. A man's being transferred to the hospital from Golden Gate Park."

Gia gasped. *No.*

"Don't worry, he doesn't match Saxon's description. Actually, sounds like it might be Dennett." Ace reached out and gripped her hand. "Saxon's damn good at what he does, Gia."

"He's been shot before."

"He has, in a warzone. Trust him to get the job done."

"He's in danger, for her. Because I asked him."

"Try to get some work done. Find a distraction."

With a nod, she moved back into her office. She sat at her desk, but the nervous energy made it impossible to concentrate.

God, Willow. This was it. Gia couldn't have Willow in her life if she kept on this destructive path.

All the work on Gia's desk blurred, then her cell phone rang. She glanced down and saw it was a blocked number.

She frowned and answered. "Gia Norcross."

"We have your brother."

The robotic voice made Gia stiffen. That was impossible. She looked out the doorway to Ace.

"If you talk to anyone, Vander is dead," the voice continued.

"Gia, don't—"

My God. It was Vander's voice. He didn't sound stressed or worried, just pissed.

"What do you want?" she demanded. "Who are you?"

Ace had her phone tapped, right? Right now, he was on his own call, and wasn't showing any reaction to her receiving the call.

"We've blocked the trace on this call," the robot voice said. "It's just us, Ms. Norcross. Remember, you tell anyone, we'll put a bullet in your brother's brain."

"What do you want?"

"You'll exit your office with no one noticing."

"I'm being watched, protected—"

"Do it, or your brother dies."

Her hand clenched on the phone, her knuckles white. "Okay."

"Head onto the street and around the corner. There will be a car waiting. A white Cadillac."

"A white Cadillac," she repeated.

"Find it and get in."

"If you hurt my brother, I'll hurt you."

The robotic chuckle was eerie and creepy. "You have five minutes, Ms. Norcross. Don't be late."

The call ended.

Fear churned in her belly, and she tasted bile in her mouth. She shoved it down.

"Focus, Gia," she whispered. She quickly typed an email and added a send delay of ten minutes. Then she turned off her cell phone and stuck it in her bra. She wiggled it around until it was the least noticeable.

Okay, now she needed to get out without Ace noticing, or Ashley getting suspicious.

Think, Gia.

Okay. The file room was close to the front doors. She'd tell Ashley she had to get in there to get something, then she'd slip out the front door. Ace had access to the building's cameras, but hopefully he wasn't monitoring them live.

Gia rose and pulled in a deep breath. Vander needed her.

She strolled out of her office. "I need some files from the file room."

Ashley swiveled in her chair. "I can get—"

"No." *Shit, that was too abrupt.* "I'm trying to keep myself busy." She tried for a smile.

Ashley sat again and nodded. "Okay, let me know if you need help."

Gia walked at a normal speed toward the file room door. God, she hoped it was normal speed. Was Ace watching her?

She reached the file room and ducked inside.

Leaning against the wall, she took some more deep breaths. How many minutes did she have left?

She peered out and saw that Ace was looking at his laptop. Ashley was on the phone.

The desks of some of her junior staff sat nearby. They were all empty at the moment, her people either in a meeting or out getting coffee. Someone's stylish, tan trench coat was resting on the back of a chair.

Gia ducked out, nabbed the coat, and pulled it on.

Tying the belt, she waited for Janine at the reception

desk to answer a call, then she walked right out the front doors of Firelight and into the hall.

Her heart hammered in her throat and her stomach felt sick. She flicked up the collar of the coat and looked at the floor. There was no time for the stairs, and she had no idea where her security building's cameras were. Were there cameras in the stairs? Who knew?

She pressed the button for the elevator.

As she waited, she thought her heart was going to burst out of her chest. Any second, she expected Ace to burst out after her.

The elevator doors opened and she stepped inside. She pressed the button for the lobby.

It was the longest elevator ride of her life.

Panic felt like barbed wire around her neck by the time she hustled through the lobby. Outside, she turned the corner, and ahead, she saw the white Cadillac idling on the street.

Please be all right, Vander.

For a second, she thought of Saxon, Willow.

Then the door of the Cadillac opened and Conrad Lex got out.

Oh, shit.

"Where's Vander?" she demanded.

"I've got no clue." The man grabbed her and shoved her in the back of the car. He slammed the door closed.

Gia swiveled, trying the doors but they were locked.

Dammit. Dammit. Dammit.

Lex got in the driver seat. "It's just you and me now, Gia."

CHAPTER SIXTEEN

S axon aimed his gun and fired.

Dennett's goon ran into the trees. Off to Saxon's right, Vander marched across the grass. Thankfully, the Golden Gate Park wasn't too busy today. A few people heard the gunshots and ran.

Vander swiveled and fired into the trees, then shook his head.

"They're gone. Couple of guys carried Dennett out. He got clipped by one of his own guys."

Saxon had zero sympathy. "Willow," he called out.

To his left, she popped up from behind some bushes. Nervously, she walked toward them, swiping her hands on her jeans.

Saxon scanned her. Disheveled, but not hurt. "You all right?"

She licked her lips.

Saxon bit back his sharp words. He wanted to call Gia. He knew she'd be worried.

Willow nodded. "Yeah, um, thanks for coming. I

appreciate it." She sent a quick glance at Vander, then back to Saxon.

"Didn't do it for you," Saxon said.

Her mouth twisted. "Right. For your precious Gia."

"For the woman who's still worried about you, despite you being a bitch. Despite you bringing trouble down on her and putting her in danger. So, don't start, Willow."

"It's best if you come with us." Vander looked like he'd prefer another option. "Give us the gems, we'll put you in a safe house, and once we've cleaned up your mess, you can get gone."

"You've always wanted me gone." She tossed her hair back. "Away from your sister."

"Yes, because you use her." Vander's tone was hard.

"Because you hurt her," Saxon added.

"None of you ever thought I was good enough for her—"

"God," Saxon snapped. "It doesn't matter what we think, it's about what you think. You think you're not worthy, so you make fucked-up mistakes, then other people think you're a waste. And that perpetuates the cycle."

She stared at him.

"They're your choices, your life. We all have shit to deal with, Willow. Shit that tries to drag us down. Don't let it. Hold on to the people who give a fuck about you." He looked at Vander. "Don't drag them down with you. If you let them, they'll help you become a better person and they'll always have your back."

Vander was silent for a moment. "Nice speech."

"Fuck you." There was no heat in Saxon's voice.

Vander slapped Saxon's back.

Willow cleared her throat and shifted nervously, and that's when Saxon's mood plummeted. He could read her body language pretty easily. "Something you haven't told us, Willow?"

She bit her lip. "I don't have the gems."

Vander and Saxon both stiffened.

"Come again?" Saxon said quietly.

"One of Dennett's dickheads, Lex or something, found me." She swiped her hand across her mouth. "The guy is *whacked*. I ran, but he took the gems."

"Fuck," Vander said.

Saxon's cell phone rang. "Buchanan."

"Saxon."

Ace's voice drove a spike of fear done Saxon's spine. "Gia?"

"I'm so sorry, man. She gave me the slip."

Saxon closed his eyes and thumbed his phone onto speaker. "Tell me."

"She got a blocked call. From Lex. Fucker lured her out by saying that he had Vander."

Vander growled. "I'm right here."

"And she believed him?" Saxon asked.

"Lex had a recording of Vander's voice. Made it seem like he did."

Especially for a loving sister, a woman with a heart so big she'd do anything for those she loved.

"Damn woman headed to the file room, stole some-one's coat, and strolled out." Ace sounded annoyed and a little in awe. "Once I realized she was missing, I tracked her movements on the building's security feed. She got into a white Cadillac, and Lex was driving. Then I got her email."

"Email?" Saxon asked.

"She sent me a time-delayed email, telling me everything."

Despite the fear and fury inside him, Saxon wanted to smile, but he couldn't. Gia was in danger.

"Fuck," he roared. Lex had Gia, and the bastard wanted to hurt her.

And the asshole had the gems too.

Willow's face was pale. "*Gia.*"

"I called Rhys," Ace said. "He's on it. I'm searching traffic cameras for the Cadillac."

"If he hurts her—" Saxon's chest was so tight he could barely breathe.

"Head in the game, Buchanan," Vander said.

Vander's voice was ice cold. Saxon could see that Vander had slipped into mission mode: cool, focused, rock steady.

Saxon had to do the same. Gia needed him.

"Right, we're headed back to the office," Vander said. "I'll call Hunt on the way. We'll find this asshole, we'll bring Gia home."

Saxon nodded.

"Then you can tan her ass," Vander added.

Saxon met his best friend's dark-blue gaze, chest tight. "Count on it."

Vander nodded. "Just don't tell me the details."

Saxon grabbed Willow's arm and tugged her toward where they'd parked. "Come on."

"I'm sorry." Her voice was a whisper. "I never thought she'd get hurt."

He had no time for Willow's realizations.

Back at Norcross, they got Willow settled in a holding room with a couch, TV, and some snacks.

Vander went straight to his office and was on the phone, one hand on his hip, barking orders at someone.

Saxon's phone rang and he saw it was Rhys. "Tell me you found her."

"Not yet, Sax. But we will."

Saxon's chin dropped to his chest.

He couldn't lose her. Not when he was realizing what a big piece of him sassy, sexy Gia Norcross owned.

Hold the fuck on, Gia. I'll find you.

LEX YANKED her roughly from the car.

They were in some alley, somewhere on the edge of Chinatown. He pulled on her arm, almost tripping her.

"Quit yanking," she snapped.

He backhanded her.

Gia blinked, tasting blood in her mouth. *Cazzo. Stronzo.*

Ace would've gotten her email. She hoped he could find her. She thought of Saxon. He was fine. She was sure that by now he would have saved Willow.

And now, he'd be coming to save Gia.

Unless she saved herself, first.

Lex opened the door of a building and pulled her inside. She looked around. It was an empty office. The blinds were drawn, there was no furniture, and the walls were bare.

His fingers squeezed cruelly into her bicep and she winced. The asshole got off on hurting people.

He shoved her toward the back of the room and that's when she spotted one small card table set up, and a suitcase on the floor. Inside it, she saw guns and her belly curdled.

"What now?" she demanded.

"Now, you shut up."

She rolled her eyes. "I can't believe your ego and your reputation are so fragile that you have to resort to this."

He shot her a venomous look. "I'm not going to let some spoiled princess ruin my career."

"One, I'm not a spoiled princess, I actually have a career. Two, you're a hired gun, and that is *not* a career."

He set something on the table.

A black velvet bag.

Gia's pulse jumped. *Oh, my God.*

He opened it and the gems scattered across the table. She gasped. They were damn pretty. "You have them." She spotted the pink diamond.

"Yes." He smiled. "Your stupid friend ran like a rabbit when she saw me. Now, I win. I have the gems and I'm going to sell them for a small fortune. And I also have you."

Fear crawled over Gia, but she tried not to show it. "And what are your plans for me?"

"I'm going to kill you."

Oh, God. Gia fought to keep her face blank.

Lex's smile widened. "Oh, I like knowing you're

afraid. I'm going to draw it out for as long as I can. Also, it's a bonus to know that your brothers are running around, afraid for their little sister."

She lifted her chin. "You're going down, Lex. Whether you kill me or not, my brothers and Saxon will take you apart, limb from limb."

There was a noise at the front door. "Good, the buyer is here."

"Dennett."

"It's not Dennett."

Alfred Sackler strode in, flanked by two blank-faced men in suits. Gia dragged in a shuddering breath. Sackler's gaze moved over her. It was calculating.

"Mr. Lex," Sackler drawled.

Lex nodded and waved a hand at the card table.

Sackler's eyes showed some emotion now. He strode over, and gently touched the gems.

Gia noted that he paid no extra attention to the pink diamond. He didn't even mention it. Interesting.

"We already agreed on the price," Sackler said. "I'll transfer one million dollars into your account."

Oh yeah, Sackler was keeping quiet about the priceless diamond.

"I also want the woman," he continued. "I'll pay you for her too."

What? Gia jolted and glared. "You can't be serious?"

"Very." Sackler smiled. "I have uses for you."

"She's not for sale," Lex said. "I've plans for her."

Gia crossed her arms. "The world is filled with assholes. I'm not happy that I seem to be capturing the attention of so many of them."

Lex swung at her, but she ducked his arm and kicked him in the shin.

He staggered back one step, pure anger on his face. "Definitely not for sale."

Gia raised a brow. "I'm the least of your problems." She swung her head around to look at Sackler. "Perhaps you'd prefer to discuss with Mr. Sackler why he's only giving you a million dollars, when there's a priceless pink diamond in that bag?"

Sackler's face didn't change, but his gaze turned frosty. His two guards stiffened.

Lex went still, his brow creased. "What?"

"She's just trying to cause trouble," Sackler scoffed.

"I heard the gems were worth a quarter of a mil," Lex said carefully.

"The rest of them are, but not the pink diamond." Gia slid a strand of her hair behind her ear. "Sackler lost it in a poker game to Dennett and wants it back."

"Bitch," Sackler breathed.

Lex whipped up his handgun, aiming it at Sackler. "She's telling the truth. You lied. You tried to con me."

"It wasn't very hard, Lex."

Gia watched with interest as Lex's jaw worked, a vein popping out of his temple. She could almost see smoke coming out of his ears.

"The deal's off!" Lex growled. "Get out of here."

"I don't think so." Sackler waved his fingers.

The two guards opened fire. The shots were deafening inside the enclosed space. Gia threw up an arm and choked on a sharp cry.

Beside her, Lex's body jerked, and blood splattered Gia's cheek. He went down, bleeding on the floor.

Oh. *God.*

She breathed in, then out, nausea fighting with a wave of dizziness. *Oh God.*

Sackler strode to the table and snatched up the stones, shoving them into the bag. Then he smiled at Gia. "Looks like you are coming with me, after all." He reached out to touch her, but she stepped back. "Thanks to you, I got an excellent deal for the gems, the diamond, *and* you." His smile disappeared. "Now move."

He shoved her ahead of him and when she got to the door, she saw a big, black Escalade parked right in front of the building.

"Castle, deal with the mess in there. Get rid of the body."

"Yes, sir."

The other guard rounded the Escalade to get to the driver's seat. Sackler opened the back door of the Escalade. "In."

If she got in, she was dead. Gia jerked back, and ran.

She heard Sackler shout. His other guard was already on the other side of the SUV. She had the advantage.

She sprinted down the alley and turned into another narrower alley between two buildings.

It was dank and smelled of rotting trash. Ahead, a chain-link fence barred the way.

She looked back over her shoulder.

Sackler's goon raced into view.

Shit. Gia kicked off her shoes. *I'm sorry, Manolo.*

Barefoot, she hit the fence, climbing upward. Her

skirt made it hard, but she made it over the top, and then jumped to the bottom, landing hard. Something pricked her foot, but she ignored it and looked up.

Sackler's thug was directly opposite her and they stared at each other through the fence.

Gia turned and ran.

She heard the telltale rattle of the fence as her pursuer climbed it. She sprinted down the alley, dodging a puddle. Her chest burned.

She was almost to the street—

An arm grabbed her shoulder and yanked her backward.

Gia lost her balance and crashed to the ground. Her hip hit hard and she cried out.

Then something touched her belly.

Her body jolted and her muscles screamed. *Ow*. Her teeth clicked together as she shuddered.

Stun gun.

The man pulled back, the device held in one hand. Gia fought to stay conscious, her head full of fog. She groaned.

The man picked her up and tossed her over his broad shoulder. Her entire body was lax, and she couldn't make it move.

Moments ticked by as he walked back, maneuvering her over the fence. Soon they were back at the Escalade.

Sackler smiled. "Ah, good. Lay her in the back seat. At least she can't cause any more trouble, now."

Don't bet on it, asshole. Gia was tossed on the seat and she lay there, fighting back tears. She hurt, and she knew this was bad.

Sackler and his man climbed into the front seats. The Escalade's engine started, and they pulled out.

Gia wasn't giving up. She was a Norcross. And she was in love with Saxon Buchanan. She wanted to live in his gorgeous house, make love with him every day, take baths in his big tub, and more.

She kept trying to move, and finally her fingers twitched.

Yes.

She slid her hand under her coat, and into her bra where she'd hidden her phone. She found the power button and pressed it, keeping the phone buried in the coat. It vibrated as it turned on. Carefully, she pulled it out, keeping it nestled inside the coat's lapels.

Glancing up, she checked on Sackler. He and his guard were ignoring her. No doubt they expected her to be groggy and cowering in terror.

Not today, Sackler.

She moved her fingers slowly over the screen. Then she sent a text to Saxon.

With Sackler. Find me.

CHAPTER SEVENTEEN

Saxon was working hard to keep a lock on his emotions. He wouldn't lose it. He refused to.

He *had* to find Gia.

"Got something," Ace yelled. He was manning the wall of flat screens in his office. "White Cadillac spotted in Chinatown."

Saxon's phone pinged and he yanked it out. His heart contracted. "Gia sent me a message."

Vander, Rhys, and Easton crowded around him.

"Dammit, Sackler has her." *Find me.* Those words speared through him.

"I'm tracing her cell now." Ace's face was serious as his hands danced over the keyboard.

Saxon forced himself to stand still and drag in a hard breath. His smart, sexy woman was busy trying to save herself. Fuck, he loved her.

Vander's phone rang. "It's Hunt." He pressed the phone to his ear. "Talk to me."

Rhys gripped Saxon's arm. "Hold it together, Sax. I know how you feel, and it sucks."

He met Rhys's dark gaze. So similar to Gia's eyes. They'd both inherited them from their mom. Rhys had suffered through Haven being taken—actually she'd been kidnapped several times.

"We'll find her." Easton's tone was firm, unyielding.

"Ace?" Saxon said.

"Working on it."

Vander strode back, his face grim.

Saxon's chest compressed. "What?"

"Lex's bullet-riddled body was found dumped in an alley on the edge of Chinatown."

Easton cursed.

"There were also reports of a man carrying a woman off."

"She's alive," Rhys said. "She sent that message. We know she's alive."

But for how long? Sackler wasn't afraid to kill.

Rhys' face hardened. "Gia's beautiful, attractive. The rumors are that Sackler likes to have private auctions with his friends and sell off women."

Fucker. Saxon's hands balled, and he watched a muscle tick in Vander's jaw.

"He's going down," Vander growled.

"He's never been caught," Rhys said. "There's nothing to prove the rumors."

"It's enough," Vander bit out.

"Got her!" Ace cried.

They all swiveled.

"Where?" Saxon barked.

"In Dogpatch." Ace leaned over and tapped on the screen. "Looks like a warehouse."

Saxon jerked. He wanted to move, jump in a car, and race there. But the soldier in him knew he needed more intel. He wouldn't risk Gia's life by racing in unprepared and out of control.

"Dammit, I lost her signal." Ace cursed. "Her phone's off, or it's been destroyed."

Shit, Sackler must have discovered it.

Vander met Saxon's gaze. In his best friend's dark-blue eyes, Saxon saw the same need to act.

"What info have you got on the warehouse?" Vander demanded.

"Pulling it up now." Ace straightened. "It's owned by a Hanes-Brown Corporation." He tapped on the keyboard, then smiled. "Which is owned by Sackler Enterprises."

"I want the schematics." Vander turned. "Gear up. We're going in and bringing Gia out."

"Fuck yeah." Saxon was already headed for the stairs to get to the locker room.

Downstairs, they geared up—black Kevlar vests, black cargo pants. From the weapons locker, Saxon strapped his Heckler & Koch to his thigh, then grabbed his M4 assault rifle.

I'm coming, Contessa.

"Wish Rome was in town," Rhys muttered.

Saxon did, too. Rome had left on the weekend for a bodyguard job in New Orleans.

"I called in Ryan," Vander said.

Good. Saxon felt a kick of relief. Ben Ryan was a

former Navy SEAL. He was married to his high school sweetheart, and did contract work for Norcross. Clean-cut, dependable, and good in a fight. Saxon was glad to hear he'd have their backs.

All kitted out, Saxon pressed an earpiece into his ear. "Ace?"

"Got you." His friend's voice was crystal-clear.

Everyone checked their comms and headed out to the X6s.

Ryan was waiting for them. Despite being out of the Navy for several years, his blond hair was still cut military short, his bearing straight. He was already kitted out.

"Good to see you, Ben." Vander shook hands with the man.

"Sure thing," Ben replied.

"We're going to breach a warehouse in Dogpatch. Fucker, with unknown backup, has Gia."

Ben nodded.

Soon, they were loaded into two SUVs. Rhys, Easton, and Ben were in one. Saxon and Vander were in the other.

Every second of the drive made Saxon's nerves string tighter. His head was filled with images of Gia. Starting with a pretty, dark-eyed teenager, to the flushed, gorgeous woman smiling at him while she wore his shirt.

"I love her."

Vander glanced at him from the driver's seat. "I know. We'll get her out. You guys have years ahead of you of driving each other crazy."

"I'm going to marry her." As soon as he could.

Vander was silent for a moment. "I'm sorry I was

pissed when I found out about you guys. It was a knee-jerk brother reaction. If my sister has to be with somebody, I'd like it to be with a man I respect. A man who'll treat her right. You two are perfect for each other."

Saxon's throat tightened. "Thanks, Vander."

They drove south and soon reached Dogpatch, nestled close to the bay. Saxon scanned the warehouses ahead. Vander parked and they climbed out, rifles in hand.

Saxon had been in a similar situation so many times—on a mission, weapon in hand, Vander beside him.

"I'll make her happy." Saxon smiled briefly. "And angry, and excited, and mad, and elated."

"I know, brother." Vander gripped his shoulder. "Now, let's go get her."

They moved in on the warehouse. Vander murmured to the others, who were coming in on the other side.

"Two bogeys at the door," Vander said quietly.

Saxon saw them. Two suited men; no obvious weapons, but clearly armed—he saw the bulging shape of the guns under their jackets.

"We have no idea how many are inside?" Vander scowled.

"Vander, I've got a drone in the air," Ace said. "Give me a minute, and I'll run a heat scan."

"Acknowledged," Vander replied.

Fuck, that meant they needed to wait for the drone. Saxon blew out a breath. Waiting was always the hardest part of any mission.

He hoped to hell that Sackler only had a few guards

with him. And Saxon hoped Gia was keeping her sassy mouth quiet for now.

"Lex had the gems," Vander said. "And Gia."

"And now he's dead, and Sackler has Gia."

"So, he likely has the gems as well."

Their gazes met.

"All I care about is Gia," Saxon said. "We get her first. The gems are secondary."

Vander lifted his chin. "Hell, yeah."

There was a click on their earpieces. "Vander, we're in position on the other side of the warehouse," Rhys said.

"Any visuals on Gia or Sackler?" Vander asked.

"No. All we can see in the warehouse is shelving stacked with boxes and other shit."

"Acknowledged."

"Drone is three minutes out," Ace murmured.

Saxon knew Vander had spent a fortune on small, high-tech, military-grade drones. Ace treated the damn things like babies. They had thermal imaging, high-res cameras, and some were even weapons-equipped.

Suddenly, gunfire broke out from inside the warehouse.

Saxon's heart stopped. He whipped up his M4 rifle.

Then he started forward.

"Saxon," Vander hissed.

"I'm *not* fucking waiting. Gia is in there and I'm going to get her."

Vander cursed and followed.

OKAY, this warehouse was creepy.

Gia sniffed. There were only a few lights on, and weak sunlight filtered in from high windows. The place was filled with shadows.

When you were terrified, you imagined all kinds of bad things in the darkness.

That said, Gia was well aware that the most dangerous thing in the place was Sackler, who was walking ahead of her.

How did someone get so twisted?

The guard behind her shoved her and she shot him a glare over her shoulder.

Asshole. She mouthed the word and watched him scowl. The prick had found her phone when he'd dragged her out of the Escalade. He'd left it crushed in pieces on the street.

They walked between two long rows of metal shelves that went almost to the ceiling. The entire place was filled with shelves loaded with boxes and crates.

They reached the end of the row, and a small table and chairs sat in an open space. There were more guards there as well.

Gia swallowed. Saxon and Vander would come. They could deal with these guys with their eyes closed.

Taking a breath, Gia followed Sackler.

Then, she spotted the cage.

She stumbled, and felt like her chest caved in. It wasn't big—waist high, made of metal.

Two women sat inside of it. Gia sucked in a sharp breath. They were both terrified. Maybe a few years younger than Gia, and it was hard to guess their nationalities. One had pale skin and long, black hair, while the other had dark-brown skin and brown hair. Both were extraordinarily beautiful.

Burning-hot rage scalded Gia's veins.

Sackler had stolen these women. Was keeping them in a cage like animals.

She pressed a hand to her thigh, her nails digging into her skin. He was going down. Whatever happened here today, Gia vowed to free these women and make sure Sackler was stopped.

He halted at the table, and eyed Gia. "I have a cage for you, too, lovely Gia."

"Fuck you."

His lips twitched. "Would you like to? I can make you enjoy it."

Ugh. Gia's stomach revolted. The bastard wasn't laying one finger on her.

With a laugh, Sackler upended the velvet bag. Colored gems spilled all over the table.

Then he lifted the pale-pink diamond.

"Ahh." He held it up.

It was beautiful. It looked wrong resting in the asshole's ugly hand.

"Yes, everything's worked out better than I'd hoped. That idiot Dennett learned a lesson, I got my diamond back, and, as an added bonus—" he stroked Gia's hair "—I got you."

She jerked her head away. "I think I'm going to vomit."

His face hardened, and he turned to the guards. "Go and check the warehouse."

With nods, his men disappeared into the shadows, and Gia's pulse jumped like crazy.

Sackler yanked her close and tried to kiss her, but as soon as his lips touched hers, she bit him.

With a growl, he shook her.

"You won't get away with this," she cried. Ugh, that sounded like a bad line in a movie. "My brothers and my man will stop you. *I'll* stop you. I'm freeing those women, I'm taking that diamond, and if I'm lucky, I'll get an opportunity to shoot you."

Sackler threw his head back and laughed. Taking her chance, Gia punched him in his soft belly.

The air rushed out of him, and he grunted in pain and surprise.

Using all her strength, she kneed him in the face, and snatched the diamond out of his hand.

With a strangled, agonized sound, Sackler fell to his knees, cradling his head.

Gia spun and looked at the women. "I'll be back, I promise." Then she sprinted down one of the rows of shelves.

She clutched the diamond, which was surprisingly warm to touch. Then she scanned the rows of shelves. *Exit.* She needed a way out.

Somewhere behind her, she heard a bellow. "Find her!"

Shit.

Then she heard guns firing, and almost tripped.

"Alive," Sackler shouted. The gunfire immediately ceased.

At least her bare feet kept her footsteps quiet. She

ran to a junction in the middle of the warehouse. Damn, the place was a maze. She needed a way out. *Come on, come on.*

She turned left, but a second later, heard someone coming down one of the rows.

She pulled back and ducked down.

A guard thundered past her. She heard the squawk of a radio.

"Anyone got a visual?"

"Haven't seen her yet."

Gia backed away, then turned and jogged in the opposite direction. Her fingers clenched on the diamond. She turned a corner.

And found herself face-to-face with a guard.

His brows drew together, and he reached for her.

Shit. Gia jumped on him.

She caught him by surprise and they fell. The guard hit the ground first, Gia's weight on him, and she heard the air wheeze out of him. Good. He was winded.

She stuffed the diamond down the front of her shirt, then rolled to the side. She got her arms around his neck in a chokehold that Vander had drilled her in about four thousand times. She didn't need brute strength to choke someone, she just had to hit the right spot before they pushed her off.

The guard stiffened, and Gia put all of her strength into the chokehold. It was the longest two seconds of her life, but finally, the guy slumped against her.

Thank you, God.

She heard his radio squawk. "Sutton, you there?"

Gia leaped to her feet.

"Sutton, respond."

Shit. She heard footsteps coming her way.

Turning, she ran and bolted down another aisle. Then she heard more voices ahead of her. Her chest locked. *Crap.* She was trapped.

She looked at one of the shelves and spotted a gap between two boxes. She squeezed into it, sliding past the two big boxes, and came out in the next row. But more footsteps were running toward her.

Shit, shit, shit.

"Sutton's down," someone yelled. "She's close."

"I want the woman and the diamond back now!" Sackler yelled.

Heart pounding, Gia ran, but at the far end of the row, a guard stepped into view. When he spotted her, he lifted his handgun and fired.

Gia ducked and squeezed through the next shelf. For a second, she got stuck, and she cursed her curvy hips, but then she was free.

Damn, they were converging on her. She looked up at the shelves. *Could it work?* She was out of other options.

She pressed her foot to the box on the lower shelf, and gripped the shelving above her head. Then she climbed. She made it up two shelves and squeezed into a space between a crate and a box.

Down below, two guards sprinted past.

Gia closed her eyes, and tried to quieten her breathing. She thought of Saxon.

Come on, Hot Stuff. Now would be an excellent time for a rescue.

CHAPTER EIGHTEEN

S axon and Vander circled the warehouse, coming up on the guards at the front door.

Saxon heard Vander murmur in his earpiece to the others, but Saxon stayed focused on getting inside.

He had to get to his Contessa. To Gia.

He jumped the first guard. With two vicious blows, Saxon brought the man down. He lowered the man's unconscious body to the ground.

Vander scuffled with the other guard. Even though the guy clearly lived at the gym, since he had a bulky body and no neck, and was probably mid-twenties, Vander didn't have to expend much effort.

With another elbow to the head, the guard slammed into the warehouse wall and slid to the ground.

Saxon and Vander stripped the men of their weapons, then Vander lifted his hand and used a hand signal. He pointed to the door.

Lifting his M4, Saxon nodded. Vander opened the door and they slid inside silently.

Scanning the interior, Saxon took in the shelves and shadows. He waited, then heard shouting toward the center of the space.

I'm coming, Gia. Be okay. She had to be okay.

He and Vander split up. Saxon had no idea how many guards were inside. In the distance, he heard Sackler barking orders.

Saxon paused, and pressed his back to the shelf.

"Anyone seen her?" a deep voice said.

"Just a glimpse. Shot at her, but she fucking disappeared."

Saxon memorized that voice. That asshole was going down.

"Any blood?" another man asked.

Saxon tensed.

"Nothing."

He relaxed a fraction.

"Can't believe that bitch got the jump on Sutton."

"One down." Vander's low murmur in the earpiece.

Vander would do what Vander did best—use the shadows, and pick off the guards swiftly and quietly.

That meant Saxon could find Gia.

He moved forward and darted across to another aisle. He jogged quietly, getting closer to where the guards were grouped together.

Suddenly, a man rounded the corner. His eyes widened. "Who the fuck are you?"

Saxon rammed into the man. The guard swung at him, but Saxon dodged, and punched the guy in the kidney.

The guard shouted, but Saxon kicked him into the shelves.

"Vander." Ace's voice. "You have five guards and Sackler inside. There are two heat signatures at the far end of the space in what looks like a cage. One smaller heat signature is up higher."

That had to be Gia since they were searching for her. She was hiding. Saxon punched the guard again, and the guy flopped facedown on the floor. *Clever girl.*

"Fuck," Ace said. "An Escalade with five more guards just pulled up."

"Rhys, breach," Vander ordered.

"Incoming," Rhys replied.

Rhys, Easton, and Ben would come in from the loading bays.

"Where's Gia?" Saxon murmured.

"Central row, close to the loading bay end," Ace replied.

Saxon moved quickly, scanning the shelves. She must be here somewhere.

"Ah, Mr. Buchanan."

Saxon spun. Sackler stood there with two guards. Both had their guns aimed at Saxon. One held a hand-gun, while the other one gripped a shotgun.

"Drop your weapon," Sackler said.

Saxon tossed his rifle to the concrete.

"I want you to call out to Ms. Norcross, otherwise my men will shoot you."

Saxon remained silent.

"She has my diamond," Sackler said. "Call her!"

Saxon laughed. "She got the diamond, took down one of your guards, and you lost her?"

Sackler's face twisted. "*Enough.* Call her."

One of the guards fired his shotgun with a boom. The round hit some crates off to Saxon's right.

"Fuck you, Sackler," Saxon said.

The man snatched the shotgun off his guard and strode to Saxon. He jammed the barrel in Saxon's gut.

"Don't test me."

"She's a hundred times smarter than you," Saxon said. "Your little empire, all the dirty things you do, that ends today."

"No, Mr. Buchanan, *you'll* end today, bleeding here on the concrete."

"Have you ever used a shotgun?"

Sackler stiffened.

"I didn't think so." Saxon snatched the weapon out of the man's hands and then punched Sackler in the face.

He cried out, blood spurting from his nose, and crashed to the floor. Saxon pumped the shotgun, spun, and fired toward the guards.

The men dove in different directions. The one with the handgun fired, bullets hitting a box above Saxon's head.

The other guard rose and pulled a knife from his belt. Then he charged.

Saxon swung the shotgun like a bat. It slammed into the guard's head with a crack and the man flew sideways, collapsing on top of a groaning Sackler.

"Don't move," a voice said.

Saxon looked up. The final guard held his Glock

aimed at Saxon's head. His eyes were steady, seasoned. He was no rent-a-cop.

All of a sudden, a shape leaped off the shelf above them and slammed into the man.

The pair crashed to the floor, and the man's gun flew out of his hands.

Gia slapped at the man's head. "No one aims a gun at my man!"

The guard tried to cover his head to protect himself but she kept slapping him.

"Okay, warrior princess." Saxon tugged her up. "I think he learned his lesson."

"He was going to shoot you." She leaned down and got in one more smack.

God, he loved her. Saxon snatched up the guard's gun. It was impossible to love her any more than he did because there was no room left inside of him. One punch knocked the guard out, and then Saxon dragged her into his arms and kissed her.

Damn, he felt weak from the rush of relief. She was okay. She was alive and in his arms. "I'm thinking I'll lock you up."

She smiled at him. "Only if you stay with me."

"I want my diamond."

They spun.

Sackler was on his feet, nose swollen, blood streaming down his face and soaking into his shirt. He aimed a gun at Gia.

Saxon stiffened. He was an idiot. He'd thought Sackler was down and had no more weapons. He'd been too distracted by his relief to double check.

Rookie mistake.

"I do know how to use this one, Buchanan," Sackler said.

Saxon stepped in front of Gia. She shoved forward to stand beside him.

He glared at her, but she just lifted her chin, her eyes defiant.

The sounds of fighting echoed from other parts the warehouse. Vander and the others were busy.

"Ms. Norcross, unless you want your brains splattered all over your boyfriend, I suggest you give me what I want."

With a sigh, Gia reached into the neckline of her shirt and pulled out the diamond.

Hell, it was big. It was the palest pink, and there was something almost otherworldly about it.

Sackler stared at it, his lips curving. "Hand it over."

"No," Gia said.

The man stepped forward and shook the gun. "Now!"

Saxon tensed, ready for anything. "Gia."

Her life was more important to him than any hunk of carbon.

She shook her head. "He can't—"

"I love you," Saxon said. "I don't give a flying fuck about that diamond."

"You love me?" she whispered.

"I think I always have. From the first time you told me I was an arrogant, know-it-all snob with my head up my ass. I think you were fourteen."

She bit her lip. "I'm sure I didn't say that."

"I think you called me that last week as well."

Her face went soft. "I love you too, Saxon. Completely." Her brows drew together. "But I can't believe you're telling me this *now*. With a bad guy holding a gun on us. Of all the times."

Saxon grinned. "Well, you won't forget it."

"Your romance needs work."

"Oh, I'll show you romance."

"Enough!" Sackler roared.

ALBERT SACKLER LOOKED FAR LESS polished and smug than he had earlier.

Gia shot him a glare. "I warned you that Saxon and my brothers would make you regret your choices. You chose to be an asshole."

Gunshots echoed at the back of the warehouse. Sackler glanced that way nervously.

"Now you have to deal with the consequences. You enslaved women, you bastard," she spat. "You've killed, all for your own greed."

"Enslaved women?" Saxon's tone was as sharp as a blade.

"There are two women in a cage at the other end of the warehouse."

She felt his big body tense. His voice lowered. "Is that what you had planned for Gia, Sackler? Were you going to put my woman in a cage?"

The man swallowed, then he waved his weapon at them. "*Stop talking*. Give me the diamond!"

The gun went off and the bullet hit the concrete at their feet.

Gia cried out and Saxon yanked her close, shielding her.

"You want the diamond?" Gia said. "Then you can have it." She aimed and using every bit of her strength, fueled by all her anger, she wound up and threw it like a baseball.

It sailed straight at Sackler and smacked him between the eyes. With a groan, he hit the concrete.

The diamond bounced on the floor and rolled away.

Sackler made a choked sound. The gun fell from his fingers.

Saxon lunged and kicked the gun away. "He's out cold." He looked at her. "Damn, Contessa, you have a hell of an arm."

"I played softball for years." She grinned. "I was good."

Saxon zip tied Sackler's hands. Next, he tied up the guards. "You're very good." He rose, stepping over the diamond.

"Saxon, the pink—"

"Don't give a fuck about it." His gaze scanned her body, his face tightening. "Any of that blood yours?"

She swiped at her stained shirt. "No. Sackler killed Lex, and I was standing too close."

Saxon swept her into his arms.

"It might be some of my blood on my feet though." She eyed her bare toes and wrinkled her nose. "I had to abandon my favorite pair of Manolo Blahniks in an alley. Then a thug chased me, and I stepped on something."

"You might need a tetanus shot or stitches, but you sound more pissed about the shoes."

"I am, Saxon. They were my favorites."

"I suspect they're all your favorites." He pushed her hair back from her face. "I'll buy you more. I'm rich, remember?"

She tugged his head close. "Hmm, so you are."

"You're safe now," he said.

"I knew you'd come for me. Willow?"

"She's fine."

"Good." Gia slid her hands into his hair.

He took her mouth hungrily. All the emotions inside her coalesced into brutal need for this man. She was alive. He was alive.

This was finally over.

He growled into her mouth, his tongue twining with hers. Gia jumped up and wrapped her legs around his waist, and his hands cupped her ass.

Mmm, this made everything worthwhile.

"God, my eyes." Easton's deep mutter.

"I need bleach," Rhys replied.

A growl that had to be Vander's. "Lucky for you two, this is only your first time seeing this."

Reluctantly, Gia lifted her head.

Her brothers all stood in a row—each one of them looking badass in black, guns in hand.

Vander surveyed the wreckage around them and bent to pick up the diamond.

"Nice to see you're all right, Gia," Easton said.

"Even if Saxon did have his tongue in your mouth and his hands on your ass," Rhys grumbled.

"Get used to it." Saxon set her down. "I'm going to marry her."

Gia's heart stopped and she stared at him. "What?"

"As soon as I can." Saxon looked at Vander. "Gia said there were two women being held in here."

Vander's mouth flattened and he nodded. "Ben has them."

Gia rounded on Saxon. "You can't ask me to marry you now! You have to make it romantic. With a ring."

"No, I'm not asking you, I'm telling you. You *are* going to marry me. Maybe we can go to Vegas to get it done quicker."

"Vegas," she hissed. "No way, Saxon Buchanan. I want a big wedding, with a designer dress that will blow your mind."

"Okay." He smiled at her.

The look in his eyes made her heart flip-flop.

"I love you, Gia," he said.

She melted. "God help us, I love you, too."

Ace's voice came through Saxon's earpiece and Gia could just make out the words. "Guys, you have company."

"What?" Vander tensed.

Saxon pushed Gia into the center of the group and the men all whipped up their guns.

"Ten men heading into the warehouse, and moving fast," Ace said.

"Fuck," Saxon muttered.

Gia swallowed. This was supposed to be over.

Two groups of five men came down the row at either end, trapping them. They were all holding guns.

The men were all stone-faced professionals. A few of them parted, and Kyle Dennett stepped forward. He had one arm in a sling.

The man smiled. "It always pays to let others do all the hard work for you." He held out his uninjured hand. "I came for the diamond."

Dammit. Gia muttered a few good Italian curse words. "If we give it to you—" she glared at him "—you'll leave me and Willow alone."

Saxon wrapped an arm around her.

"You aren't in a position to bargain, Ms. Norcross. Willow needs to be punished."

God, what an asshole.

Dennett's gaze flicked to Saxon, then Vander. "You're outnumbered. If you fire, someone will get hurt."

Vander held up the diamond.

Even in the low light, there was something amazing about it. Gia felt like she could stare into it forever.

Dennett's face took on a sharp edge. "Finally."

Damn. Gia didn't want this asshole to get his hands on the gem.

Suddenly, bodies dressed in black dropped from the shelves above them, landing all around.

Gia swallowed a scream.

The newcomers attacked.

The sound of punches and grunts, and bodies hitting the concrete, filled the air. In seconds, Dennett's men were down and disarmed.

One tall, muscular man in black body armor, with a mask over the bottom half of his face, stepped up behind

Dennett. He pressed a gun to the back of Dennett's head. His gold eyes glittered above his mask.

Gia shivered. He had fascinating, frightening tiger eyes.

"Who the fuck are you?" Dennett yelled. "I'll—"

With a quick move, the man slammed the butt of the gun against the back of Dennett's head. With a sharp gasp, Dennett collapsed.

Gia scanned around. The team in black had taken down all of Dennett's men—quickly and efficiently.

"Nobody move," a sharp, female voice said.

Gia blinked. One of these badasses was a woman? She studied them more carefully, and then decided that three had more slender builds and were probably women.

"It's nice to see you, Lachlan," Vander said.

The golden-eyed man inclined his head. "Vander."

"I'm guessing you're here for this." Her brother held up the diamond.

CHAPTER NINETEEN

Vander's covert, black-ops friends had come to pay a visit.

Saxon's Ghost Ops team had been black ops, but this team had always been just a whisper. The tall leader shoved his mask down his rugged face. He shook hands with Vander.

"You're just going to give them the diamond?" Gia asked.

The man, Lachlan, glanced at Gia. His eyes were intense, assessing. "Yes."

A tall, fit woman with blonde hair in a braid strode forward.

Vander handed the woman the diamond. "It's their job, Gia."

She straightened. "But—"

"They're the good guys," Vander said. "And the diamond is safer with them."

Gia frowned, but stayed quiet.

"I assume you'll leave us to clean up the mess?" Vander said dryly.

Lachlan's lips moved in what might have been a slight smirk. "We were never here."

"Right." Vander nodded. "I heard you got engaged."

Now Lachlan smiled. "If you're ever in Vegas, give me a call. We'll go out, because I wouldn't recommend my fiancée's cooking."

A few of his team snickered. The blonde snorted. "I'll tell her you said that."

"She's a hell of a baker, though, so you'll have to try her desserts." Lachlan pulled his mask back into place. "Thanks for the assist."

"You too, Lachlan."

In seconds, the team pulled back and was gone.

Gia blinked. "Did I just imagine that?"

"Nope." Saxon pressed her face to his chest. It was damn good to hold her. "You just met Team 52. You can't tell anyone about them."

"The diamond—?"

"Was likely from the Great Table diamond, and is probably dangerous."

"Dangerous? How can a diamond be dangerous?"

"Don't ask, Gia. It's in safe hands." He slid his fingers into her hair, and nudged her face up. "And so are you."

She smiled, her face softening. She was a mess. Clothes stained and torn, her hair a wild tangle, no shoes, and dried blood on her face. She'd never looked more beautiful.

Somewhere in the warehouse, a door banged open. "Police! Nobody move."

"Uh-oh," Gia murmured.

"Hunt, it's Norcross," Vander called out. "All threats are neutralized."

A second later, Detective Hunt Morgan strode toward them. He was wearing dark slacks, a blue shirt with a shoulder holster, and his badge strapped to his belt. Several officers in uniform were two steps behind him.

Hunt's gaze swept over the space and his jaw tightened. "Fuck."

"The bad guys are all down," Vander said. "You should thank me."

Hunt shot Vander a glare. "Gia, are you all right?"

She nodded. "One of Vander's guys is with two women that this asshole—" she pointed at a groggy Sackler on the ground "—had in a cage."

Hunt's jaw tightened. He waved at two officers. They hauled Sackler up, while other police officers checked the downed guards.

"There's also a bag of gems," Gia added.

"You've all been busy," Hunt drawled.

She smiled, and Saxon shook his head.

"Okay, well, get comfortable," Hunt said. "I need everyone's statements, and I need to give Vander my weekly speech about running around San Francisco, wreaking havoc, and not alerting the police to what's going on."

Vander swung his rifle up on his shoulder. "I owe you a beer."

"You owe me an entire brewery," Hunt countered.

They gave their statements to the detectives, and

paramedics checked Gia's feet. There was nothing that needed stitches, and her tetanus shot was up to date.

The women were also checked over and taken to the hospital. The authorities would reunite them with their families.

Best of all, Albert Sackler was behind bars, and Hunt was getting search warrants to search his home and other properties.

Whatever happened, the man was going down.

"I want a shower," Gia said.

"Come on, warrior princess." After waving at Vander and the others, and waiting while her brothers hugged her, they headed out to the X6.

"A shower and food are on the horizon for you." He buckled her seatbelt, and soon, they were driving back to his place.

She turned in the seat. "By the way, I do not accept your half-assed marriage proposal. You do it properly, Saxon Buchanan. With a big ring and a bottle of champagne."

He grinned at her. His Gia wasn't shy about asking for what she wanted.

Back at his place, he carried her up the stairs.

"Why do I feel so drained?" She rested her head against his shoulder.

"You've been running on adrenaline all day. You've been stressed all week. It's normal to crash."

He carried her into his bathroom

Saxon started running the bath, then helped to strip her clothes off.

"Saxon, I can do it—"

"Let me look after you, Gia."

She nodded. He noted that she had a few new bruises, but all in all, she was fine. He kissed her shoulder, then her elbow, ran his fingers down her side.

"I want to shower the grime and blood off first before I get in the bath," she murmured.

"Go shower, then get in the tub. I'm going to sort out some food." And a few other things.

She stepped into the shower stall and blew him a kiss.

Saxon grabbed his phone, and in the kitchen, he made a call. Thankfully, money could make almost anything happen, and fast. Then he pulled out some mixed nuts, stuffed peppers, and cheese and crackers. He set them out on a board. Next, he pulled out two champagne flutes.

The doorbell rang. On the way down, he checked to make sure that Gia was in the tub, then headed down to collect what he'd ordered.

Once he had that, he grabbed a chilled bottle of Moët & Chandon, the champagne flutes, and the board of snacks.

When he entered the bathroom, she was lying in the tub, damp hair piled on top of her head, and her eyes closed. Her beautiful breasts were peeking through the bubbles, and his cock flared to life.

He set everything down beside the tub and she cracked one eye open. "Moët, my favorite."

"I know." He filled the flute and handed it to her.

"What are we celebrating?" she asked.

"Being alive. You being safe." He filled his glass and then clinked it to hers. "Sackler behind bars."

"Those are very good things."

"Me loving you more than I thought I could love anyone."

She stilled. "Saxon..."

"I've never loved a woman before. You're it for me, Gia Norcross."

She reached out and tugged his head down. She kissed him, long and deep.

"We're celebrating one more thing," he said.

"Did you buy me a new pair of Manolo Blahniks?"

"No. We're celebrating you marrying me." He held out his hand.

Gia blinked and stared at the ring. "Where did you get that? How can you do that so fast?"

"I have my ways." It was a large, pear-shaped, pink diamond, surrounded by smaller, white diamonds. "You're going to marry me, Gia."

"Still no question." Emotion shimmered in her eyes. "But you have the ring, the champagne, and most of all, you're the man I love." She beamed at him. "Put that ring on my finger, Hot Stuff."

Elation and a happiness that he'd never known rushed through him. He set the flute down, then climbed into the tub.

"Saxon, your clothes!"

Water sloshed and his saturated clothes clung to him as he straddled her.

Then he slid the ring on her finger.

"All mine now, Contessa."

Smiling, she dragged him close and kissed him. "Now, I get to drive you crazy for a lifetime."

"GIA, YOU AREN'T CONCENTRATING."

No, she wasn't, because she was sprawled on top of a naked Saxon, her head facing his feet, and her legs on either side of his head.

Mostly, she couldn't concentrate because his far-too-clever mouth was between her legs.

She moaned. His hand bit into her ass and she rolled against him. "God, Saxon—"

His tongue plunged inside her, then he sucked on her clit.

"You're too good at this," she moaned.

He bit her thigh. "Is that possible?"

"*No.* Don't stop."

His chuckle made her shiver. Then his hand pressed between her shoulder blades, pushing her down.

Gia's gaze fell on his hard cock. *Mmm.* She circled it with one hand and her gaze snagged on her engagement ring. Smiling, she closed her mouth over the head of his cock.

Saxon grunted, his fingers digging into her skin. She sucked him deep, bobbed, and sucked again.

A groan rumbled out of him and then his mouth was back between her legs, licking and sucking roughly.

Gia pumped his cock, licking and lavishing it with attention. This could become her new favorite pastime.

His hips pumped up, driving his cock deeper into her mouth. She moaned, clamping her legs on his head. Then he was sucking her clit again. She threw her head back, his cock popping free.

"Saxon, God, yes."

Gia's climax rocked through her, leaving her shaking and crying his name. With pleasure still rushing through her, he rolled her over.

She found herself on her back. Saxon grabbed a condom—his moves jerky and desperate—then he pushed her ankles onto his shoulders and thrust inside her.

Oh, God, yes.

"Eyes, Gia. Look at me."

She met his gaze. He was so damn handsome.

He moved inside her, never once looking away. His hands found hers, pushing them into the bed.

The look in his eyes, the love... Gia whimpered. There was so much feeling inside her. Too much and never enough.

"You have no idea how beautiful you are," he murmured.

"Saxon."

"I'm gonna make you come again, then I'm going to come deep inside my Contessa."

He picked up speed, finding an angle that vibrated through her clit. Soon, she was crying out and bucking against him.

"Get there, Gia."

With one more thrust, her climax hit, shockwaves washing over her. Her back arched.

He didn't look away. She felt the intensity of his gaze watching her as she rode through her pleasure.

Then his lunges lost their rhythm, his breathing harsh pants. He let out a deep groan, and his big body shuddered as he came.

Gia closed her eyes and stroked her hand lazily over his sweat-dampened back.

"You alive?" he asked.

She managed a hum.

He chuckled and she felt it in her belly. He kissed her chin and pulled out. He sauntered into the bathroom and she rolled over to watch. She'd be happy just to stay right here for the foreseeable future.

As Saxon headed back to the bed, the doorbell rang.

Gia groaned.

"They'll go away," he growled.

The bell rang again. Then again, and Saxon made a frustrated noise. Gia laughed.

Saxon's cell phone rang on the bedside table and he snatched it up. "It's Rhys." He thumbed the phone and Rhys' voice came through.

"Answer the door," Rhys said. "My woman wants to see her best friend, and we brought dinner."

Saxon growled again, and Gia giggled. She scrambled off the bed, snatched up his shirt, and pulled it on. She hunted around for some leggings to wear with it. Meanwhile, Saxon tugged on some jeans and a T-shirt.

Downstairs, he pulled the front door open.

Rhys stood there with a stack of pizza boxes.

"Those better be from Tony's Pizza," Gia said.

Haven shoved past Saxon and threw her arms around Gia.

"I'm fine," Gia reassured her friend.

Haven just hugged her tighter.

Vander appeared behind them. "I brought beer."

"I don't drink beer," Gia said. "Rhys is my favorite brother now."

"Your man has a wine cellar," Vander said. "And Easton is on his way. He was stopping at Tartine for dessert."

"Ooh! Easton's my favorite brother," Gia cried, grinning.

Vander pulled on her hair.

"What is that?" Haven squealed and grabbed Gia's hand. "Oh, my God, oh my God."

Gia smiled at her ring, then Saxon. No, her fiancé. "I decided that Saxon wasn't quite as annoying as I'd always believed."

Her man smiled at her, and she felt it in her heart. She planned to make him smile, make him happy, as often as she could.

"How did he propose?" Haven asked.

"Well, if we ignore the declaration while the bad guy was pointing a gun at us in some shady warehouse—"

Haven laughed.

"—I was naked in the bath and there was Moët."

"If we're discussing Gia naked, I need a beer." Vander headed for the stairs.

"And I'm joining you," Rhys announced.

Vander slapped Saxon on the back. "Congrats, brother."

"Thanks," Saxon replied.

"Good luck," Rhys added.

"Not my favorite brother anymore," Gia snapped.

Easton appeared in the doorway. "What did I miss?" He was holding a white bakery box.

"Gia and Saxon are engaged," Haven said.

Easton smiled, and kissed Gia, then gripped Saxon's hand.

"Happy for you guys." He met Saxon's gaze. "And good luck."

Gia mock scowled. "I no longer have a favorite brother."

Easton touched her nose, then headed up the stairs.

"Come on," Saxon said. "I have another bottle of Moët chilling."

Gia smiled. "Look, he's even well-trained."

Haven linked her arm through Gia's. "I'll remind you of that the next time he's pissed you off."

They headed up the stairs.

"Gia, this house," Haven breathed. "It's like it was designed for you."

"I know." Just like the man.

CHAPTER TWENTY

Saxon leaned back in his desk chair, phone pressed to his ear. "Yeah. Okay. Thanks, I'll be in touch."

He ended the call and swiveled to look through the glass wall. He was back on his regular cases, and as always, Norcross Security had plenty of work to keep them busy.

He spotted Ace talking with Rhys and Rome across the Norcross office. In the two days since they'd rescued Gia, Albert Sackler had been charged with a string of offences, and his dirty little empire was being dismantled. Dennett hadn't been charged with anything, but he was laying very low.

Gia was safe.

She was back at work, his ring was on her finger, and she was as sassy as ever.

They'd had dinner with her parents the night before. He grinned. Mrs. Norcross had cried...then started in on when she could expect her first grandchild.

Vander appeared in the doorway and gave Saxon a

faint smile. "You look like a king whose kingdom is exactly as he likes it."

Saxon rested his hands behind his head. "Sounds about right. Hey, you available to help Gia move into my place this weekend?"

Vander raised a brow. "Saxon Buchanan is well and truly off the market."

"Think I always was, just took me a while to realize it."

"I can help her move. I'll round up Easton, Rhys, and Dad, as well. That woman has enough shoes and clothes that it'll take us all day."

And Saxon had a closet for her to fill.

"Only person with a similar amount of clothes to her is you, with all your fancy suits."

Saxon shot his best friend the finger.

"I got word that Dennett has decided to relocate to a different city," Vander said.

Saxon rested his arm on his desk. "How did you manage that?"

"Easton put some business pressure on him, and I spoke to a few people. Dennett found his opportunities in San Francisco drying up rapidly."

The idiot had really messed up by going up against the Norcross family.

"Wonder where the diamond is now," Saxon mused.

Vander shrugged one shoulder. "Locked up somewhere safe in Nevada. Now, I hope we can be drama-free for a while."

Saxon heard the tap of heels and looked up. His fiancée powered across the Norcross office. It was a little uncomfortable to feel his cock take notice with her brother, his best friend, standing right beside him.

She wore a tight, black skirt, with a silky red blouse. Her hair was pulled back tightly, with just a few wisps escaping.

She looked smooth, polished, and professional, until he saw her shoes. They were very sexy stilettos with red soles that gave him some X-rated ideas.

Vander shook his head. "Whipped."

Saxon grinned. "Yep, and I am not complaining about it." He drank her in. Oh yeah, he planned to fuck her later while she wore those shoes.

"I know that look." Vander scowled. "I'm out of here."

"Hey, it's my favorite brother." Gia kissed Vander's cheek.

"Why am I your favorite today?"

"Life is good, so you're all my favorites today."

Shaking his head, Vander tugged on a loose strand of her hair, then headed toward his office.

"Hello, love of my life," Gia said.

Saxon smiled. "Hello, Contessa. To what do I owe this pleasure?"

She sauntered closer. "Just wanted to see my man."

When she got close enough, he spun and pinned her against his desk. Her hands clamped onto his forearms and he rose, then closed his mouth over hers.

She hummed in pleasure, a sound he loved hearing from her. The kiss took a while, and he heard someone wolf whistle outside his office.

Saxon pressed his forehead to hers. "Damn, I wish

my walls weren't made of glass, because then I could push up this sexy skirt and fuck you on my desk."

"My office walls aren't made of glass," she murmured.

His cock throbbed. Images of what he could do to her on her desk bombarded him.

She smiled. "Visit me close to closing one day, Hot Stuff."

"I'll add it to my agenda."

She stroked her hand down his shirt. "Have you got time for lunch?"

"Hell, yeah."

Rome appeared in the doorway, his face composed as always. "Guys, you've got a visitor."

Saxon swiveled, then felt Gia stiffen.

Rome stepped back to show Willow standing just outside Saxon's office.

Hell. She wore jeans and a simple shirt. Her hair was pulled up in a ponytail. She didn't look strung out or high, just pale and tired.

Saxon moved. "I'll get rid of her—"

Gia put her hand on his arm. "No, it's okay."

"It's my job to protect you, Contessa. From anything that could hurt you."

Her face warmed. "I know. I want to talk to her, and just knowing you're here gives me the strength to do it."

He sighed. "Okay, but I'm staying."

She rolled her eyes.

Willow stepped inside the office, fidgeting. "Hi."

"Hi," Gia said.

Willow fiddled with her hair. "I came to say I'm sorry. For everything."

Gia eyed her for a second. "Okay."

"I'm in a rehab program, I..." She looked at both of them. "I want to make better choices."

Gia's mouth softened. "I'm glad, Willow."

The woman's shoulders sagged. "You've given up on me."

With a sigh, Gia stepped closer to her friend. Saxon took her hand and squeezed. She smiled at him before looking back at Willow.

"Willow, you've made me promises before. After everything that's happened, you're going to have to *show* me that you've changed, not tell me. But I believe in you, I always have."

"No one else ever did." Willow straightened. "That's not an excuse, I'm just saying. Thank you, both of you, for helping me. I'm sorry you got dragged into my mess and I put you in danger."

Gia nodded, then hugged her friend.

Saxon wasn't willing to trust Willow yet, but he'd give her a chance.

They'd have to wait and see.

"Oh, look at that ring." Willow smiled. "I always knew you two would end up together. Like a matching set. Congratulations."

Gia beamed. "Thanks, Will."

"All right, I'd better go." With a nervous wave, Willow headed out.

Saxon pulled Gia into his arms. "Okay?"

"I want her to make it," Gia said. "I want her to find her happy, like I have."

"It's up to her. You can't find it for her." He kissed the top of Gia's head. "My girl's got such a big, gooey heart."

She looked up. "And it's all yours."

"How about lunch at home?" he said. "And a quickie on the hall table?"

Heat flickered in her eyes and she shifted against him, purposely brushing his cock. "I like that idea."

He leaned close, his chest full of love for his woman. "And Gia?"

"Yes?"

"Make sure you leave those heels on."

PUTTING a diamond stud in her ear, Gia hurried into Saxon's bedroom. "Sorry, I know we're late."

No wait, not Saxon's bedroom, *their* bedroom. An excited shiver ran through her.

They were officially living together. She'd moved in the previous weekend.

She glanced sideways into her closet. Ooh, so beautiful. All her clothes were hanging in there, and looked gorgeous.

"Let's get a move on," Saxon grumbled. "I'm not sure we can be late for our own party."

He was standing by the bed, wearing a gorgeous blue suit. *Oh, yum.* She stared at him—from the top of his dark-blond head to his shiny shoes. All hers.

He looked up. "Fuck."

He stared at her, hunger in his eyes. It didn't matter that they'd made love in the shower an hour ago.

She smiled and posed. "You like the dress?"

It was tiny, black, with lace in strategic places, and lots of silver shimmer. And her silver Badgley Mischka shoes were pure sex kitten.

"I like the dress, but I like the sexy body in it even more."

"Well, you can show me how much later, because we're late. And I promised we'd pick Easton up from his office on the way."

Haven had organized a little engagement celebration for them at ONE65. Her parents were coming, the Firelight PR staff, and the guys from Norcross.

Saxon strode to her and gripped her hips.

"No," she said. "Don't get distracted, and don't mess me up."

"I get distracted any time I look at you."

She smiled. "And don't be sweet right now, either. Let's move, or Easton will stay at the office, working all night. He works too hard."

"He needs a woman."

Gia snorted. "They're either intimidated by the great Easton Norcross, or they fawn all over him with dollar signs in their eyes."

"True."

They drove to Easton's office building, and security let them into the elevator.

The Norcross Inc. floor was empty, except for raised voices coming from Easton's office.

"Okay, Mr. Slave Driver, I'm heading home now."

Harlow's voice. *Uh-oh.*

"Hot date?" Easton drawled.

"None of your business."

Harlow stalked out of Easton's office, her face flushed and a smile on her lips. Then she spotted Gia and Saxon. "Oh, hi."

"Hello, again." Gia smiled. "We're here to pick up Easton."

"Good. I was worried I'd have to bean him with a stapler so I could make my getaway."

"Well, how about we distract him so you can escape?" Gia winked.

Harlow smiled and opened her mouth to answer, just as her cell phone pinged. She pulled it out. Whatever was in the message wasn't good. Her smile fell, and all the color drained from her face.

Gia frowned. "Harlow? Is everything all right?"

The woman's head whipped up, and she pinned a fake-looking smile in place. "Fine. All fine."

Gia looked at Saxon. He was frowning. It wasn't all fine.

Harlow glanced at her phone again and her chest hitched. "Um, I'd better get going. Have a great night." She started shoving things in her handbag.

Gia headed toward Easton's office. When she glanced back, she saw Harlow's shoulders slump, and Gia thought she saw the glimmer of tears in the woman's eyes.

She looked so dejected and alone.

Easton stood behind his desk, the city skyline his backdrop as he shrugged into his jacket.

"Hi," he greeted them.

Her brother was so damn handsome, and he did work too hard.

"Busy day making squillions?" she asked.

He smiled. "Always."

"Well, time to go and get a drink," Saxon said.

"Good. I've had so many meetings today, so I've earned it."

Gia frowned. "Did you stop to eat lunch?"

"My dragon of an assistant forced me to eat a sandwich. If I recall correctly, she threatened to hit me with my keyboard if I didn't."

"Speaking of Harlow, she just got a message." Gia chewed on her lip. "She looked pretty upset."

Easton stilled. "What?"

"Just now, she—"

Her brother stormed past her. Gia raised a brow and saw Saxon trying to hide a grin.

"What?" she said.

He shook his head.

Gia spun and reached the doorway.

Easton had Harlow pinned against her desk.

"What's wrong?" he demanded.

"Nothing."

"Carlson—"

"You can grumble all you want, Mr. Glower, I'm not telling you."

"Mr. Glower? That's not one of your best."

Harlow huffed out a breath. "I know. It's been a long day, because my demanding boss is a workaholic."

Easton lifted a hand, like he wanted to touch her, but then let it drop. "Tell me, Harlow. I can help."

"No one can help." Harlow's voice was soft, edged with something sad. Then she shoved Easton back. "I

268

have to go." She snatched up her coat and bag. "Have a great weekend." She almost ran out of the office.

Easton stared after her, frowning.

Hmm. Gia bit her lip. She wanted to rub her hands together.

Harlow was neither intimidated by her brother, nor in awe. And her brother had that look in his eye, the one that said he wanted something.

Easton never let anything stop him from getting what he wanted.

Saxon gripped her shoulder. "No meddling, Gia Gabriella," he whispered.

She smiled at her man. "Who, me?"

He sighed.

"Saxon?" Easton said. "I want you to run Harlow's background. See if you find anything concerning."

Gia stiffened. "Easton, I'm pretty sure she wouldn't be happy about that."

"I don't care. If she's in trouble..."

"I'm on it," Saxon said.

"Men." Gia threw her hands in the air.

Saxon slid an arm around her. "Let's get you some champagne, Contessa."

"I know when you're trying to distract me, Saxon Buchanan."

He smiled at her.

Dammit, he was so handsome, and he knew it.

"You're the smartest, sexiest woman I know, Gia Norcross, soon to be Gia Buchanan."

She gasped. "Oh God, Gia Buchanan."

He lowered his head. "You like that?"

"Yes," she whispered.

"Me, too." His mouth covered hers.

And then there was just Gia and Saxon.

They were safe. They were happy and in love.

She knew they'd fight, make up, laugh, love, and have each other, always.

I hope you enjoyed Gia and Saxon's story!

There are more Norcross stories on the way. Stay tuned for **THE SPECIALIST**, starring Easton Norcross, coming in 2021.

If you'd like to learn more about the mysterious, covert team in black, **Team 52**, then read on for a preview of the first Team 52 book, ***Mission: Her Protection***.

Or for a little adventure with your romance, you can check out the treasure hunting former Navy SEALs of

Treasure Hunter Security in the book,
Undiscovered.

Don't miss out! For updates about new releases, free books, and other fun stuff, sign up for my VIP mailing list and get your *free box set* containing three action-packed romances.

Visit here to get started: www.annahackett.com

PREVIEW - MISSION: HER PROTECTION

It was a beautiful day—ten below zero, and ice as far as the eye could see.

Dr. Rowan Schafer tugged at the fur-lined hood of her arctic parka, and stared across the unforgiving landscape of Ellesmere Island, the northernmost island in Canada. The Arctic Circle lay about fifteen hundred miles to the south, and large portions of the island were covered with glaciers and ice.

Rowan breathed in the fresh, frigid air. There was nowhere else she wanted to be.

Hefting her small pickaxe, she stepped closer to the wall of glacial ice in front of her. The retreating Gilman Glacier was proving a fascinating location. Her multi-disciplinary team of hydrologists, glaciologists, geophysicists, botanists, and climate scientists were more than happy to brave the cold for the chance to carry out their varied research projects. She began to chip away at the ice once more, searching for any interesting samples.

"Rowan."

She spun and saw one of the members of her team headed her way. Dr. Isabel Silva's parka was red like the rest of the team's, but she wore a woolen hat in a shocking shade of pink over her black hair. Originally from Brazil, Rowan knew the paleobotanist disliked the cold.

"What's the latest, Isabel?" Rowan asked.

"The sled on the snowmobile is almost full of samples." The woman waved her hand in the air, like she always did when she was talking. "You should have seen the moss and lichen samples I pulled. There were loads of them in area 3-41. I can't *wait* to get started on the tests." She shivered. "And be out of this blasted cold."

Rowan suppressed a smile. *Scientists.* She had her own degrees in hydrology and biology, with a minor in paleontology that had shocked her very academic parents. But on this expedition, she was here as leader to keep her team of fourteen fed, clothed, and alive.

"Okay, well, you and Dr. Fournier can run the samples back to base, and then come back to collect me and Dr. Jensen."

Isabel broke into a smile. "You know Lars has a crush on you."

Dr. Lars Jensen was a brilliant, young geophysicist. And yes, Rowan hadn't missed his not-so-subtle attempts to ask her out.

"I'm not here looking for dates."

"But he's kind of cute." Isabel grinned and winked. "In a nerdy kind of way."

Rowan's mouth firmed. Lars was also several years younger than her and, while sweet, didn't interest her in that way. Besides, she'd had enough of people trying to set her up. Her mother was always trying to push various *appropriate* men on Rowan—men with the right credentials, the right degrees, and the right tenured positions. Neither of her parents cared about love or passion; they just cared about how many dissertations and doctorates people collected. Their daughter included.

She dragged in a breath. That was why she'd applied for this expedition—for a chance to get away, a chance for some adventure. "Finish with the samples, Isabel, then—"

Shouts from farther down the glacier had both women spinning. The two other scientists, their red coats bright against the white ice, were waving their arms.

"Wonder what they've found?" Rowan started down the ice.

Isabel followed. "Probably the remains of a mammoth or a mastodon. The weirdest things turn these guys on."

Careful not to move too fast on the slippery surface, Rowan and Isabel reached the men.

"Dr. Schafer, you have to see this." Lars' blue eyes were bright, his nose red from the cold.

She crouched beside Dr. Marc Fournier. "What have you got?"

The older hydrologist scratched carefully at the ice with his pickaxe. "I have no idea." His voice lilted with his French accent.

Rowan studied the discovery. Suspended in the ice, the circular object was about the size of her palm. It was dull-gray in color, and just the edge of it was protruding through the ice, thanks to the warming temperatures that were causing the glacier to retreat.

She touched the end of it with her gloved hand. It was firm, but smooth. "It's not wood, or plant life."

"Maybe stone?" Marc tapped it gently with the axe and it made a metallic echo.

Rowan blinked. "It can't be metal."

"The ice here is about five thousand years old," Lars breathed.

Rowan stood. "Let's get it out."

With her arms crossed, she watched the scientists carefully work the ice away from the object. She knew that several thousand years ago, the fjords of the Hazen Plateau were populated by the mysterious and not-well understood Pre-Dorset and Dorset cultures. They'd made their homes in the Arctic, hunted and used simple tools. The Dorset disappeared when the Thule—ancestors to the Inuit—arrived, much later. Even the Viking Norse had once had communities on Ellesmere and neighboring Greenland.

Most of those former settlements had been near the coast. Scanning the ice around them, she thought it unlikely that there would have been settlements up here.

And certainly not settlements that worked metal. The early people who'd made their home on Ellesmere hunted sea mammals like seals or land mammals like caribou.

Still, she was a scientist, and she knew better than to make assumptions without first gathering all the facts. Her drill team, who were farther up on the ice, were extracting ice core samples. Their studies were showing that roughly five thousand years ago, temperatures here were warmer than they were today. That meant the ice and glaciers on the island would have retreated then as well, and perhaps people had made their homes farther north than previously thought.

Marc pulled the object free with careful movements. It was still coated in a thin layer of ice.

"Are those markings?" Isabel breathed.

They sure looked like it. Rowan studied the scratches carved into the surface of the object. They looked like they could be some sort of writing or glyphs, but if that was the case, they were like nothing she'd ever seen before.

Lars frowned. "I don't know. They could just be natural scoring, or erosion grooves."

Rowan pushed a few errant strands of her dark-red hair off her face. "Since none of us are archeologists, we're going to need an expert to take a look at it."

"It's probably five thousand years old," Isabel added. "If it is man-made, with writing on it, it'll blow all accepted historical theories out of the water."

"Let's not get ahead of ourselves," Rowan said calmly. "It needs to be examined first. It could be natural."

"Or alien," Lars added.

As one, they swiveled to look at the younger man.

He shrugged, his cheeks turning red. "Just saying. Odds are that we aren't alone in this universe. If—"

"Enough." Rowan straightened, knowing once Lars got started on a subject, it was hard to get him to stop. "Pack it up, get it back to base, and store it with the rest of the samples. I'll make some calls." It killed her to put it aside, but this mystery object wasn't their top priority. They had frozen plant and seed samples, and ice samples, that they needed to get back to their research labs.

Every curious instinct inside Rowan was singing, wanting to solve the mystery. God, if she had discovered something that threw accepted ancient history theories out, her parents would be horrified. She'd always been interested in archeology, but her parents had almost had heart attacks when she'd told them. They'd quietly organized other opportunities for her, and before she knew it, she'd been studying hydrology and biology. She'd managed to sneak in her paleontology studies where she could.

Dr. Arthur Caswell and Dr. Kathleen Schafer expected nothing but perfection from their sole progeny. Even after their bloodless divorce, they'd still expected Rowan to do exactly as they wanted.

Rowan had long-ago realized that nothing she ever did would please her parents for long. She blew out a breath. It had taken a painful childhood spent trying to win their love and affection—and failing miserably—to realize that. They were just too absorbed in their own work and lives.

Pull up your big-girl panties, Rowan. She'd never been abused and had been given a great education. She had work she enjoyed, interesting colleagues, and a lot to be thankful for.

Rowan watched her team pack the last of their samples onto the sled. She glanced to the southern horizon, peering at the bank of clouds in the distance. Ellesmere didn't get a lot of precipitation, which meant not a lot of snow, but plenty of ice. Still, it looked like bad weather was brewing and she wanted everyone safely back at camp.

"Okay, everyone, enough for today. Let's head back to base for hot chocolate and coffee."

Isabel rolled her eyes. "You and your chocolate."

Rowan made no apologies for her addiction, or the fact that half her bag for the trip here had been filled with her stash of high-quality chocolate—milk, dark, powdered, and her prized couverture chocolate.

"I want a nip of something warmer," Lars said.

No one complained about leaving. Working out on the ice was bitterly cold, even in September, with the last blush of summer behind them.

Rowan climbed on a snowmobile and quickly grabbed her hand-held radio. "Hazen Team Two, this is Hazen Team One. We are headed back to Hazen Base, confirm."

A few seconds later, the radio crackled. "Acknowledged, Hazen One. We see the clouds, Rowan. We're leaving the drill site now."

Dr. Samuel Malu was as steady and dependable as the sunrise.

"See you there," she answered.

Marc climbed onto the second snowmobile, Lars riding behind him. Rowan waited for Isabel to climb on before firing up the engine. They both pulled their goggles on.

It wasn't a long trip back to base, and soon the camp appeared ahead. Seven large, temporary, polar domes made of high-tech, insulated materials were linked together by short, covered tunnels to make the multi-structure dome camp. The domes housed their living quarters, kitchen and rec room, labs, and one that held Rowan's office, the communications room, and storage. The high-tech insulation made the domes easy to heat, and they were relatively easy to construct and move. The structures had been erected to last through the seven-month expedition.

The two snowmobiles roared close to the largest dome and pulled to a stop.

"Okay, all the samples and specimens to the labs," Rowan directed, holding open the door that led inside. She watched as Lars carefully picked up a tray and headed inside. Isabel and Marc followed with more trays.

Rowan stepped inside and savored the heat that hit her. The small kitchen was on the far side of the rec room, and the center of the dome was crowded with tables, chairs, and sofas.

She unzipped and shrugged off her coat and hung it beside the other red jackets lined up by the door. Next, she stepped out of her big boots and slipped into the canvas shoes she wore inside.

A sudden commotion from the adjoining tunnel had Rowan frowning. *What now?*

A young woman burst from the tunnel. She was dressed in normal clothes, her blonde hair pulled up in a tight ponytail. Emily Wood, their intern, was a student from the University of British Columbia in Vancouver. She got to do all the not-so-glamorous jobs, like logging and labelling the samples, which meant the scientists could focus on their research.

"Rowan, you have to come now!"

"Emily? What's wrong?" Concerned, Rowan gripped the woman's shoulder. She was practically vibrating. "Are you hurt?"

Emily shook her head. "You have to come to Lab Dome 1." She grabbed Rowan's hand and dragged her into the tunnel. "It's *unbelievable*."

Rowan followed. "Tell me what—"

"No. You need to see it with your own eyes."

Seconds later, they stepped into the lab dome. The temperature was pleasant and Rowan was already feeling hot. She needed to strip off her sweater before she started sweating. She spotted Isabel, and another botanist, Dr. Amara Taylor, staring at the main workbench.

"Okay, what's the big issue?" Rowan stepped forward.

Emily tugged her closer. "Look!" She waved a hand with a flourish.

A number of various petri dishes and sample holders sat on the workbench. Emily had been cataloguing all the seeds and frozen plant life they'd pulled out of the glacier.

"These are some of the samples we collected on our first day here." She pointed at the end of the workbench. "Some I completely thawed and had stored for Dr. Taylor to start analyzing."

Amara lifted her dark eyes to Rowan. The botanist was a little older than Rowan, with dark-brown skin, and long, dark hair swept up in a bun. "These plants are five thousand years old."

Rowan frowned and leaned forward. Then she gasped. "Oh my God."

The plants were sprouting new, green shoots.

"They've come back to life." Emily's voice was breathless.

THE CLINK of silverware and excited conversations filled the rec dome. Rowan stabbed at a clump of meat in her stew, eyeing it with a grimace. She loved food, but hated the stuff that accompanied them on expeditions. She grabbed her mug—sweet, rich hot chocolate. She'd made it from her stash with the perfect amount of cocoa. The best hot chocolate needed no less than sixty percent cocoa but no more than eighty.

Across from her, Lars and Isabel weren't even looking at their food or drink.

"Five thousand years old!" Isabel shook her head, her dark hair falling past her shoulders. "Those plants are millennia old, and they've come back to life."

"Amazing," Lars said. "A few years back, a team working south of here on the Teardrop Glacier at Sverdrup Pass brought moss back to life...but it was only four hundred years old."

Isabel and Lars high-fived each other.

Rowan ate some more of her stew. "Russian scientists regenerated seeds found in a squirrel burrow in the Siberian permafrost."

"Pfft," Lars said. "Ours is still cooler."

"They got the plant to flower and it was fertile," Rowan continued, mildly. "The seeds were thirty-two thousand years old."

Isabel pulled a face and Lars looked disappointed.

"And I think they are working on reviving forty-thousand-year-old nematode worms now."

Her team members both pouted.

Rowan smiled and shook her head. "But five-thousand-year-old plant life is nothing to sneeze at, and the Russian flowers required a lot of human intervention to coax them back to life."

Lars perked up. "All we did was thaw and water ours."

Rowan kept eating, listening to the flow of conversation. The others were wondering what other ancient plant life they might find in the glacial ice.

"What if we find a frozen mammoth?" Lars suggested.

"No, a frozen glacier man," Isabel said.

"Like the Ötzi man," Rowan said. "He was over five thousand years old, and found in the Alps. On the border between Italy and Austria."

Amara arrived, setting her tray down. "Glaciers are retreating all over the planet. I had a colleague who uncovered several Roman artifacts from a glacier in the Swiss Alps."

Isabel sat back in her chair. "Maybe we'll find the fountain of youth? Maybe something in these plants we're uncovering could defy aging, or cure cancer."

Rowan raised an eyebrow and smothered a smile. She was as excited as the others about the regeneration of the plants. But her mind turned to the now-forgotten mystery object they'd plucked from the ice. She'd taken some photos of it and its markings. She was itching to take a look at them again.

"I'm going to take another look at the metal object we found," Lars said, stuffing some stew in his mouth.

"Going to check for any messages from aliens?" Isabel teased.

Lars screwed up his nose, then he glanced at Rowan. "Want to join me?"

She was so tempted, but she had a bunch of work piled on her desk. Most important being the supply lists for their next supply drop. She'd send her photos off to an archeologist friend at Harvard, and then spend the rest of her evening banging through her To-Do list.

"I can't tonight. Duty calls." She pushed her chair back and lifted her tray. "I'm going to eat dessert in my office and do some work."

"You mean eat that delicious chocolate of yours that you guard like a hawk," Isabel said.

Rowan smiled. "I promise to make something yummy tomorrow."

"Your brownies," Lars said.

"Chocolate-covered pralines," Isabel said, almost on top of Lars.

Rowan shook her head. Her chocolate creations were gaining a reputation. "I'll surprise you. If anyone needs me, you know where to find me."

"Bye, Rowan."

"Catch you later."

She set the tray on the side table and scraped off her plates. They had a roster for cooking and cleaning duty, and thankfully it wasn't her night. She ignored the dried-out looking chocolate chip cookies, anticipating the block of milk chocolate in her desk drawer. Yep, she had a weakness for chocolate in any form. Chocolate was the most important food group.

As she headed through the tunnels to the smaller dome that housed her office, she listened to the wind howling outside. It sounded like the storm had arrived. She sent up a silent thanks that her entire team was safe and sound in the camp. Since she was the expedition leader, she got her own office, rather than having to share space with the other scientists in the labs.

In her cramped office, she flicked on her lamp and sat down behind her desk. She opened the drawer, pulled out her chocolate, smelled it, and snapped off a piece. She put it in her mouth and savored the flavor.

The best chocolate was a sensory experience. From how it looked—no cloudy old chocolate, please—to how it smelled and tasted. Right now, she enjoyed the intense flavors on her tongue and the smooth, velvety feel. Her mother had never let her have chocolate or other "unhealthy" foods growing up. Rowan had been forced to sneak her chocolate. She remembered her childhood friend, the intense boy from next door who'd always snuck her candy bars when she'd been outside hiding from her parents.

Shaking her head, Rowan reached over and plugged in her portable speaker. Soon she had some blood-pumping rock music filling her space. She smiled, nodding her head to the beat. Her love of rock-and-roll was another thing she'd kept well-hidden from her parents as a teenager. Her mother loved Bach, and her father preferred silence. Rowan had hidden all her albums growing up, and snuck out to concerts while pretending to be on study dates.

Opening her laptop, she scanned her email. Her stomach clenched. Nothing from her parents. She shook her head. Her mother had emailed once...to ask again when Rowan would be finished with her ill-advised jaunt to the Arctic. Her father hadn't even bothered to check she'd arrived safely.

Old news, Rowan. Shaking off old heartache, she uploaded the photos she'd taken to her computer. She took a second to study the photos of her mystery object again.

"What are you?" she murmured.

The carvings on the object could be natural scratches. She zoomed in. It really looked like some sort of writing to her, but if the object was over five thousand years old, then it wasn't likely. She knew the Pre-Dorset and Dorset peoples had been known to carve soapstone and driftwood, but this artifact would have been at the early point of Pre-Dorset history. Hell, it predated cuneiform—the earliest form of writing—which was barely getting going in Sumer when this thing had ended up in the ice.

She searched on her computer and pulled up some images of Sumerian cuneiform. She set the images side by side and studied them, tapped a finger idly against her lip. Some similarities...maybe. She flicked to the next image, chin in hand. She wanted to run a few tests on the object, see exactly what it was made of.

Not your project, Rowan. Instead, she attached the pictures to an email to send to her archeologist friend.

God, she hoped her parents never discovered she was here, pondering ancient markings on an unidentified object. They'd be horrified. Rowan pinched the bridge of her nose. She was a grown woman of thirty-two. Why did she still feel this driving need for her parents' approval?

With a sigh, she rubbed a fist over her chest, then clicked send on the email. Wishing her family was normal was a lost cause. She'd learned that long ago, hiding out in her treehouse with the boy from next door— who'd had a bad homelife as well.

She sank back in her chair and eyed the pile of paper-work on her desk. *Right, work to do.* This was the reason she was in the middle of the Arctic.

Rowan lost herself in her tasks. She took notes, updated inventory sheets, and approved requests.

A vague, unsettling noise echoed through the tunnel. Her music was still pumping, and she lifted her head and frowned, straining to hear.

She turned off her music and stiffened. Were those screams?

She bolted upright. The screams got louder, interspersed with the crash of furniture and breaking glass.

Team 52

Mission: Her Protection
Mission: Her Rescue
Mission: Her Security
Mission: Her Defense
Mission: Her Safety
Mission: Her Freedom
Mission: Her Shield
Also Available as Audiobooks!

PREVIEW: UNDISCOVERED

One former Navy SEAL. One dedicated archeologist. One secret map to a fabulous lost oasis.

Finding undiscovered treasures is always daring,

dangerous, and deadly. Perfect for the men of Treasure Hunter Security. Former Navy SEAL Declan Ward is haunted by the demons of his past and throws everything he has into his security business—Treasure Hunter Security. Dangerous archeological digs – no problem. Daring expeditions – sure thing. Museum security for invaluable exhibits – easy. But on a simple dig in the Egyptian desert, he collides with a stubborn, smart archeologist, Dr. Layne Rush, and together they get swept into a deadly treasure hunt for a mythical lost oasis. When an evil from his past reappears, Declan vows to do anything to protect Layne.

Dr. Layne Rush is dedicated to building a successful career—a promise to the parents she lost far too young. But when her dig is plagued by strange accidents, targeted by a lethal black market antiquities ring, and artifacts are stolen, she is forced to turn to Treasure Hunter Security, and to the tough, sexy, and too-used-to-giving-orders Declan. Soon her organized dig morphs into a wild treasure hunt across the desert dunes.

Danger is hunting them every step of the way, and Layne and Declan must find a way to work together...to not only find the treasure but to survive.

Treasure Hunter Security
Undiscovered
Uncharted
Unexplored
Unfathomed
Untraveled

Unmapped
Unidentified
Undetected
Also Available as Audiobooks!

ALSO BY ANNA HACKETT

Norcross

Team 52

Treasure Hunter Security

Undetected

Also Available as Audiobooks!

Eon Warriors

Edge of Eon

Touch of Eon

Heart of Eon

Kiss of Eon

Mark of Eon

Claim of Eon

Also Available as Audiobooks!

Galactic Gladiators: House of Rone

Sentinel

Defender

Centurion

Paladin

Guard

Weapons Master

Also Available as Audiobooks!

Galactic Gladiators

Gladiator

Warrior

Hero

Protector

Champion

Barbarian

Beast

Rogue

Guardian

Cyborg

Imperator

Hunter

Also Available as Audiobooks!

Hell Squad

Marcus

Cruz

Gabe

Reed

Roth

Noah

Shaw

Holmes

Niko

Finn

Theron

Hemi

Ash

Levi

Manu

Griff

Dom

Survivors

Tane

Also Available as Audiobooks!

The Anomaly Series

Time Thief

Mind Raider

Soul Stealer

Salvation

Anomaly Series Box Set

The Phoenix Adventures

Among Galactic Ruins

At Star's End

In the Devil's Nebula

On a Rogue Planet

Beneath a Trojan Moon

Beyond Galaxy's Edge

On a Cyborg Planet

Return to Dark Earth

On a Barbarian World

Lost in Barbarian Space

Through Uncharted Space

Crashed on an Ice World

Perma Series

Winter Fusion

A Galactic Holiday

Warriors of the Wind

Tempest

Storm & Seduction

Fury & Darkness

Standalone Titles

Savage Dragon

Hunter's Surrender

One Night with the Wolf

For more information visit www.annahackett.com

ABOUT THE AUTHOR

I'm a USA Today bestselling romance author who's passionate about ***fast-paced, emotion-filled*** contemporary and science fiction romance. I love writing about people overcoming unbeatable odds and achieving seemingly impossible goals. I like to believe it's possible for all of us to do the same.

I live in Australia with my own personal hero and two very busy, always-on-the-move sons.

For release dates, behind-the-scenes info, free books, and other fun stuff, sign up for the latest news here:

Website: www.annahackett.com

Ingram Content Group UK Ltd.
Milton Keynes UK
UKHW011312160523
421839UK00001B/151

9 781922 414137